DEATH IN THE RED DIRT

ALICE CADD

DW.MAIAHOUSE@OPTUSNET.COM

Copyright © 2024 by Deborah Wearne. All rights reserved.

Created with Vellum

PROLOGUE

Bathed in the velvet light of the early sun, the man's body lay arched in death. Jaw and fists clenched against the injustice. A film of vomit covered his face and torso. Eyes blank.

Nothing revealed the cause of his death. No stab or gun wounds. The red soil showed claw marks from death spasms, but no reason for his passing.

An easterly wind moved the hot, arid dust around him, teasing the body, wanting to take it back.

A scream sounded, shattering the landscape.

1

Day 1 Post Death

Maya was stuck. Running the worst debriefing session in her short career. Five clients, sitting in a circle clamouring to be heard. Their shouting voices melded into chaos. She was training to be a goddamn psychiatrist. She should be able to get control.

Everyone agreed that Daniel Comstock died in suspicious circumstances. But how? Why?

The group's psychiatrist Dr Ted had been arrested that morning. Justice or not? Who knew? So much noise. It was intense.

'Group therapy twice a day and Daniel would not shut up. It would've driven anyone to murder him,' said the woman with the Barbie pink name badge—Lydia— a mass of gold curls. Her voice sharp and loud. A poster girl for white privilege.

Maya stared at her, trying to force some oxygen into her own tired brain. Her mind was blank.

The man with grey hair, grey eyes, grey shirt and shorts leaned forward —Eamon. 'That's ridiculous. Of course, Dr Ted didn't kill Daniel. It was an accident. I don't understand why they arrested him'

'He's an idiot. The way he ran this retreat was criminal. All those damn drugs. He deserves to be in jail.' said Sarah, thin and coiled, a florid face with clenched jaw. A knot of anger about to explode.

Maya's head was giddy and her face flushed. It was like swimming in an emotional tsunami. They kept going at each other, ignoring her. She pushed herself forward and leaned into the centre of the group. 'This is all new to me. Could anyone give me an overview of what happened?'

Eamon had a motor tic in his right hand, a ramped-up, irregular tremor. He said, 'We've been here four weeks, as part of a mental health program, run by Dr Ted. It's been intense. We went on retreat to a remote station on the weekend and Daniel was found dead at his campsite.'

Lydia thrust her arms into the group circle, bracelets jangling. Taking up as much space as possible. Beautiful, but loud and grating.

She said, 'Daniel was obsessed with self-diagnosis, obsessed with medical sites on the Internet. He diagnosed everybody else with narcissistic personality disorder, but himself with ADHD, presumably as a built-in excuse for being a pain in the arse.' She sighed, and leant forward in the chair to stare at Maya, like a cat basking in her attention. 'I think he killed himself and framed Dr Ted to take the fall.'

'I think Dr Ted finally cracked,' said Sarah, rocking back and forth in her chair, slamming her feet into the floor, fists clenched. 'Anyone would've after all this crap.'

Maya studied Sarah, looking for clues to help her distress. She was striking, high cheek bones and almond eyes. Short, black bob. Dressed head to toe in khaki. Tattoo sleeve on her right arm, curled snakes and dragons.

Eamon leaned towards Sarah, reaching out to touch her knee. Maya cringed. It was never a good idea to touch someone so agitated. The potential for disaster was high.

'Fuck off you pervert.' Sarah sprang to her feet, tore across the floor and left the room, slamming the door.

Maya's throat filled with acid. What the hell was wrong with her? The room was cold, but her butt stuck to the squeaky couch. Everything was painted white, floor, walls, ceiling. It was creepy. Who'd buy white leather sofas, in the red, dust capital of the world? No wonder the participants were irritable and shrieking at her. So much for guiding the group, she couldn't focus.

The man named Steve was talking to unseen voices and having a good time with them. He laughed, nodded and waved to his invisible audience, appearing psychotic. He was chubby and wore orange/brown cheesecloth, better suited to the 1970s.

The last member of the group was an older man, dressed in black. Graham had a force field around him, repelling any attempts to make contact. He moved like a robot, in a hostile environment. How in the world did Dr Ted think that he would participate in group therapy? His eyes glared at the group with frown lines chiselled in granite.

Maya realised she wasn't going to achieve much in this setting. They were too keyed up. Getting them to work together was impossible. They were used to an older, male guru therapist. She was the opposite, young, inexperienced and female.

She said, 'Let's break for lunch and I'll set up meetings with everyone individually.'

The participants rose as a whole and moved out of the room. Maybe the food was excellent? Or perhaps they needed to escape as much as she did?

Maya's headache cut a swathe through her skull. The noxious smell of diesel spread through the room from the outside generator. She prayed she wouldn't vomit from the fumes.

Maya closed her eyes. Her day had been a disaster. A grumpy hospital transport driver dumped her at the Homestead that morning. She'd been hustled straight into the group room by the resident chef. A chubby, middle-aged woman in a flowery dress. All energy and busyness.

How the hell was she to run a debriefing session with no background on the participants? Everyone hysterical after Dr Ted's arrest. No wonder it was a disaster.

Her bastard of a supervisor had offered her up like a sacrificial lamb. He was friends with Dr Ted and had jumped to send her to this hellish place for the debrief. Then he'd gone on extended leave. Uncontactable.

She hadn't had time to empty her bladder. And she was starving. Could things get any worse?

Bladder sorted, Maya entered the dining room. She stared wide-eyed. It was beautiful, so different from the white group room.

Rammed earth walls, with a pleasant musky smell. Floor to ceiling windows, which opened on to a covered veranda, surrounded by strong green plants. Maya's mood lifted. The room was powerful and domineering, matching the striking environment outside. Maybe it was going to be alright?

A large Jarrah table ran along the window. Both sides were lined with wooden church pews, giving the setting a religious feel. With her recent group work disaster, perhaps the Last Supper? She tasted the relentless heat in the air.

The manic chef from the morning slowed down. She introduced herself to Maya. 'Welcome to our Homestead dear. My name's Joy. I'm sorry I had to hustle you through to group, when you'd only just arrived.'

Rotund and warm, Joy radiated enthusiasm and care. She called out everyone's name, as she moved around the table presenting delicious and healthy platters. She placed a plate of green radicchio, fresh mozzarella, bright orange mango and ripe cherry tomatoes, in front of Maya. Her mouth watered. Add in the fresh bread, and it was Maya's dream lunch.

Joy leaned in towards Maya and said, 'You are kind to help us out. We're so grateful. I've made up a room for your stay. Come and get me after lunch and I'll show you.' Maya's anxiety dropped. She loved a bit of mothering.

Maya took her food outside to have a break from the intensity of the therapy group interaction. There were three iron wrought tables, each with three stiff, cold iron chairs, and an outdoor couch. The seats in this place looked like torture implements. At least it provided a reasonable opportunity to eat alone.

The veranda was covered, but Maya was enveloped by a wave of heat. Exmouth doesn't trifle when it comes to heat, and it was over forty degrees Celsius.

There are two seasons in the Pilbara, the wet and the dry. Wet did not mean cool. In fact, it was oppressively humid. The heat increased Maya's sense of being trapped and overwhelmed. The air was hard to breathe.

After lunch, she found Joy who took her to her room. Joy burbled away, like an exuberant, winter stream. 'We're so grateful for your help dear. It's just been terrible. Dr Ted's such a good man. It's so awful that they think he could've hurt anyone. I hope you'll be settled here. If you need anything you can always find me in the kitchen. It's my happy place.' It was hard keeping up with her.

Joy opened the door to Maya's room and said, 'You need to know that we don't have mobile or internet reception here. It might seem strange to you young ones, but I like the peace of it. There's a satellite phone, in the small room, near the kitchen. You have to stand outside to use the phone. It won't work under the tin roof.'

Maya's chest tightened. More isolation. Her hand twitched to touch her mobile. She gulped back the acid in her throat.

Maya's room was white, but a softer white than the group room. Less hostile. A single bed framed with wood and made up with white sheets, and a small wardrobe. Monastic. Even a visitor's chair, perhaps stolen from the local hospital? Something out of the 1950s? She sat on the bed, overwhelmed and lost. How was she going to survive this placement?

She barely had time to unpack and wash her face, when Joy bustled back. 'I've found you a key to the group room. I moved Dr Ted's filing cabinet and a small desk there. It can be your office.'

What was this woman? Superhuman?

Maya was jostled back to the blinding, white group room by Joy. She sat her next to the new, shiny cabinet on the sticky white couch. Keys propped in her hand.

Joy nodded and smiled. 'I hope you've got everything you need, dear. I know Dr Ted is now your direct supervisor, but give me a shout if you have problems. It's such a nuisance he's in jail.' She turned and whipped out of the room. Off to sort out more problems?

Maya blinked twice, trying to force some blood flow to her brain. She turned to open the filing cabinet, with her shiny, new key and took out the participants' files.

They'd been dumped in a pile, papers everywhere. On the front of each individual's file was written a diagnosis, in thick black Texta. Maya's stomach clenched. She hated people being reduced to a simple one-liner.

Lydia Buchanan (26years) 'Borderline Personality'
Eamon Rogers (44 years) 'Chronic Depression'
Sarah Ng (19 years) 'Complex PTSD'
Steve Harris (34 years) 'Schizophrenia'
Graham Davies (50 years) 'Depressed. Avoidant Personality'
Daniel Comstock (32 years) 'Narcissistic Personality'

She sighed and picked up Lydia's file. Shiny, beautiful, glittery Lydia. She'd sucked up most of the oxygen in group.

Lydia accumulated psychiatric diagnoses, like Kardashians amassed shoes. Borderline/emotionally unstable personality disorder, bipolar disorder type 2. Whatever was the most popular, in the moment. Every psychiatrist has their 'heart sink' patients and stunning women with an enormous range of diagnoses, were Maya's kryptonite.

She'd started on Eamon's file - chronic depression due to significant childhood trauma - when a knock sounded. Maya jumped and opened the door to Eamon. She smiled at him and invited him in.

She recognised a fellow people pleaser behind his grey, anonymous clothing. He'd give the best overview of the last few weeks, and was probably the most motivated to help. Maya was sick of the files already.

Eamon said 'I want to give you some background but it's hard to know where to begin.'

Maya waited. She knew you learnt more, when the person found their own way and wasn't led to information.

Eamon said, 'This's the first time I've ever tried anything like this retreat. I was nervous from the start and a bit overwhelmed by everyone's personality. Dr Ted was off-putting. He wanted to be adored by fabulous people, and I didn't make the grade.' Eamon sighed and slumped in his chair.

Maya asked, 'What did you think of Daniel?'

'He was an entitled bastard, constantly arguing with Dr Ted. It made the sessions tedious. He was the male version of Lydia, gorgeous looking, but self-centred and annoying'

'Can you describe what happened?'

'I don't know if anyone told you about Dr Ted's treatment. He's a big believer in psychedelics,' Eamon said, his right hand starting to shake and both knees jigging in sympathy. 'Part of the retreat involved driving to a remote station and taking psilocybin, magic mushroom powder, Dr Ted bought off the internet. I've tried everything and I was desperate to have a go at cutting edge treatment.'

'No, no one told me about that,' said Maya. She gritted her teeth to suppress her horror.

'We went out to Omar Station. Took a day to get used to our surroundings, then the second and third night, used psilocybin to have a trip.' Eamon blinked, gulped, looked at Maya. 'Everybody took the stuff, including Dr Ted. I thought that was wrong. Some of the experiences were pretty bizarre and frightening. I didn't see much of Daniel.'

Her nausea intensified and Maya's heart rate quickened. God, just what she needed, illegal drugs. She sweated despite the freezing air conditioner. What nightmare had she walked into?

Eamon's tic increased in intensity. 'I was told that Daniel argued with Dr Ted that night. Lydia's the one who overheard. Daniel could've died from an accidental overdose of the drug concoction we took. Or any of the group members could've killed him, but it seems bizarre to even consider it.'

Maya managed to pull herself together and said, 'Are you coping okay?' Focusing on Eamon's mental state was the right thing to do.

'I'm okay. I'm used to death. I lost both my parents in a car accident when I was very young. I barely knew Daniel and I certainly couldn't say that I liked him.'

Eamon and Maya stared at each other. Eamon's face was grey and drawn. Maya said, 'You look exhausted. Thank you for filling me in, but go and get some rest now.'

Maya sat and stared at the ceiling. Her head hurt. What the hell was she supposed to do with that? The whole treatment program directed by Dr Ted was farcical and non-professional. For God's sake he got drugs off the damn internet and took them himself.

With her supervisor gone, Dr Ted was now in charge of her placement. She didn't know what to do. There was no one she could contact in Perth. Her bloody mobile didn't work here anyway. She was isolated.

Steve wandered through the door, looking distracted, in a hippy dippy manner. He was freshly showered, with green apple shampoo. The same one Maya used as a child. A reassuring, warm, friendly scent.

Maya skimmed his file. He'd been diagnosed with borderline IQ, in his early school years, and with schizophrenia in his late teens. Poor man couldn't catch a break. His mother was determined to cure him of his illness, so kept sending him on treatment courses.

Maya enjoyed working with people who had a diagnosis of psychosis. They struck her as more real and down-to earth than everyone else. At least in this situation her role was clear. Steve was unwell and had probably deteriorated with all the stress. God knows whether he'd taken psilocybin or not. He needed medication and reassurance.

Maya started the conversation. 'Hi Steve, would you like to talk to me?'

Steve sat down and slumped forward in his chair. 'Yes. I have a problem with voices. I can't think. I need some wafers to help me. I haven't slept much.'

'Are the voices trying to hurt you? Have you had any suicidal thoughts?' said Maya, in a low voice.

Steve looked her in the eye and said, 'No, nothing like that. They just won't shut up. They go on and on. It's annoying.'

'Did you use the magic mushrooms on Omar station?' said Maya, keeping her movements slow and relaxed.

'I'm not sure. I drank a lot of liquid. I was very confused why we were there. It got frightening by the third day,' Steve said, his eyes darting all over the room. 'I worry my parents will find out and be mad with me. Do you have to tell them?'

'Let's just sort it out together for now. I've got some olanzepine wafers and will start you on one 3 times a day. It's a medicine that will help you fight the voices. If you don't get some sleep let me know and we can change the dose,' said Maya. She opened her locked briefcase and shuffled through, to find a few medicine samples.

As she gave them to Steve, Maya said, 'Did you know Daniel well? Did you see anything on Omar Station that upset you?'

'I just wandered around on my own. It seems messed up in my head now. I didn't like Daniel but I'm not happy that he's dead,' said Steve, standing to leave, distracted. Maya smiled at him, wishing him well.

She was left in the creepy-white, group room pondering the whole grubby situation. It was clear to her that Dr Ted 'the Guru' had failed his clients miserably. Whether he was guilty of murder however, was less certain.

A sun-worn face poked around the door. Maya startled to see a broad, crinkly smile. She stopped her impulse to grab on to this person, like a raft on the Titanic.

'Hi I'm Jack Stevenson, the local senior sergeant and I'm in charge of this investigation. I hear that you're going to help us out.'

Maya's eyebrows shot up. She wasn't there to help the police. The skin on her neck bristled. 'My understanding's that I'm here to debrief Dr Ted's clients first and provide you with information second. My primary obligation is to look after the participants.' She avoided assertion unless she was fighting for clients.

Jack smiled and refused to bite back. 'Can we have a coffee together so we can discuss your boundaries with the clients and how we can work together? I know it's difficult but I really want the situation to be as comfortable as possible.'

Maya reddened, embarrassed by her initial reaction. She was not great with anger and tended to avoid the emotion. When she did react, she got it wrong, either over doing the anger into outright hostility or failing to make her point.

Jack was the dustiest person, Maya had ever seen. As if he'd crawled through a field of red dirt to get there. He was wearing the grey-green police uniform of the outback, but he'd mismatched his buttons. Like a 5-year-old failing to dress himself. He was chubby. Maya liked that in a man. Reminded her of her dads. He looked strong, physically confident and had unusual green eyes. Distracting.

Maya knew she was attractive in her own way, but she was very different. Unusually tall with long pale limbs, that she hated. She leaned forward when listening to others, paying close attention, but ended up looking like a giant question mark. She was very angular, all corners but no curves. She had long Titian red hair which was far too thick for the climate. She'd wound her hair into a French knot in an effort to stay cool. She couldn't appear more foreign in this environment, like a latent Boadicea who had lost her way.

Jack stared at her in silent appraisal. He was competent with spaces in the conversation. Impressive.

An awkwardness grew between them, as they waited each other out. Jack broke first. He smiled and moved to sit opposite Maya. 'I'm sure you've met Joy, the resident super mum.'

'Yes,' said Maya leaning back. 'She was the first person I met here.'

'Well, she's the one who suggested I team up with you,' said Jack. 'She thinks we're both struggling on our own and wants us to help each other out.'

Maya's eyes widened. 'Really? She barely knows me,'

'We've both been abandoned by our bosses,' said Jack. 'My boss can't help it. He had a fall and was airlifted to Perth. He'll be in hospital for at least a week.'

'Oh my God. How did she know all this?' said Maya.

"Who knows?' said Jack. 'She seems to know everything. Maybe she's psychic?'

'My bastard boss has gone on holidays to Europe for a month. Dr Ted's the only direct supervisor left for this placement. And he's in jail. I really am on my own,' said Maya, looking down and flipping through the papers on her lap. 'Is your boss going to be okay?

'Yeah, he'll be fine. But I'm stuck acting up as senior sergeant for this case,' said Jack. 'I need all the help I can get.'

'Isn't there anybody else at the station in Exmouth who can help?' said Maya.

'They've sent me out here with two constables, Mitch and Dave. They're city boys who've been disasters. They're always falling over themselves and breaking stuff,' said Jack sighing. 'I know this probably seems weird for a city girl, but in the bush, we're used to helping each other out in any way we can. We worry less about the hierarchy and rules.'

Maya's mind was blank. She stood to indicate Jack should leave. Her head hurt. She needed time to think about her response.

Jack followed her lead and stood as well. He said, 'Maybe we could eat outside together tonight? They've made room for us police officers to stay here. We want to avoid the long drive to Exmouth each day.'

Maya laughed. 'I couldn't believe it when I came. Hospital transport in a 4-wheel-drive. Driven in silence, by the grumpiest person, I've ever met. It took nearly 2 hours to get here, with the Yardie Creek Crossing,'

'Wait until it rains. If the creek floods you can get stuck and have to go the long way round. It'll take at least twice as long.' said Jack.

Silence. They were back to staring at each other. Jack jumped up, shook her hand, and left.

What the hell had happened here? What had she walked in to? Should she tie herself to Jack's lifeboat or not?

2

Maya stood at the window in her bedroom and stared at the bush alive with sound. Cicadas, bird songs, laughing kookaburras. Kangaroos wandered onto the grass around the house. The rich, red earth and olive-green scrub stretched to the horizon. Ancient, foreign, but maybe hostile? Like she'd been dropped on Mars. How the hell was she going to cope?

She watched the clouds gather. Dark and foreboding. The heat and humidity grew, until the clouds burst with heavy rain. The drops so large and heavy, they bounced in the dirt. Maya clenched her jaw. The change was violent.

Maya's body hurt. Nausea ebbed and flowed. Memories of her secret shame drifted into view. She buried it deep, wrapped in a tight shield, locked in a compartment in her unconscious. But it kept threatening to escape. Like a toothache, building in the background. If she thought about what'd happened, she'd cry.

A kangaroo and her joey wandered in front of her open window. Hopping along, taking their time, ignoring both Maya and the rain. That helped. She smiled.

Maya's busy mind obsessed over Sgt Jack's suggestion that they work together. The whole situation was disorientating. She was isolated and there were real threats. Daniel had died. Perhaps murdered? She needed to ally with someone.

But she said yes far too easily and got stuck with uncomfortable obligations, not wanting to cause waves. She was a people pleaser. Working with a police sergeant was a big step. The boundaries for her patients worried her. Should she agree or not?

Maya's salivary juices flooded her mouth, grabbing her attention. She smelled lemongrass, ginger and the rich scent of well-aged soy sauce. She followed her nose. Joy's masterpiece was calling.

Everyone arrived in the eating area early. Hungry, and maybe a bit lost?

There were four whole baked barramundis in the centre of the table and a series of salads, shiny red, green, orange. Doors to the covered veranda were opened. Enticing them outside to witness the forces of nature.

The veranda tables encouraged intimate, if uncomfortable, dining. Sgt Jack was sitting at one, trying to manoeuvre his knees under the badly designed, tiled top. Maya took her food and went to sit with him.

The constables, Mitch and Dave, were on the furthest table to Jack, whispering to each other and taking turns to glare at him. Jack's down turned mouth and glum expression, underlined his lack of enthusiasm for being the boss.

After dwelling on his proposition, Maya had a little speech prepared. She drew up to her maximum height and said, 'Sgt Jack I'm prepared to work with you, but only if it doesn't interfere with my primary responsibility towards my patients. I have to prioritise their mental health.'

'Great. Call me Jack,' he said smiling. 'We can stop each other from crashing around here, like idiots. I want to keep everyone well, but we can keep our eyes open and figure out what the hell happened.'

Maya began to eat. The barramundi melted in her mouth. She closed her eyes to focus on the flavourings.

'It's delicious, isn't it?' said Jack. 'Maybe we could get to know each other, while we eat, and focus on the case afterwards.'

Maya nodded, too busy enjoying the food to talk much.

Jack started. 'I'm Exmouth born and bred. I grew up running around town beach and snorkelling on the Reef. My childhood was super boring. I'm the third in a tribe of boys and my dad was the local cop.'

Maya's eyes widened. 'That sounds like the most amazing childhood.'

Jack smiled, then lowered his eyes. 'I want to let you know I have ADHD,' he said, fiddling with his buttons. 'You've probably already recognised it, but it's why I'm so keen to work with someone. It helps with the structure.'

Maya gazed at the chaos surrounding Jack and said, 'Thanks for letting me know. I'll help out where I can.'

'What about you? Where did you grow up?' said Jack, looking up.

Maya laughed. 'Country people have such a different perspective on life. No one would ask that in the city. They focus on what you do for a living. It's about money and power.'

'No one cares in the country. The richest people are the station owners, who come into town, red and dirty,' said Jack leaning towards her, and running his hands through his hair. Maya's heart sped up. Was she attracted to him? Did something about his dusty aura, so opposite to her, charm her?

'I've a different background,' said Maya. 'My mother passed away when I was a baby. I was adopted by my uncle, her brother, and his partner Peter. I call them my gay dads.'

'Jeez that is unusual. I've not met anyone raised by two dads,' said Jack.

'They were wonderful to me. They took me into their home and adored me. I was really lucky,' said Maya.

'I can see that. It's a gift to be loved by your parents,' said Jack. Maya caught his face dropping. What was that about?

'Peter's Kenyan. He's a black man, who wears traditional dress. He'd play with me and dance with me,' said Maya. 'And my uncle's a huge person, like an overgrown bear. Full of warmth and hugs. It was a happy household.'

'I can see you dancing, like an African tribeswoman. You'd be good at it,' said Jack laughing.

'I dare say, I was good dancer at the age of three. I could certainly twerk,' said Maya.

Loud voices attracted their attention. Lydia sat with Mitch and Dave. She said, in a theatrical whisper, 'She getting all his attention. I think he's attracted to her. He's neglecting the case.'

Maya couldn't hear the reply, but Mitch and Dave appeared engrossed in the conversation. She blushed and tried to hide her embarrassment.

Jack shrunk into his chair and scuffed his feet. His eyes darted around the area. 'I hate to say it but we should probably go and do some work.'

Jack and Maya went to the white group room, which they agreed could be their office, despite the squeaky, creepy, smelly chairs.

Jack said, 'Let me fill you on what has happened so far in. I became involved on the Sunday, when Lydia Buchanan called me on the phone. She lived in this area for a year when we were in high school, so we know each other a bit.'

Jack stood up and started pacing. Tense, too much energy. 'Dr Ted led them out to Omar Station. I don't know if anyone has told you, but he's a bit of a Guru. He believed in the healing powers of psilocybin and got them all high on a mixture of magic mushrooms, LSD, opioids and God knows what else.'

'I heard from Eamon. I was horrified,' said Maya, curling her legs in her chair, eyes wide. Like a cat.

'It's obviously illegal, but you have to wonder about his common sense, as he took this stuff too.' Jack's jigging increased. 'Daniel Comstock passed away some time early Sunday morning. We arrested Dr Ted immediately. You can't go around giving people concoctions of drugs, that you find on the dark web.'

Jack sat down looking Maya straight in the eye. 'We assumed it was a simple accidental overdose due to Dr Ted's mad brew of psychedelics. Unfortunately, we were wrong. The lab told me this afternoon, he was poisoned with strychnine. Where the hell he got that from, is beyond me?'

Maya's blood froze. That sick, queasy feeling in her stomach recurred. Maybe the creepy sense of doom was her unconscious saying something was wrong here, not guilty secrets pushing to escape. She tried to think what to say, but couldn't come up with anything.

'This means that we have a murderer in the group,' Jack said. 'Or Daniel took the strychnine himself. Or even a murderer came and found them on the Station.'

'Oh God, what the hell are we going to do? And we're isolated, no mobiles,' Maya said, her whole body starting to tremble. 'I'm responsible for Dr Ted's clients.'

'This's one of the strangest situations I've ever been in,' said Jack, reaching out to touch Maya's arm. 'I worry about everything too. The Homestead's isolated. If it floods, Yardie Creek crossing is vulnerable. I'm inexperienced, but need to figure out what happened. And I have trouble focusing and concentrating at the best of times. It's stupid, but these thoughts go round and round my head with no solution.'

Maya said, 'I can see why you want my help. But every part of me is screaming, run. Get the hell out of here.'

'I will help you leave if that's what you want, but I'm really hoping you stay and help me find out what happened,' said Jack.

Maya looked Jack, full in the face and thought for a moment. She had to choose. She wanted to run, but she wouldn't leave her job. People depended on her. She'd stay and try to help Jack figure it out. She nodded at him. 'I'll stay.'

Jack said, 'I think we're going to have to be upfront with the participants here. If nothing else they may need to be aware of protecting themselves. Dr Ted might be the murderer, but it's hard to understand his motivation. He loved running these retreats and really believed they help people. This situation will stop his work.'

'It seems even less likely that Daniel killed himself. So far everyone has described him as narcissistic, full of himself. No one has mentioned suicidal thinking,' said Maya, frowning.

'I want you to withhold the fact that Daniel died from strychnine poison? It's such an unusual way to kill, it could be useful in finding the perpetrator.'

Maya nodded. She was busy suppressing her strong instincts to scream. What had happened out there? She said, 'It could be anyone. All you'd need to go to Omar station is a good four-wheel-drive.'

Jack nodded and said, 'Yep, you're absolutely right. We're keeping an open mind but will be investigating everybody, except you of course.' He grinned. A weak attempt at humour?

Jack left to report to his bosses in Perth. Maya sat in silence trying to absorb the whirling changes. Strychnine for God's sake. Who would do that to a person? Where would they get that sort of poison?

Maya saw a floor plan of the Homestead in the filing cabinet and photos of the renovations undertaken. She decided to find her bearings in these surroundings. Maybe that'd help her sense of total disorientation and stop her feeling lost?

The Homestead was a strange mix of expensive renovations in the main rooms, and forgotten functional rooms hidden behind. It was shaped like a three-pronged fork. The offices, group room, kitchen and eating areas were in the head of the fork. These rooms were modernized. The improvements appeared excellent except for the creepy white room.

The central prong of the fork held Dr Ted's living quarters. Who knows what that was like? The North prong was occupied by male participants and the southern prong, female participants. In the female quarters everyone had their own room which was lockable. The bathroom area and two toilets were shared. These areas were functional but harked back to the 1950's. Unrenovated.

On her return to the female corridor, Maya was met by chaos. Lydia had locked herself in the bathroom. Sarah and Joy were banging on the door to get in.

Sarah was riled up. 'Lydia's so selfish. She's been in there for over an hour. She said she had to relax in a bath. But we need time to clean up too.'

Joy was calmer and focused. 'My main issue is making sure she's safe. Since the disaster with Daniel, I'm worried someone else will kill themselves.' She paused for a moment. 'Although that might prove Dr Ted's innocence.'

Maya gestured at them both to come away from the door and led them to her room. She could hear Lydia moving about in the bathroom. She wasn't dead.

Maya said, 'If banging on the door doesn't work, it's usually a good idea to withdraw attention. Let's give her 15 minutes and see if she comes out on her own.'

Maya turned towards Joy and asked, 'Do you really think that Daniel committed suicide?'

'Well dear, I'm not sure what happened. The only thing I know is that Dr Ted's a good man and would never hurt anybody,' said Joy. 'I guess it could've been an accident on the station.'

Sarah was listening through the crack in the door for any change in activity from the bathroom. She said, 'I think Daniel was the least likely person in the world to self-harm. He had an ego the size of an elephant.'

They heard Lydia come out from the bathroom and slam the door. Sarah was quick on her feet. She rushed into the bathroom and crashed the door closed.

Joy stared out the window. 'Sarah's right. Suicide does seem unlikely. We've been running retreats here for more than a decade. Dr Ted's been working with psychedelics for all of them. We had a few problems the first year but after that everything settled down. Murder's just so unlikely.'

'I guess it's up to the police to figure out the whole situation and what happened,' said Maya, sitting on the bed with a yawn.

'Yes.' said Joy, 'But they were so rude to Dr Ted and there really isn't any need.' She bustled out. Probably looking for more work to do. Some people were only happy when busy.

Maya sat on her bed trying to centre herself. She took some deep breaths. She'd been out of home living with friends for the last four years but right now she really missed her dads. She tried to imagine what they would say to her. They'd be horrified by the whole situation and want to spirit her away. She longed for the familiar nurturing and support.

She took out a tiny woven doll, with a shock of black woollen hair, out of her luggage. A worry doll. It'd belonged to her mother. She stroked the hair with her finger, trying to settle herself. The hidden secret that she didn't want to touch, ached in her gut.

Maya waited for sleep to come. Her busy mind, tried to settle on what she should do. She didn't have many options. She was stuck at the Homestead at least for the next week. It'd probably take that long to organise transport out anyway, even if she had her phone. She missed her phone. The distraction of technology. An itch she couldn't scratch.

Maya sat up and stared out the window. She heard the cicadas chirping in a chorus. The sheets were crisp, taunt and smelled freshly laundered. She liked the pillow, soft under her head. There was an old-fashioned clock on the small side table. Everyone she knew used their phones to tell the time. But here, out of mobile range, time went slower. Like the minutes on the clockface were dragging their feet.

She closed her eyes and began to review the day. The first person to come to mind was Graham. She could see him as if in front of her, fully dressed in black with a black cloud obscuring his face. Maya had the least interaction with him. She knew angry middle-aged men were at high risk of suicide, but she was scared of him. Could he be the murderer? She needed to read his file.

She liked Eamon, recognising a fellow people pleaser. He'd been helpful to her and to his fellow participants. Dressed in grey to blend into the background, he appeared well versed in the psychiatric system. Maya had the feeling, he'd be fine. But was he covering up a dark shadow?

Lydia in her bright colours, and energetic jangling movement, loved being the centre of attention. She was a survivor and could easily strip attention away from more vulnerable others. Was she capable of murdering someone?

Steve was an unwell man. Schizophrenia was a severe illness, but Maya was capable of caring for him. He would need her attention and she was happy to give it to him. He was likeable. But madness could lead to killing. Should she be more scared of him?

Lastly Sarah was at risk. Maya visualised this small, yet furious woman dressed in khaki green, physically tying herself in knots, willing herself to disappear. Fighting at shadows. Maya knew she would have to watch Sarah closely.

Maya let go, limbs spread like a starfish. She'd find a way to work it out. Perhaps she couldn't fix her own problems, but it helped to focus on the others.

3

Day 2 Post Death

Maya stumbled out of her room and into the eating area, the next morning. Her only thought was coffee. The large table laid with bright flowers in several vases. There was fresh fruit and yoghurt. Joy came through from the kitchen and asked if Maya wanted home-made blueberry pancakes.

Maya laughed. 'How on earth do you manage to get all of this done? You're like an earth mother packaged with an angel. That smell of coffee's intoxicating.'

Joy smiled. 'I've always loved cooking. Looking after people gives me such pleasure. Sit down with your coffee and I'll go and make your breakfast. I find that delicious food always makes everything feel better. It's healing in itself.'

As Maya ate, the heat of the day started to build, and her head throbbed. She decided to swim in the ocean. Cold water was the best solution to the humid weather. She'd been told that the Ningaloo reef formed a natural lagoon, two kilometres just south of the Homestead.

She covered her pale skin with sun lotion and copious cotton layers. Then grabbed a bike to transport her snorkelling gear. In the sweltering heat of the wet season, the biking was hard going. Her legs hurt and she started to sweat.

Arriving at the lagoon, Maya heart sank as Graham emerged from the waters, looking dark and angry. Her stomach gripped. The heat was messing with her brain. It was stupid, being on her own, with a murderer on the loose. It was far too easy to forget there was a killer

Graham moved in a rigid, robotic manner, warding off any approach. A dark energy surrounded him. But he spoke to her for the first time. 'There're three turtles sleeping in the seaweed about 150 m south-west from this point. They're usually active in the morning. I always come down early to see them.'

Maya blinked. That was the last thing she'd thought he'd say. He remained gruff and turned away, not keen on conversation. She was torn between treating him as a client and running in fear. 'Are you ok after what happened to Daniel?'

Graham's jaw clenched. 'I don't want to discuss any of this with you. Just leave me alone. I'll only talk to Dr Ted.'

Maya gripped her snorkel tightly, and watch him leave, with his jerky, mechanised movements. She started swimming in the direction of the turtles. One hundred and fifty meters was a long way. The further out she swam, the deeper the waters. But she was confident. The heat might be messing with her brain but she could swim well.

The first thing to grab her attention were the parrot fish chomping on the green blue coral. Crunch, crunch. She laughed out loud at the sound, drew back salt water and choked. She didn't expect them to be so loud.

A brown and white spotted groper, about one meter in length, was slowly spinning around minding its own business. She smiled at its huge, downturned mouth. One of Maya's dads would call her a grumpy, grumpy groper, when she was an irritable teenager. She wondered if he knew what he was saying?

There was a giant clam a mottled grey colour with an iridescent blue wavy opening. The coral fish were stunning colours, blue/orange, stripes/spots. It was a wonderland.

Before she realized how far she had swum, she saw the turtles. They were in a little group of grey/green, bushy sea grasses and had rammed their heads in the centre of the stems with their bottoms sticking out. As the ocean moved with the current, the turtle bottoms swayed back and forth. Maya's body undulated in unison, giving her a sense of peace and connection. SShe relaxed for the first time since she'd arrived. Maybe it'd be okay after all?

After her shower, Jack appeared dressed in his police uniform. Haphazard and disorderly. Maya smiled to herself, he must drive his bosses to distraction. He shuffled his feet, looking down. 'Can I ask you to help me out this morning? I'm interviewing both the female participants and I need an impartial witness to my propriety.'

Maya laughed. 'Don't tell me you are afraid of two young women.'

'You've no idea how dangerous my job can be. Two young females are far scarier than a whole battalion of mad, bad bikies,' said Jack grinning back.

They left together and came across Sarah. She'd been swimming laps on the sandy ocean beach, north of the homestead. Her body was less tense, not as curled in on herself. Her bathers were khaki. Maybe she shopped exclusively in Army surplus stores?

Maya took the lead and said, 'Is it possible for us to talk to you? We'll be speaking to everybody over today. There's information that has come to light and it's best that we give it to you individually.' Sarah stiffened and Maya lowered her voice to continue. 'I'll support and advocate for you. Sgt Jack will be asking the questions.'

To Maya's surprise, Sarah agreed to the interview, as soon as she'd showered. Maya had expected her to protest.

Jack led the way to the office Joy had opened for him. It was the mirror image position to the white cell where Maya was working. The personal office for Dr Ted. Male testosterone came with power round this place.

Maya's eyes widened when they opened the door. This office was colourful and well decorated, in complete contrast to the white group therapy room. There were wooden floors and exposed beams. The walls were a gentle green. Like walking into a forest. Tasteful. The art on the walls was modern, an explosion of colour. Pinks, purples and blues. All the framed photos were of landscapes. No pictures of Dr Ted or his family. Who knew why?

The desk and floor were covered in files, papers, journals and pens, suggesting a man addicted to chaos. Maya knew from her review of the case files that Dr Ted was a careless and casual note taker. Thankfully, at the beginning of each participant's file there was a clear typed summary outlining the patient history, hospital admissions, psychological treatments, diagnosis and medications. Maya needed all the help she could get. She sat in the soft auburn chair and sighed.

Sarah was an enigma. All her previous therapists agreed that she presented with symptoms of complex PTSD, despite the fact that she denied memories of abuse. She was raised in a volatile home; unknown father, drug addled mother and a procession of potentially abusive stepfathers.

Maya knew the importance of respecting the unconscious and not stomping around in someone's psyche to uncover the past. Certainly not under the current circumstances. Denial can be lifesaving.

Sarah was strong and seemed determined to keep going against the odds. Maya wasn't sure that treatment with psilocybin was sensible in these conditions, but she understood Sarah's courage to try a risky treatment to emerge from her past.

Sarah marched into the room. 'What do you want to tell me?' Loud and officious.

Jack jumped, perhaps nervous of offending? 'We've just been told by the Medical Examiner that Daniel's death wasn't accidental, he was murdered or committed suicide.'

Sarah absorbed this information Her eyes faded. She seemed to bury it deep, maybe to examine later? She sat and physically shrunk back into the chair, a tight ball of dark, angry clothing.

Jack continued. 'We wanted to get more information from everybody who was present on Omar Station where Daniel died. Can you tell us about your experiences over those three days?'

Maya smiled to herself at his wariness. She wondered if Sarah ever recognized her own power.

Sarah mumbled into her chest. Maya strained to hear. 'I hated Dr Ted and everybody in the whole group. I'd come to the retreat to try psychedelic treatment. We went out in the desert, and slept in swags. It was a bizarre experience. I really hadn't thought it through.'

She rocked back and forth. 'I had one hell of a trip, but that involved bad, as well as good. At times I thought I was flying. Thank God there were no high-rise buildings because I understand how people jump off. Other times it was like I was being attacked and I was fighting ghosts in the red dust.'

She looked straight at Jack. 'To be honest, it's a miracle no one else died. The whole thing was so chaotic. Dr Ted was irresponsible and stupid. By the end he'd totally lost control.'

Sarah clenched her fists and bashed them against her legs. 'I saw Daniel many times during the night. He spent hours lying on top of his swag laughing hysterically at the stars. He told me it was the greatest fucking experience he'd ever had. But this changed by about 2 AM. He vomited behind the portable loos and said he thought he was going to die. I ran off to get Dr Ted but became so distracted by the starlight I just forgot about it.'

They all jumped when Jack's satellite phone rang, calling him out of the room. Maya decided to take the opportunity to find out more about Sarah.

Maya said, 'How did you originally get involved with this retreat?'

Sarah leaned back in her chair and unclenched her fists. 'I've been in and out of private hospitals for many years. I'm just sick of being a revolving door patient. I found out about Dr Ted on the Internet. There were group chat rooms talking about new treatments and I got hooked by the idea of trying psychedelics.'

Maya said, 'I'd expect it to be quite expensive. How did you manage to afford staying here?'

'Everyone has private health insurance which covers most of the retreat. The psychedelic treatment was extra. Dr Ted got the stuff off the internet, but it's all readily available and not that pricey.'

'Are you okay? It must've been frightening waking up to a friend's death,' said Maya.

'I was terrified. Lydia was hysterical, running around screaming. Dr Ted was asleep and we couldn't raise him. I worried he was in a coma.' Tears came to Sarah's eyes. 'No one could remember how to do CPR and Daniel had vomited everywhere making it even worse. He was rigid, his muscles so tense. The whole thing was a nightmare.'

Sarah let out a huge sigh and slumped in her chair. 'Can I go? I'm exhausted.'

Maya nodded. Sarah had exhausted herself. Jack and Sarah passed each other in the doorway, with no comment.

Jack's words tumbled over each other in a rush to get out. 'I've been speaking to the Omar station owner Gary. He said that strychnine is used on stations around here to control the wild dogs.' Jack's face was animated and he swept his arms about. 'The station owners put out traps for the dogs, but because of the distances they take weeks to check them. To stop the dogs dying slowly, they put strychnine on the jaws of the trap so that the animal licks the poison around the wound and dies quicker.'

Maya grimaced. 'That's just horrible.' Disgusted by the deliberate killing of these animals.

Jack said, 'It's by far the most likely source of the poison. The strychnine on the station is in powder-form, kept in a box in a locked gun cabinet. The keys are in the shed and easy to find. Anyone could've accessed it but Dr Ted's the one most likely to know about it.'

Jack stood to continue, as if in lecturer mode. 'According to Gary, the poison makes people become agitated and distressed. It affects the muscles of the body, causing spasms. The victim dies from respiratory failure or coma.'

Maya said, 'This matches the stories about Daniel's death but who in hell would do such a thing? Why would another human choose to torture someone in this manner? Or did he do this to himself? That's even more unbelievable.'

Jack shrugged his shoulders and sat back down. 'I can't understand it either. I doubt it was suicide. It sounds like a horrible death. No one had any inkling he was suicidal. There's no letter and the use of strychnine implies planning.' He leaned towards Maya. 'We have to treat it as murder. The planning involved and access to strychnine, point the finger at Dr Ted.'

They stared at each other in silence.

'Let's go and interview Lydia, maybe she can help.' said Jack

They found Lydia sitting outside, under the shade of a giant eucalyptus tree. The sun was glowing and she was lying on her back staring up at the branches moving against the deep blue sky. Maya smelled the pungent scent of marijuana. Lydia had stopped her incessant jiggling. She gave a half-hearted smile and said 'Medicinal use only.' At least the weed slowed her down a bit.

Jack sighed in frustration. 'We have important information so we're telling you all. Daniel didn't die from the combination of substances you took on the station. The Medical Examiner is very clear that Daniel was murdered or committed suicide.'

Lydia started to giggle almost uncontrollably. She gasped for air, hyperventilating. A panic attack. Very familiar territory for Maya, who moved forward to hold Lydia's hand, trying to ground her.

Maya said, 'Take some deep breaths. Count to 4 as you breathe in, hold for 4, breathe out for 4 and then hold for 4. I'll breathe with you so you can follow my lead.' Box breathing was taught to soldiers. Simple and effective. Easy to remember when panicked.

Lydia started to get some control and then began sobbing. 'I loved him. We'd really great sex. This whole thing's so fucked up.' Jack started at Lydia's mention of sexual intimacy. But Maya hesitated. Lydia was dramatic. Who knew the truth in what she said?

As Lydia calmed, Jack took over questioning. 'I know it's difficult but what can you remember about the night Daniel died.'

Lydia said, 'Everyone's been gossiping about the psychedelic treatment on the station. I was so angry with Dr Ted about what happened. We were there for three days but the whole thing was out of control. It's difficult to put it together. I'd taken LSD before, but I was the only one. It's important to control the environment so you have a good trip. Dr Ted didn't even try.'

Jack said 'Did you see Daniel over that last night?'

'Yes. We'd set up away from the campfire. Bloody Sarah followed us over. She always has to be the centre of attention. Daniel had a rotten time the night before, so I wanted to try and help him have a good trip. We both drank the concoction put together by Dr Ted. I don't really know what was in it, but Daniel had about twice as much as me.'

Jack interrupted. 'Was the mixture in one bowl and then ladled out to participants?'

'Yes. I thought that was strange,' said Lydia. 'Usually, the psilocybin comes as dried mushrooms and each individual dose is measured out specifically for the person. You know, body weight and size. Dr Ted had a powder which he just dumped in a big bowl, added lemonade, stirring it up. He then measured out individual glasses for everybody.'

'Initially Daniel was having a great time. We lay on the swags and watched the Milky Way together. I fell asleep. I was really tired from the night before. When I woke up, I could see Daniel arguing with Dr Ted.'

Jack said, 'Could you hear what they were arguing about?'

'No but it was pretty animated. They were both gesturing at each other and seemed really pissed off. I know that Daniel was having money problems. We paid extra for the psilocybin treatment. Daniel was finding it hard to keep up with the costs,' said Lydia. 'I think his private health insurer had threatened to pull the plug. Dr Ted was always tough on keeping up payments. He was terrified of not having enough money.'

Lydia picked at the burrs stuck to her leggings. 'Daniel was annoyed with him. He thought that Dr Ted was sleeping with Sarah, so she was getting treatment for free. I didn't believe Daniel at first.' She hesitated, looking sideways at Jack. 'I shouldn't say, but that night

I definitely saw Sarah and Dr Ted together, and they were pretty bloody close.'

Maya knew that Lydia could make things up, but she was losing her ability to be shocked by Dr Ted's behaviour. It seemed inevitable that he was having sex with a patient. He lacked any sort of moral compass to guide him.

Dr Ted was still in jail, but Maya dreaded meeting him when released. She worried about Sarah, who was already so confused regarding sexual intimacy from her childhood issues.

Maya stopped for a moment trying to earth herself in this beautiful landscape. The red dirt glistened with sweat. She looked at the gigantic eucalyptus, broad, tall, white trunk, rising in defiance against the harshness of the world around it. Powerful in its endurance.

Jack moved away, scowling and muttering. They'd got no useful information from Lydia. They left her under the tree, giggling on the ground.

A GONG SOUNDED from the veranda. Joy called out, 'Lunch'.

Jack and Maya walked in to a wall of angry faces. Even Lydia had dragged herself back from the tree. Sitting bolt upright like an infant bird expecting its feed.

Steve put his hand up. An overgrown hippy child, dressed in loose, orange cotton, mimicking a school room. He said, 'What do you want to tell us about Daniel's death?' They'd all been gossiping. No secrets here.

Jack took a deep breath and said, 'We've heard from the medical examiner that Daniel was murdered or deliberately committed suicide. It was not an accidental drug overdose.'

Graham glared at Jack. 'I knew it couldn't have been a drug overdose, because you can't die from too much psilocybin.'

Jack tensed, red in the face, and shouted, 'Did you read that on the Internet? None of you knew what you were taking. There were all sorts of things in the powder including LSD, MDMA, opioids and meth. It wasn't just psilocybin. You're lucky it didn't contain bleach.'

By now everybody was staring at Jack, who gestured wildly and kept going. 'I know there wasn't poison in the psilocybin mix, or more people would've been affected. But you were still all stupid.'

The participant's previous reactions to Daniel's death had been so superficial, that Maya considered the possibility nothing would affect them. But this news and Jack's fury did. They looked shocked. Serious. Eyebrows raised and wide-eyes.

Maya realised that all, bar Graham, had assumed Daniel died from an accidental overdose of the psilocybin mixture, no matter what was said. They'd been ignoring the possibility of murder. Jack's comments meant they simultaneously realised this really could be homicide.

The stunned silence started to become uncomfortable. Maya said, 'We still don't know what happened. He may have killed himself or the murderer may not be in this group. The station is accessible by four-wheel-drive. Did anybody see a car approach on the third evening?'

No one said anything. There were headshakes, but they seemed to have lost the power of speech.

Lydia put up her arm, and said, 'What did kill him?'

Jack said, 'We aren't going to release that information at the moment. We always keep certain details from the general public in any investigation. You need to stay at the Homestead to help us with our investigation. No one can leave to go back to Perth'

Lydia grumbled 'I bet she knows.' Pointing at Maya, 'I bet you're sleeping with her.'

Inwardly Maya sighed. Lydia appeared to believe everyone was having sex with each other. She said, 'Lydia this is inappropriate. This situation's already tense enough.'

Sarah was moving in a frantic, distressed manner. Rocking back and forth.

Maya knew she'd dissociated. That distant, unresponsive staring was unmistakable. But it was difficult to manage in this situation.

She spoke to Sarah in a low, gentle tone. 'Sarah they're working on getting us out of here. It'll probably take a few days but you'll be back home before you realise it.'

Maya was well trained in the basic rules of dissociation management. The person is unlikely to process verbal information but you can ground them using the five senses. Maya picked up a wrapped chocolate and made as much noise opening it as possible. She spoke about the taste of chocolate in a low clear voice. She made suggestions about the smell and taste, then placed the chocolate on the plate in front of Sarah. She then moved slowly to pour Sarah a peppermint tea again talking gently and working to re-orientate her.

Graham grimaced. 'I guess I'll be blamed for this disaster. Everyone always blames me. I'm going to my room and I don't want to talk to anyone.'

Eamon hadn't made a comment. He'd faded into the background and appeared to be processing the whole situation. Grey clothes, undercover. Maybe thinking how to be nice? He said, 'Suicide just doesn't make any sense. Daniel was the least suicidal person I've ever met. He was careless and clumsy with words but he had no desire to die. Even murder seems crazy. There really isn't anyone in this group who had any reason to murder him. Yes, he was annoying at times but it's a huge jump to plan to kill someone.'

Lydia said, 'I loved him. We had such a special relationship. We'd hooked up by the time we went to the station. I would've known if he'd been suicidal. But he wasn't.'

Eamon glared at her. 'Lydia, you'd say you were having sex with anyone if it made you the centre of attention.' Maya agreed with Eamon, she'd started to discount Lydia's boasts of secret knowledge regarding relationships. She was annoyed by Lydia's implications regarding Jack.

Steve had been staring into space the whole time, engrossed by the unseen voices around him. Maya moved towards him. She said 'Steve have you been taking the extra tablets?' Steve nodded. 'Why don't we give you an extra wafer now? It might help if you go back to your room. It'll be quieter.

Steve said, 'I'd like to be on my own. I want a sleep.'

Everyone got up from the table and wandered off. Their movements were automatic. Like 'group think'. Robotic. The meal spoiled. Maya sat staring into space. Her heart quickened and her breath shallow. Something had gone very wrong here. But the menace was unknown. How can you protect the innocent from a hidden, shadowy threat? Was it even possible?

4

Joy buzzed in from the kitchen and began stacking dishes. Maya jumped to her feet to help her. Practical, physical work always made Maya feel better. Helped her think. She loved cleaning, even enjoying the clinking of the cutlery and clattering of the plates.

Joy said, 'What a shame this happened on this retreat. It's such a disappointment for poor Dr Ted. He works so hard to make these groups a success.'

'Are you worried about the whole situation? It must be frightening hearing that Daniel might've been murdered,' said Maya moving down the table, setting things straight.

Joy laughed. 'I'm 63 years old and have lived a very strange life. Nothing surprises me anymore. I haven't been shocked about anything much for years. To be honest I don't even believe he was murdered. I know the participants and they're not killers.'

Maya followed Joy into the kitchen. The cooking area was Joy's domain. She had the latest appliances and cookware. Everything was well maintained and shiny clean. There was a wonderful smell of new potential for dinner. The rich yeasty dough. Fresh bread.

Maya knew she missed her mother. She'd died in labour, so Maya hadn't known her. But she liked to imagine talking to her, being loved and reassured.

Both her dads were loving and adored her. However, they were medical specialists and worked long hours. This meant that Maya spent time in after-school care or with nannies. The nannies were young girls who had no more skills with cooking, than either of her dads.

Maya grew up on the finest, healthiest takeaway the area could provide. But she'd never seen anyone cook from scratch. Even now, she shared a unit with three other doctors. They were working 50-hour weeks and rarely sat down together, let alone ate anything home-made.

Watching Joy was like being in a movie with Mrs Doubtfire. Joy uncovered a bowl and pulled out risen dough. She showed Maya how to knead, sending out yeasty, rich scents. The smell was intoxicating. It was relaxing pulling and pounding the soft, warm dough.

'What was your home life like growing up?' said Joy turning to stare at Maya.

Maya blinked in surprise. Her gaze was too intense. A bit awkward.

'I was lucky in many ways. I was adopted by my uncle and his partner after my mother died. My dads are wonderful, genuine people who really loved me,' said Maya.

'I've never met anybody who was raised by two dads.' said Joy.

'Well, I've never met anyone who cooked everything from scratch. My dads are both busy gynaecologists, so I never learnt homemade cooking,' said Maya, moving to load the dishes in a large space age dishwasher. It was fantastic. She'd love to have one at home.

Joy stopped moving. 'That must've been hard for you. A child needs a mother.'

'I was shy growing up and found it hard to make friends. My dads both had big personalities whereas I was quieter. Sometimes I felt alone,' said Maya, slowing down to look at Joy. She wasn't sure why she trusted Joy. Maybe she did need some nurturing?

'Did you ever get angry as a child?' said Joy, frowning. Maya flinched Perhaps Joy was trying some homespun psychotherapy on her?

'No, I'm the opposite type of person. I've always been a people pleaser,' said Maya. 'My dads used to criticise me for being way too nice. They're right. I'm not good at dealing with anger, which is a nuisance for a training psychiatrist.' Moving the cutlery. Keeping the conversation light and bright. Who needs extra psychotherapy when cleaning?

'I get angry and I always know what to do about it,' said Joy. Maya was surprised by her darker tone and turned to look at Joy. Joy's jaw was gritted and her eyes tense. The temperature in the kitchen dropped.

'I'm sorry to hear that. You must've suffered in the past. It's never easy living with sad memories,' said Maya.

There was an embarrassed silence. Maya tried to get the conversation back on track by asking, 'Do you have any children or grandchildren?'

Joy's face was unreadable, but she answered quickly. 'Yes, I have a boy called Samuel. I'm so proud of him. He's at university and is studying engineering. He's such a bright boy. I was a single mum but I brought him up right. He's always done me proud.' She returned to her work, busy, concentrating.

Maya followed her lead. She was absorbed in the dough when Joy's voice boomed in her ear. 'Would you like to come and see my vegetable gardens?'

Maya tensed but said, 'Yes. Definitely.'

The garden faced North East and was shaded from the afternoon sun. There was a large shade house covering an abundance of greenery, next to a small shed.

'This is huge. Someone has put in a lot of work,' said Maya.

'Yes dear, Nathan our station manager spent a lot of time helping me. He's been a real help to me growing food for the table,' said Joy.

Maya moved forward to examine the vegies.

'We use a no dig garden method,' said Joy puffing out her chest and smiling.

'I can't believe how much food you grow,' said Maya eyes wide touching the tiny growing cucumbers. The raised beds were over flowing with greenery. Tomatoes, capsicums, lettuces. Rich healthy colours in all corners. No wonder the food was good.

'Come and see the shed,' said Joy, leading the way. The shed was air-conditioned. Inside were the more delicate fruit and vegetables.

'Lydia showed a lot of interest at first, but when she discovered we don't grow marijuana, her enthusiasm faded,' said Joy, relaxed enough to joke.

'Where did you learn to do all of this? Did you grow up on a farm?' said Maya.

'Yes dear. I grew up on a farm at Three Springs. Wheat and sheep.' Joy was busying herself, collecting vegetables and fruit. 'My mother was an amazing woman. She was a fantastic cook.'

'I'd have to say that you have the same talent as your mother,' said Maya following Joy, imitating her and trying to help.

'Thank you dear, but my mother had five children and a good husband. Unfortunately, I was blessed with only one child,' said Joy.

Something changed in the atmosphere between them. Perhaps an unsaid secret? Maya hesitated for a moment, then said, 'Yes, Samuel. You seem very proud of him.'

'True enough dear,' said Joy who then bustled back to the kitchen followed by Maya. A duckling following the mother duck.

Joy started working on a complicated vegetable lasagne for dinner, requiring layers of thinly sliced sweet potato and pumpkin. She used a julienne for the vegetables, and showed Maya how use a pasta maker to make the lasagne sheets. Maya was gripped by the skills in feeding people.

Joy had calmed and relaxed with Maya. The rhythms of the kitchen would soothe anyone. Chop, chop, the squelch of the pasta. The smells of dough and fresh vegetables giving up their juices.

They were twisting the pasta into flat sheets. Maya found the procedure complicated, so she had to concentrate. The opportunity to talk faded.

After helping Joy, Maya decided to check up on Steve. He was vulnerable, in this uncertain situation. She found him in his room. Distressed, standing in the corner, talking to the voices in the ceiling. She gave him some extra medication and a cool glass of iced water.

'Do you like music or would you like to watch a DVD? It might help if you're distracted,' said Maya.

'I'm worried about my parents. They'll be so angry with me. I've disappointed them again. The voices keep shouting at me and are giving me a headache,' said Steve. He rocked on his feet, moving back and forth, back and forth, as if he could turn back time and fix the past

'Steve, would you like me to contact your parents and explain the situation?' said Maya. 'You did nothing wrong and I'd be very pleased to tell them that.'

Steve stopped swaying. He looked Maya full in the face. 'Yes, that's a good idea.'

'Would you like to go downstairs and have a cup of tea and a piece of cake with me, while I ring your mum and dad?' said Maya 'It's nice and fresh in the kitchen and dining room. We could see what Joy's doing and help her.'

Steve turned away from Maya. 'I don't like that woman,' he said. 'I think she's bad.'

Maya startled. Was Joy part of Steve's delusional system? And if that was true could his delusions have involved Daniel and led to violence?

Maya said, 'Has Joy upset you in some way?'

Steve lay down on his bed. 'Yes, I can hear her voice in my head a lot of the time. She goes on and on, even when she isn't here.'

Maya wondered if Joy reminded Steve of his mother. She needed to go through the files to read something of his family history.

'What about Daniel? Can you hear his voice?' said Maya.

'Not since he died, that would be stupid.' Steve turned his back to her, but Maya was left thinking.

Maya said, 'No worries, you stay here and I'll put on the soothing music. Take your time and come down when you feel ready'

Maya went back to the white office. She pulled Steve's file. Like all of Dr Ted's efforts, the file was disorganised and difficult to read.

She found a psychology report which discussed his family background. The psychologist described the parents as odd, but kind and gentle towards Steve. All this did not explain his anxiety regarding Joy. It was possible for anyone to be caught up in a person's delusional system. Maya was interested that Steve's illness might involve Joy, who appeared so caring. And what about Daniel's voice? Could Steve's illness explain the murder?

Maya made her way to the 'telephone room'. She found the sat phone easily. It was in a large yellow plastic case. On the outside was written, "Take outside, the tin roof interferes with reception" in large letters. The instructions for the call were on the phone via a purple sticky note.

Maya was terrible with technology, and sat phones made her anxious because of the expense of the call. But she had promised Steve, so pushed herself through.

She walked outside into the middle of the paddock. Red dust and prickly weeds. Thank God the heat was fading. She sweated, as she pushed the numbers instructed and was rewarded with a ring tone.

'Good afternoon, Mrs Harris speaking,' said the phone.

Maya said, 'Hi it's Dr Maya Donaldson ringing from Exmouth. I'm the new doctor looking after Steve.'

'Thank God you called. We've been worried about him,' said Mrs Harris. 'The police told us about the death and we don't know what to think.' Her voice sounded caring, if stilted.

'Steve's been very worried that you're angry with him,' said Maya, stamping her feet to kill the bull ants surrounding her.

'No not at all. We just want to know he's safe. Tell him we love him and will see him soon,' said Mrs Harris.

'Look I'm on a sat phone so we don't have much time, but is there anything I need to know about Steve,' said Maya. She needed to get as much information as possible.

Mrs Harris said, 'I think we've been worried about him because Steve used to be violent when he first got ill about 15 years ago. He was using drugs at the time. Self-medicating to get rid of the voices.' Her words tumbled over themselves. 'He's only been physical with me and my husband. I hate to think he could hurt someone but his illness is so unpredictable.'

'I understand why you're worried. The murder didn't involve a physical attack. There was planning involved. Do you think that Steve is capable of that?' said Maya.

'Probably not, but I was especially worried when I heard about the psychedelics. Everyone seemed to know about this treatment apart from me and my family. Steve signed the consent form but he'd sign anything you put in front of him,' said Mrs Harris, her voice breathless.

'I understand your concern and I'll keep a special eye on Steve. It's not clear to me whether he took psychedelics or whether he's stressed by everything else,' said Maya.

Maya was left standing in the field thinking. What the hell had happened here? Who'd give psychedelics to a vulnerable person with schizophrenia? This place was crazy. At least she could give Steve reassurance that his parents weren't mad with him.

Maya was tired and numb. The evening meal passed quickly. She went to her room, and sat on her bed in her blue cotton pyjama shorts and shirt. Neat and tidy. Stomach full of vegetable lasagne and fresh bread.

She sighed. Who the hell went to bed at 9pm? Her brain wouldn't stop. Staring at the blank white wall. Frustrated and bored.

Soft, padding footsteps stopped outside her room. There was a tentative knock.

She opened the door despite her clothing and peered out. She saw Lydia in a short, hot pink nightie and Sarah in grey-green shorts and T-shirt. Nothing in Maya's training had prepared her for managing boundaries when she and her clients were in pyjamas.

'Do you want to come and see the puppies?' said Lydia grinning.

Maya hesitated. That was a temptation.

'Dr Ted has a therapy dog on site,' said Lydia, 'Her name's Lucy.'

'Yes, and she's had two puppies,' said Sarah, over the top of Lydia.

'They're really cute and so much fun.' Sarah was relaxed. Smiling even. A complete change.

The thought of a newborn, puppy smell, hooked Maya. She jumped at the chance. 'Of course, I want to. What sort of dog is she?'

'They're kelpies out here. Working dogs. But Lucy's job is to make us feel better,' said Lydia laughing.

The dogs were on the veranda with Graham standing by. Dressed head to toe in black. Strange to see him cuddling puppies.

The veranda was lit with bright lights. Dazzling. Like they were putting on a stage production for the kangaroos. The three tables pushed to the side and chairs sprawled everywhere. Sarah took the couch and everyone else perched on the iron chairs. Cold and uncomfortable. The person who'd furnished this place was a mad sadist.

Graham looked gruff and stared at the ground. He said, 'The puppies need socialisation.' He was petting Lucy, and passed Maya one of the puppies. 'This is the boy pup. The other's a girl.'

The puppy smelled like cinnamon, caramel and sugar rolled up in one warm ball of chocolate, brown fur. He licked her palm. Maya laughed. The touch ticklish, gentle and soft.

Aware she was in her pyjamas in front of all these people, Maya just let go. Thank God she'd invested in well-covered sleepwear. The scent of the puppies brought new life and hopefulness. It was fun.

'Where are Eamon and Steve? The puppies could help them both,' said Maya. Everyone else was there, laughing and relaxed.

Lydia, holding the other puppy, said, 'Steve had a bad experience with dogs as a child. He was bitten when he was seven years old and ended up in hospital.'

Graham frowned. 'And Eamon doesn't like dogs. I can't trust anyone who doesn't like animals.'

'Maybe he just had a bad experience and doesn't want to talk about it,' said Sarah, curled up on the outdoor couch.

Lydia said, 'I don't think so. We've all been taking turns to look after the puppies while Dr Ted's in prison but Eamon won't help. Graham's right, you can't trust a person who doesn't like dogs.'

Maya didn't care for the narkiness of Lydia's opinion. But she was in puppy heaven, so didn't challenge her. She said, 'I'd love to take a turn looking after them.'

Graham hesitated. 'Okay. I'm the one who's organising the care. I'll put you on the list and take you through the routine.' His voice was tight but this was the most he'd ever said to Maya. Maybe a connection? But did she want one? Was it safe?

'They've a closed-in area that's fenced around the back of the property,' said Sarah. 'I worried about the heat, but Dr Ted says they have to get used to it if they're going to be working dogs.'

Eamon opened the veranda door to come outside. He saw the puppies and his face darkened. He gritted his teeth and turned away.

How could someone hate puppies that much? What was wrong with him?

'It's pretty easy to care for them. They're still with their mum who does most of their care. You fill up their water bowls in the morning and give them their puppy food. The biggest risk's dehydration if they run out of water.' Graham smiled to himself, as if warming at the memory of the routine. The first emotion he had shown other than hostility.

'The most fun bit's socialising them. Dr Ted likes them to have at least an hour with people per day,' said Lydia, playing with the other puppy.

'If we had music and wine, it would be like a party,' said Sarah from her couch-throne.

Graham frowned. 'Dr Ted keeps this Homestead dry. He's totally against alcohol.' An acolyte of his adored Dr Ted.

'But he's not against psychedelics,' said Lydia, turning towards Maya, 'Do you have the key to the drug cabinet?'

'Absolutely no way,' said Maya, tensing her jaw. 'The police have taken all the psychedelics and psychostimulants. I'd never have agreed anyway.'

Maya focused back on the puppy but some of the joy was taken from the situation. She wasn't their friend. She was there to do a job.

Jack peered through the door. He smiled at Maya and came outside.

Lydia sat up straight and started moving her arms widely. 'Jack we were just discussing the fact that Eamon doesn't like puppies. Do you think that makes him a murderer?'

Maya was struck by the thought that Lydia appeared attracted to Jack. Maybe she was attracted to all men in general? Thirsting for approval?

Jack sighed and rolled his eyes, not answering the question.

'I think Eamon's just sad,' said Sarah. 'He lost both his parents when he was seven years old. He was brought up in foster care. He would've never had a puppy.' She sighed and closed her eyes. Perhaps thinking about her own experiences?

'Did you have a dog, Lydia?' said Jack.

'Yes. We had a Jack Russell cross called Winks who was my best friend,' said Lydia, grinning. 'She had so much energy and was always up for a good play.'

'I had a golden retriever called Lila as a boy,' said Graham.

Maya turned to look at him immediately. She was stunned. He'd offered private information. Graham glared at the ground

Maya was out of kilter in this situation, trying to walk the tightrope between professional distance and the friendship being stuck in a strange situation together. She remembered her childhood Labrador, Fred. Loyal and loving. She'd been very lucky.

'I don't like the bigger dogs,' said Sarah from her royal seat. 'But these puppies are amazing. Best antidepressant ever.'

Graham stood to collect the puppies. 'Well, it's their bedtime now and their mum needs a rest. Maya, would you like to learn the routine?'

'Yes, that'd be great,' said Maya.

The heat abated with the sunset and there was a pleasant breeze. The set up with the puppies was easy to learn. Graham didn't speak but showed the routine with gestures. Shut off and irritable again. Graham and Maya returned.

It was pleasant lolling over the chairs and couches on the

veranda, despite the hard, iron frames. 'I'll never forgive my mother for putting Winks down,' said Lydia in a low voice.

'Oh God Lydia, you were so spoiled,' said Sarah arcing up. 'You were lucky to have a dog. I bet she was put down due to old age.'

'No, she wasn't. She was old but they could've treated the cancer. She didn't have to go,' said Lydia.

'Well, you're not a child now. Grown-ups understand that the pain and suffering for an older dog in cancer treatment can be intolerable. Your mum made the right decision,' said Graham. His voice heavy and tight.

'People don't like you because you're selfish,' said Sarah glaring at Lydia.

Maya intervened. 'You can't tell another person's pain or suffering. It's like the old proverb. Don't judge another until you walk a mile in their shoes.'

'Well, I think that some people choose to be sick to get attention,' said Sarah, glowering in Lydia's direction.

'Mental illness is a private journey. I don't believe that anyone chooses this path only to draw attention to themselves,' said Maya. 'I've seen all sorts of suffering. We're not here to judge anybody.'

Lydia said nothing. She looked at the ground. Shoulders slumped, turned inward. Maya wanted to bring back the antidepressant puppies.

The silence was awkward. Jack said, 'Have any of you found out something useful about Daniel's death?'

'You should be telling us. Not the other way around,' said Graham scowling at him.

'You know each other and have been hanging around with nothing to do. You must've thought of something,' said Jack, swinging back on the chair legs and rocking.

'The only thing I know for sure is that Dr Ted had nothing to do with it,' said Graham slumped forward.

'If you say that, it means one of us is a murderer,' said Lydia projecting her voice more than necessary.

'Why couldn't someone have come to the campsite under the

cover of darkness to murder him?' said Graham. 'Who knows who he annoyed?'

'The thing that strikes me the most, is that none of us really knew Daniel,' said Sarah. Maya smiled. When not dissociated, Sarah was perceptive. Clever.

'I knew him. We were lovers,' said Lydia, clinging to the centre stage.

'Then tell me one thing about his family,' said Sarah. 'I've spent weeks in therapy with Daniel, but I know nothing about his background. That's just weird.'

'She's right. I could tell anyone about Sarah and Lydia's families, but I know nothing about Daniel. He only ever talked about himself,' said Graham. 'I thought it was the narcissism.'

'Come to mention it, I don't know much about you either, Graham,' said Lydia.

Graham's face reddened and he clenched his jaw. He stood up and went back into the house, slamming the door.

Stunned silence. The cricket chirping escalated as if they were the chorus in a Greek tragedy. Gossiping about the human drama in front of them.

A man appeared out of the shadows on the west side of the property. Maya jumped. So quick and silent. Jack called out. 'Hey Nathan. Great to see ya."

Nathan smiled and approached the light. He was dressed in jeans and a T shirt. Dusty with a slouch hat and dark complexion. A First Nation's man. Lydia puffed out her cheeks and sat up tall in her skimpy nightie, staring at him. Thrusting her chest forward.

Nathan backed away from her and moved to sit with Jack. He said, 'Hey Jack. I heard you might be snooping around up here.'

Jack turned to Maya and said, 'Nathan's an old mate. We went to school together.'

'Yeah. He was crap at it. Just couldn't sit still,' said Nathan, laughing, a real warmth in his voice.

Maya smiled and said, 'Hi. Nice to meet you.'

'Nathan lives on site and manages this property for Dr Ted,' said Jack.

Lydia leaned forward, playing with her hair, and said, 'It's 150 acres of prime bush land. Dr Ted isn't practical. Nathan knows everything about the land. He's amazing.'

Jack rolled his eyes and Nathan looked at his feet. Scuffed his shoes.

Nathan said, 'Do any of you lot, wanna go fishing tomorrow morning? We'll be leaving around 5 AM. It'll be an early morning but you'll be back in time for work.'

'I'll ask around and let you know. But put me down as a yes,' said Jack.

'I'd like to come too,' said Maya. She wasn't great in the mornings but she'd partnered up with Jack and was sticking with him no matter what. She knew he had ADHD, so it might be a wild ride. The thought of the creepy, white room without Jack, in a house full of potential murderers, was awful.

'Me too. It'd be a privilege,' said Lydia preening. She turned to Maya. 'Nathan's one of the Yinigudura clan. He has a link to the land going back more than 30,000 years.'

Maya sighed. It was like listening to a school presentation. Lydia was exhausting.

'Yeh but I grew up in town. My dad's a truck driver and my mum's the school librarian. I had the most middle-class life you could imagine,' said Nathan, now glaring at Lydia.

'Wanna beer? There's only lite of course. Bloody Dr Ted hates alcohol,' said Jack pulling a face. He moved his chair to further block Lydia's view of Nathan, 'Pull up a pew.'

Lydia scowled, sending daggers towards Jack.

'Are you looking into the death of that bloke on Omar Station?' said Nathan.

'Yeah,' said Jack. 'But don't worry. We don't think that it isn't any of your mob.'

'Black man's paranoia. We worry you lot will try to pin everything on us,' said Nathan looking straight at Jack, not laughing. Maya was struck by how difficult it could be to grow up indigenous in the Australian country.

'This is a weird one. But we don't think that your mob are involved,' said Jack staring back, face open. Boundaries established, the men sipped their beer in companionable silence.

Lydia jiggled and jangled but didn't seem to have anything to say. Sarah looked at the floor. Maya sat as if in suspended animation. Watching from the outside in. Not sure what to say or do. Trying not to squirm on the uncomfortable chair.

'We're planning on going out to Omar Station over the next few days. Are there any of your family out there?' said Jack.

'Yup. Auntie Nell helps out with the children sometimes and Jimmy's the station manager,' said Nathan.

'Yeah. I remember Jimmy. He's a top bloke,' said Jack.

Lydia stood up and Sarah copied her. Lydia said, 'I'm off to bed. I'm tired.' Glowering. Sarah said nothing but followed Lydia.

Maya moved to leave but Jack grabbed her arm. He leaned towards Nathan and said, in a low, quiet voice, 'I'm glad they've gone. I wanted to ask you if you'd heard any rumours. We're pretty sure it was murder. You can trust Maya here.'

'There're always rumours about this place. Attracts some strange people. And they do weird things. Lots of gossip,' said Nathan. 'We heard you'd arrested Dr Ted.'

'Yeah, we did, but we need more evidence to hold him. Anyway, it's not making sense that Dr Ted's the murderer,' said Jack. 'To tell the truth I don't have any idea what happened at the moment.'

'No one seems to know what happened to the dead bloke,' said Nathan.

'You're right. I haven't got much information out of anyone here. Hopefully tomorrow when we're fishing, we can have a more casual chat.' Jack turned to Maya. 'I often get better information when I'm just hanging around with people rather than formal interviews.'

'That Lydia's a handful. She'd try to crack on to anything that moved,' said Nathan, shrugging his shoulders. 'But I guess that doesn't make her a murderer.'

'Yeah, I'd give her a wide berth if I were you. Way too much trouble,' said Jack. 'Do you remember her from school? She was only there for a year.'

'You betch ya. You don't need to warn me. I remember,' said Nathan.

They both went quiet and sat there staring out to the horizon.

'I'm tired,' said Maya. 'I'm going to turn in.' It was a lot to process. She wanted time to herself, to wind down and centre.

5

Day 3 Post Death

Dawn was not a time of day, familiar to Maya. She was a night owl. A lot more comfortable with midnight, rather than 5 AM. Maya scowled at the world as it lightened. The golden pink colours of the early day peeped through the clouds but Maya was far too grumpy to appreciate them.

Maya was determined to hold it together, going on her first fishing adventure. Her stomach had other plans, twisting and turning. She took slow deep breaths hoping to settle. Jack was her lifeboat in this strange world of murder. She was sticking with him, no matter where he led her.

The fisherfolk met in the kitchen, lured by hot coffee. The smell drifted straight into Maya's heart, giving her hope for survival. She liked her coffee straight black. Throwing it down her gullet, like an American cowboy swilling whiskey. The taste bitter, yet sweet. The warm liquid spread throughout her body, invigorating her.

'Who's coming?' said Nathan, peaking through the flywire with a beaming smile. How the end could anyone be cheerful at this hour?

'Just this lot,' said Jack, frowning like every decent person should at this time. 'Sarah and Steve complained of seasickness. Graham glared at me. I don't think he likes people.'

The boat ramp was a 5-minute drive. Nathan and Jack hitched up the large aluminium dingy, while Maya, Eamon and Lydia hopped into the car.

The ramp was an unlikely piece of engineering. Someone cobbled together rocks, discarded bricks and chipped pieces of concrete. They'd fashioned a path from the wet sand into the sea pointing like an arrow. Maybe thinking positive would get them out there?

Maya said, 'You'd need the most stunning sense of optimism to believe that'd work as a ramp. It's full of ruts and edges.'

'It's pointing straight out to sea. Couldn't be more encouraging,' said Jack grinning. He'd perked up after multiple cups of coffee.

Nathan laughed. 'You only believe it'll work because you've seen me do it.'

Maya, Eamon and Sarah stood on the beach. Jack rolled his shorts up as high as possible, and waded into the water along the ramp, wobbling with care to avoid a fall on the rough surfaces. Nathan drove the trailer back and forth, making bunny hops in reverse. Jack pulled on the rope from the boat, trying to shift it into the water.

Everything looked hopeless until the trailer let go with a jerk. Jack stumbled back and the boat flew into the water. The watchers cheered and clapped.

Jack laughed. 'You lot have to get wet. You have to wade out to me. We can't come in closer.'

Despite the ungodly hour, the land was heating up. Maya rolled up her pants and plunged into the cool waters. The others were wearing shorts but she'd entombed herself in linen. Pale skin was annoying.

It was trickier getting in the boat then she'd anticipated. She laid along the aluminium side and rolled as if she were a sausage. Embarrassing. The others followed. Eamon struggled more than she did. Like trying to beach a small whale.

Maya tasted the clean salt water and freshness on the breeze. A misting fan for her personal use. The sun was warm and welcoming, rather than the fiery beast it grew into as the day passed. Life was looking up.

Nathan leapt in the boat, in the most athletic, competent fashion. He appeared half man, half sea-god. His limbs long and rangy. Arms hanging loosely. Muscles relaxed in the sun. Moving with poise, like he was built to stand on a rocking ship.

Nathan grinned. 'Great day for fishing. The water's flat. The weather's perfect so we're going to go on the outer reef.'

'Fantastic,' said Lydia. 'The fishing's so much better out there.' She formed a cushion from her towel on the bench. She smiled to herself taking a deep breath of the salty sea air. Maya noted that she'd calmed overnight. Her excessive behaviours towards Nathan were gone.

Eamon took the opposite approach. He clutched at the side of the boat with white knuckles and wide eyes. Taking short, breathy gasps of air. He'd make himself faint if he kept it up.

Nathan moved back to control the motor, and set off. The boat flew along the surface. Planing, Nathan told them. Skimming the surface like a thrown stone. The bottom of the boat bumped on the ocean, like it was having hiccups. Maya grinned. She was having fun.

The trip was short, maybe 30 minutes. Even Maya in her ignorance, could see they had reached the open ocean. The colour of the water changed to a deep blue- green.

'Okay,' said Nathan standing, balanced on the waves, 'we're going to drift with the swell. Bait up your rigs, then drop your line. Don't cast or we're going to get tangled. It's about 40 m to the bottom here. Good luck.'

Lydia and Jack hustled forward. Eager to begin fishing. Eamon eyes glazed over. Not sure how to proceed. Nathan slowed down so he could mimic his actions. Maya followed along.

Maya dropped her line and held her breath. The fishing line bounced along the seabed. She felt the nibbles of fish on her bait. Then a tug, strong and purposeful. The fishing rod bent in half. Jack shouted, 'Pull, Maya, pull.' She jerked back on the rod and started to wind.

It was hard work. Her muscles burned. Everyone was shouting now. 'Colour', 'I see red', 'quick you'll lose it'. They all had a bloody opinion.

Nathan was quieter and a lot more help. He didn't yell at her. He moved to grab the line and used a net to pull the largest fish Maya had seen into the boat. It was a vibrant orangey-red colour and a circular shape like a dinner plate. It flopped about on the floor of the boat. Nathan picked it up, pulled out the hook and knifed the gills. It was over in seconds.

Jack grabbed Maya's arm and said, 'You caught a red Emperor. It's the best fish we have up here. It's delicious.'

Everyone was grinning at her. Nathan said, 'It's about 60 cm, a real beauty. Lines down. This's a hotspot. Let's get another one.'

Maya leaned back against the cool aluminium of the boat. She was exhausted by the effort. The dingy rocked with the swell. Stomach acid rose in her mouth. Her throat burned.

'Lift your head and look at the horizon.' said Jack leaning towards her, 'You look green about the gills.'

Nathan passed her a wrapped sweet, 'Suck on this ginger lolly and sip water slowly. It'll help'

Maya took slow, deep breaths and the queasiness settled. She watched the others.

Lydia sighed multiple times and used large sweeping arm gestures. It came across as aggressive. Maybe sending a message to the others or just angry with the fish?

Nathan moved in silence. His balance suggested a trained athlete. Perhaps he was a swimmer?

Eamon, clunky and clumsy, stumbled about making a mess, with Nathan gliding behind him cleaning up. Eamon was uncomfortable in his own skin.

Jack was efficient. He liked his food and was competent at getting it. His line went in and out, in and out. It jagged and he yelled, 'I'm on.'

Everyone stopped to watch the drama. Jack stood, secured the rod to his left side and wound the spinner, like a demon. He appeared strong and capable on the boat. He knew what he was doing.

'Colour,' said Lydia.

Nathan leaned over and scooped up another large fish.

'Ooh a blue bone, my favourite fish,' said Lydia, leaning forward almost in the water.

Jack's taut face cracked into a grin. He leaned towards Maya. 'You have to eat the blue bone fresh. It's delicious. We've had a few here. Joy'll be thrilled.'

Maya smiled at him. 'Sounds like a real treat. She's a great cook.'

Lydia returned to fishing with renewed vigour. Her line bent and she screamed, 'I'm on. I'm on.' She thrashed all her limbs as she stood to bring in the fish. Nathan moved to balance her chaotic swings and stood ready to grab her, if she fell.

She took a lot longer than Jack, but another fish tossed onto the floor of the boat. This fish was grey, with occasional bright blue stripes, and a prominent forehead. Lydia said, 'A Northwest snapper.' She glared at Maya. 'Pretty good but not as good as a red Emperor.'

Nathan sat down and looked at the group. 'We've got three large fish. As much as we can eat in the next couple of days. I don't want to take more than we need.

'Yes,' said Lydia, staring at him and nodding. 'We need to respect the cycles of nature.' She was over the top.

Jack cut her short and said, 'Fair enough. This's an excellent feed. Does anyone want a cheese sandwich as a snack?'

Maya and Eamon paled. Nathan passed them both another ginger lolly. 'Just suck on these, breathe slowly and look towards the horizon.'

Maya smiled. 'I can't believe how many fish we've caught in such a short time.'

'This area's not fished out like back in Perth. It's precious and I want to keep it that way,' said Nathan.

'What's that?' said Eamon pointing to the North East. A black shadow was making its way towards the boat. Maya's heart sunk. Her first thought, shark. Gliding, sliding in the water. But its movements were slow, playful and smooth. Looking curious. Not aggressive. Just the same, its size was huge.

Nathan stood and pointed, 'Can you see the dark body with the large white spots? It's a whale shark.' No trouble balancing on the rocking boat.

Jack got up to look. 'Oh yes. It's a young one. About 6 m. Typical teenage male wandering off and getting into trouble.'

Maya's heart rate increased. She'd heard of these animals, mythical giants of the deep.

Lydia moved to stand but the dingy lurched sideways. 'For God sakes Lydia. Sit down you'll tip us over.' said Jack trying to balance the watercraft.

'Exmouth's famous for the whale sharks,' said Lydia rocking the boat even while sitting. 'It's why thousands of tourists descend on the town during the dry months. A bloody nightmare'

'Yes, but it's unusual to see them this close in. And it's so early for the season,' said Nathan. 'I think Jack's right. This one's young and curious.'

The whale shark swam the length of the boat. The comparative size emphasised the whale shark's hugeness in all directions.

'Once he passes you can jump in with goggles and follow him,' said Nathan. 'Keep a 2m boundary around so you don't scare him.'.

'Is it safe? You said it's a whale shark. What's the shark bit mean?' said Eamon, voice shaky and high pitched.

Nathan laughed. 'They eat plankton which are microscopic. They're very gentle. My mother told me that the islanders call them grandmother spirits They're kind, gentle and bring good fortune.'

'And you wouldn't be scared of a grandmother.' said Lydia, lunging for the facemasks.

Maya was thrilled. She'd heard of these amazing animals but never thought she'd have the chance to swim with one. Her hands trembled as she put on the mask.

The whale shark was dawdling. Taking his time. When he was metres past them, Nathan said, 'Slide off the edge of the dingy. Two at a time to keep us balanced. Don't splash or make big movements. It might scare him.'

Maya slid in the warm water. Fully dressed in her fishing clothes, apart from shoes. She put her face under and looked forward. The giant whale shark was swimming slowly. She started off and kept up.

They split into two groups either side of the tail. It was an incredible experience. The whale shark was large, and beautifully patterned. Swimming through enormous trenches of coral. Like a giant's wall garden. The proportions were staggering.

Maya heard a shout and looked up. Nathan brought the boat around and was waving his arm in a circle. He shouted, 'Time to come in. Let's leave the poor bastard alone.'

They swam back to the boat. Maya grabbed the side and tried to enter. As did everyone. The dingy lurched in chaos from the forces on each side. Despite his size, Jack was the only one who managed to board.

He and Nathan stayed low in the boat and reached out their hands to help the others. It was a demeaning situation. Jack physically pulled Maya out of the water and dragged her over the side as she cringed in embarrassment. But he was strong to lift her. Her stomach fluttered.

'Well, that was one of the most remarkable experiences of my life.' said Lydia, showing her typical flair for the dramatic.

'We were so lucky.' said Eamon glowing, 'He was huge.'

'They grow three times that length in adulthood,' said Nathan. 'But it's unusual to see them swimming so slowly. You were lucky you could keep up.'

Maya felt her face shining in the sun, and grinned into the warmth. She did feel blessed by the wandering spirit. However pathetic that might sound.

They leaned back in the dingy as Nathan took them back to shore.

The process of getting the boat back in the boat ramp, was easier than going out that morning. They stood in the water and helped Jack line the boat up with the trailer.

Maya went with Nathan to clean the fish. Away from the ramp, to rocks in the shallow water.

Nathan gestured to the surrounding audience of shrieking seagulls. He said, 'Your job is to protect the good fish we caught from this lot.'

Maya watched him open a green canvas tote filled with surgical-looking instruments. He began by scaling the fish. His movements were precise. He then gutted fish and threw the rejects to the seagull audience.

'I don't like waste,' said Nathan looking down and peering at her sideways.

'If we all thought like that, there'd be fewer problems in the world,' smiled Maya.

Back in the car, Jack said, 'It's only 9 AM. I feel like we've done a full day's work already.'

Eamon grinned and said, 'If we hurry back Joy will resuscitate us. Her breakfasts are legendary.'

True to form, Joy had the table laid. Pink, embroidered tablecloth with hydrangeas in a glass vase. She said, 'I'll whip up some scrambled eggs. The chooks have been laying a lot. And fresh toasted bread with butter.'

Maya sunk into the deep wooden pew that lined the table. Exhausted, but tingling from the excitement of the experience.

Her clothes and skin were salty and scratchy. She smelt the fish on her hands. Not unpleasant but foreign.

Jack was walking past and said, 'Wash your hands with toothpaste before you shower. It really shifts the fishy smell.'

Maya laughed. Jack came to sit next to her. She felt a tingle of shared energy. That sense of attraction. Was it mutual?

Everyone was starving and shoveled the food down their throats.

Jack said to Maya, 'Will you help me with the interviews after breakfast? I'd like to catch up with all the participants prior to Dr Ted's return. He's coming out on bail. It sounds like he'll be back today, if the bosses in Perth have it right. '

'OK I'll meet you in the white group room in half an hour,' said Maya.

She scrubbed her hands with toothpaste. It did work to get rid of the fish scent. She turned on the shower. It creaked and groaned, but the warm fingers of water massaged her whole body. Magical. She scraped off the sticky salt and sand, her own exfoliation treatment. Transporting her to luxury. She closed the experience by slathering on rich, silky cream. Heavenly.

Maya arrived early to the group room and moved around the furniture in an effort to soften the atmosphere.

Her attempts were not successful. The room fought back against her. Still giving off a ghoulish, funeral vibe. Perhaps because of the intense white walls. The smell of diesel in the background and the scent note of human sweat made the whole thing even more unpleasant. Her queasy stomach returned.

Jack arrived with Steve in tow, both fidgety and restless. He said, 'Steve and I know he's not well. We thought we'd record his interview while you're here to help. I've already got statements from him about the night Daniel died. We just want to know if he's got anything to add.'

Steve was dressed in pink/purple, cheesecloth shirt and trousers. Having a conversation with voices in the corner. He turned to smile at Maya. 'I like you. You make me feel safe.'

Maya smiled back. 'I like you too, Steve.' She sat down keeping her body language open and welcoming. Steve sat mimicking her.

'OK Steve do you want to tell us what happened the night of the murder?' said Jack keeping his voice low and steady.

'We went away camping for the weekend and Daniel died,' said Steve. Maya bit her tongue to stop from laughing. It was the perfect answer to Jack's question. Accurate but void of useful information.

Jack paused and looked at Maya, before rephrasing. 'That's true and I'm investigating his death. Did you see anything that might've been important or give us clues about what happened to him?'

'He looked awful when he died. All his muscles were stretched and tight. He was arching his back,' said Steve, closing his eyes and gritting his teeth.

'It must've been horrible for you. Did you see anyone behaving strangely?' said Maya leaning in, helping.

'The whole thing seemed strange to me. Everyone took drugs which is a bad idea. I've had trouble with drugs in the past and it's important not to start again,' said Steve. He was a practical, concrete thinker and had the gift of focusing on his most relevant issue.

'Did you see Daniel arguing with anyone?' said Jack, leading his witness but pushing for detail.

'Daniel argued with everybody all the time. He had opinions about everything and wouldn't stop talking,' said Steve. Another accurate but useless answer. Jack looked stuck.

Maya stepped in. 'Steve do you ever feel paranoid?'

'Yes,' said Steve.

'Can you tell me more about that?'

'Well, I worry people will hurt me. The voices talk about it a lot.'

'Did these thoughts ever involve Daniel?'

'Oh yes. He was always gossiping. Sometimes I heard him yelling at me when he wasn't around. The voices didn't like him, so neither did I.'

'Did you ever think of hurting him?'

'Of course. I think everyone thought about it.' Steve looked straight at Maya. 'But I didn't.'

'Do you know how he was killed?'

'It looked like evil spirits had entered him and twisted his soul. If I'd killed him, I would've stabbed him in the side like Jesus on the cross,' said Steve, starting to rock his body. 'I've had enough. Can I go now?'

Steve did look pale.

Jack's shoulders slumped. He looked at the floor and sighed. 'Thanks for your help, mate. You can go now.'

Maya smiled. 'You were terrific Steve. Thanks so much for helping us.'

Eamon was waiting in the hot corridor. He'd found himself a

plastic chair and was sitting ramrod straight, like an A grade student waiting for the headmaster.

Maya grinned at him. Her fellow people pleaser. He'd even combed his hair flat, and giving a '1930s shoeshine boy' vibe.

'Graham asked me to tell you that he can't come for an interview this morning. He has too many commitments,' said Eamon, his voice tight.

'That man's avoiding me,' said Jack, glaring at Eamon as if he were the source of the trouble.

Eamon cringed. His tremor started in his right hand but he covered it.

Jack said, 'I'm talking to everybody to see if you have anything to add to your original statements after Daniel died. Given that we think he was murdered, the stakes have risen. '

'I've gone over and over that night in my mind but I can't think of anything that might help you,' said Eamon. 'It was such an awful experience. Whenever I try to think logically about it, I get flashbacks of Daniel's face grimacing in death. It makes me feel sick.'

They sat still, staring at each other. Maya leaned forward and said, 'Does Sgt Jack know about Lydia's report that Dr Ted and Daniel were arguing.'

'Yes, I've told him everything I told you. There's no point keeping secrets. You're trying to help us,' said Eamon, shoulders shrugged, staring at the floor.

'It must be frightening, not knowing what happened.' said Maya keeping her voice low and slow.

'Definitely. It just seems unreal. Like a dream world where I'll wake up and find Daniel alive,' said Eamon.

'Do you have any idea how he died?' said Jack.

'You told us it wasn't an accidental overdose, so I thought he might've had a seizure and hit his head.' Eamon stared at the floor in silence. 'I've spent weeks with the others. It's hard to see any of them as murderers except maybe Dr Ted or Graham. They were the angriest and most bitter.'

They sat in the quiet again. Nothing to add.

Jack said in a low voice, 'You can go now. Thank you.'

Eamon left, silent as a monk. Jack turned to Maya frowning. 'We're still stuck. No one saw or heard anything that gives us a clue.'

Maya said, 'I spoke to Steve's mum. He has a history of violence when unwell. She's worried he took the psychedelics and hurt Daniel.'

'They've told me already. If Daniel was stabbed or beaten to death, I could've believed it, but poisoning is really elaborate for a psychotic man.'

'Yes that's true, and I doubt it's Eamon.'

'Why?'

'He seems so nice and normal.'

'You can't think like that in a murder. Everyone's a suspect until proven otherwise, even if they're nice.'

Lydia poked her head around the door. Her bracelets jangled with excitement. She was breathless. 'Dr Ted's made bail. He's on his way back.'

Maya's stomach clenched and acid rose in her throat. How would she cope with Dr Ted? Was the killer? The thought frightened her.

6

Day 3-4 Post Death

Maya laughed when she saw all the participants out the front and lined up, like they were meeting the Queen. Everyone had made an effort, clean, neat and tidy. Last she'd heard, they'd been furious with Dr Ted.

Maya was tingly and nervy. She was tired of being the most qualified person present. The isolation and lack of supervision was stressful. It was getting to her. But she had no respect for Dr Ted. He was going to be her supervising psychiatrist and could make things difficult for her at this placement.

Oh God, he might even know her secret. Her stomach gnawed.

The police car drove up the long, red, gravel driveway. Constables Mitch and Dave had gone to Exmouth to get Dr Ted, and he disembarked like a royal.

Maya gasped in shock. Dr Ted was tall, at least 6 foot 5, and wearing a long yellow tunic, consistent with the guru vibe. He had black/grey hair and a splendid beard that he'd plaited. He glided rather than walked and behaved as if he were doing the police a favour. Portraying a magnificent disinterest in those escorting him.

What astonished Maya the most, was that Dr Ted was black

African, regal. Almost a mirror to her adoptive dad's skin tone. Maya was always aware of her dad's skin colour. They were an odd pair, with him so dark and her so pale and red. Unusual in Western Australia.

Dr Ted smiled at the reception committee and moved slowly along the line, hugging and talking to each person individually. His reflection, like the sun, appeared to warm those in his orbit. His attention appeared to mesmerise his clients. No matter their previous comments about him.

When he reached Maya, she saw he had unusual dark green eyes. He said, 'Welcome to our Homestead. I've been told that you came from Perth to comfort and care for everyone here. I'm grateful for your kind assistance.' His voice was deep and sonorous. Maya had never thought about the tone of another voice. He had a resonance that made it sound like everything would be all right.

Maya said, 'Thank you. I've been sent here by the college as part of my forensic training. Everyone's been lovely but I'm not sure how much help I've offered.' Her voice sounded pale and unnatural in comparison.

Dr Ted nodded graciously and moved forward into the house.

Lydia jingled over, laughing at Maya. 'You should see your face. Now you know why all this chaos happened. It's impossible to say no to him. '

Maya hesitated. She could not shake her sense of nausea. 'Do you know where he comes from? I've never met anyone who looks so much like my adoptive father before. '

Lydia said, 'I know he's a mixture. He was born in the Congo but is much taller than the average Congolese. He's always talking about how grateful he is, to be in Australia and not hear the sounds of gunfire every night.' She stabbed her toe in the red dirt, killing a trail of ants. 'I think he likes being different. It gives him power.'

Maya didn't see Dr Ted again until the next morning. She was up early, showered and came into breakfast. She joined him at the long wooden table on the opposite church pew.

Maya took a deep breath and said, 'I was wondering where you're from? I was adopted by a man from Kenya. He's been wonderful to me my whole life.'

Dr Ted glowed and took his time to tell his tale. 'I was born in the Congo. My mother was part Congolese but part Arabian. I never knew my father but he apparently came from the Tutsi tribe. There must some European genes because of the colour of my eyes.' His voice was hypnotising. 'Your dad sounds like a remarkable man taking you on as a small child.'

Maya smiled, feeling a connection with him despite all the fears she had. 'He really is special. I love him very much.' The threat of murder felt distant and unreal.

Mitch and Dave hustled in like overgrown puppies. Panting in delight at more food. Fresh toasted muesli. Too busy to talk, they loaded their plates high with deliciousness.

They joined Maya at the long table and looked at her sideways.

Maya said, 'How long have you both been working in Exmouth?'

'We went through the Police Academy and graduated together,' said Mitch, rocking backwards and forwards with excess energy. Failing to answer the question.

'We're from Perth but are stuck here for two years,' said Dave, moving side to side. They were like over-wound energiser bunnies. Perhaps more ADHD in the ranks?

'We saw you talking to Sgt Jack the other night. He's our new boss,' said Mitch.

'He's angry with us but we don't like the bastard anyway,' said Dave, finishing the thought.

Maya nodded. She didn't know what else to do. The two of them were an unstoppable force of nature. Dr Ted ignored them and their excess energy.

She said, 'Do you like being in the bush? I've been sent here as part of my training, and I think it's amazing.'

'We're both footy players. 'A' division for Claremont. It's too hot to play properly here,' said Dave.

'Yeh we're sick of it and want to go back to Perth,' said Mitch, echoing his friend.

Jack came into the room, eyes bleary. He took some muesli and sat on the other side of Maya.

'Were you working late last night?' asked Maya.

'Yes,' said Jack sighing. 'There's a hell of a lot to organise. The bosses in Perth are micro-managing me. The paperwork takes forever.'

He looked at Mitch and Dave. They glared at their muesli, as if it offended them.

Jack said, 'I need you two to drive out to Omar Station today. You have to fingerprint one of the gun lockers and collect a box to send to Perth for forensics. Gary, the station owner, knows about it and will guide you through it.'

Mitch and Dave groaned. It was rude if not insubordinate.

'Can we stay in Exmouth once we drop off the box?' said Dave.

'Yes,' said Mitch, 'we're really sick of this place. You can't get Internet reception. We're cut off from the world.'

'Yeah, we want to follow the sport,' said Dave.

'And it's really stupid that you have to do walk out to the middle of paddock to make a phone call,' said Mitch. They were on a roll. They'd only been at the Homestead for a couple of days and had lists of complaints.

Jack rolled his eyes and said, 'Yes you can both go back to town. At least you'll cause less damage.'

'It wasn't my fault that the photos didn't work,' said Mitch stabbing at the muesli. 'No one trained me on procedures with that camera.'

'And it wasn't my fault that the axle bent on the four-wheel-drive,' said Dave. 'I didn't grow up driving in these sorts of conditions.'

'Yes, yes, yes,' said Jack. 'It's never your fault. It was wrong of us to assume either of you could work a car and camera.'

Mitch and Dave reddened, and glared at Jack as if he were to blame.

After he finished eating, Dr Ted stood and said to Maya, 'Will you come to my office to give a handover on the clients?'

Maya went clammy and hot. Nervous, as she walked with him.

She entered the elegant, green office, as if condemned. Her thoughts towards Dr Ted confused her. Was he the murderer? Was she safe with him?

'Thank you once again for helping us. Have there been any problems in my absence?' said Dr Ted, sitting in the largest chair.

Maya said, 'Given the circumstances, everyone's coping as well as possible. I'm keeping my eye on Steve because of the psychosis and Sarah who's dissociating more.' She took the smaller, humbler chair at his feet.

Maya found it difficult to address her concerns about psychedelic treatment directly so hinted. 'I was concerned about Steve's psychosis when I heard about the psilocybin. I know there's experimental work in the area of PTSD and treatment resistant depression, but I wasn't aware of any trials in Exmouth.' She shifted back and forth with nerves. 'My only experience with these drugs is in the area of addiction. I've seen a lot of suffering. It worries me.'

Dr Ted said, 'I consider myself one of the great world leaders in this area. As you already know so many people do not get better from their mental illnesses. All the medications we use have side-effects and problems. Patients are dying from the weight gain and suicidal thinking that the drugs can cause. We just have to do better.' He moved his arms expansively. Performing for an unseen audience.

Dr Ted stood to continue. 'Psychedelic research began in the 1950s. The only reason it stopped was because of Reagan's mad war on drugs. It's absolutely clear he failed to win this war. My goal is to heal people, particularly when they've experienced trauma. You know there is no ideal treatment for these people. Were you aware that psychedelics increase serotonin levels like the antidepressants?'

Jack had already told Maya that Dr Ted was going trial for his unregulated use of psychedelics. Dr Ted gave the impression he was in training for the court. Maya had to admit, he was damn magnificent.

There was a knock and Lydia burst into the office. She was coy and preening, dressed in florescent pink hot pants and her signature, jingly bracelets. She said, 'Hi Dr Ted. I just feel so upset about the whole situation. It seems so unfair to you. I think everyone's jealous of you and they're trying to cancel out the good that you do. '

Maya laughed to herself. This certainly wasn't what Lydia said to her. Gone were her criticisms of Dr Ted. It was like watching a peacock fan its tail and stride around.

All this blundering about made Maya again question whether Dr Ted had a sexual relationship with any of his patients. Perhaps even Lydia? The whole situation was unclear and confusing. Her gut churned. Could she trust any of them?

Graham opened the door and came in, just stopping himself from falling on top of Lydia. He was dark and angry, still wearing black jeans, black T-shirt, black glasses and black boots. Why anyone would come to the heat of Exmouth with only black clothing, was beyond Maya's comprehension?

He spoke the longest sentence Maya had heard from him. 'When you have time Dr Ted, I need to see you. I've been struggling since the death. I was so worried about you and everything you must've gone through. I remember the shock when I was first arrested and went to jail. I thought it might shatter you.'

Maya heart quickened and nausea rose, the now familiar flow of shock through her body. Graham had a history of jail time? No one had told her and it wasn't in the files. What the hell was going on in this place?

Dr Ted replied, 'Graham it's not your job to look after me. You have to trust me to manage my own difficulties. If you can't manage that, I don't know how I can help you.'

Dr Ted got up and ushered both Lydia and Graham out, reassuring them he would see them later. He closed the door and turned his full attention onto Maya. She experienced the intensity of his gaze as a blow to her chest.

Maya was uncomfortable but recognised how intoxicating this attention could feel. It reminded her of a childhood poem her dads had performed for her, "Won't you walk into my parlour? said the spider to the fly. Tis the prettiest little parlour, you ever did spy."

She'd never worked with anybody who had survived a cult, but she had read about how often smart people found themselves trapped. The problem was the difference between intellectual knowledge and intuitive gut feeling. Her stomach was giving her hell, while her brain confused her.

'Please call me Ted, we are colleagues after all. I've always wanted to teach to pass on my knowledge. This seems to be a unique opportunity for you to learn a non-Western approach to healing. Western psychiatry is obsessed with biology and using drugs to heal people. This is not working. My approach is to integrate the mind and body using every option available.' Dr Ted towered over her. His speech was overly formal. Perhaps it was his background, but it intimidated her.

Maya was an archetypal 'good girl' and people pleaser. His deep voice seduced her and she wanted to 'be nice'. She tried to focus on facts that she knew. For example, giving unregulated psychedelics to vulnerable people was never going to end well and she was sure that sleeping with your patients was wrong. The rules she learnt in psychiatry, definitely limited creative healing, but controlled the amount of harm.

Maya had a good moral compass. When working, she'd follow her intuition. But Dr Ted looked so like her dad. It was confusing. Her instincts had gone on strike, and her unconscious was busy whining.

She tried to bring the conversation back to things she knew. 'I've put Steve on olanzapine 10 mg wafers three times a day. I'm not sure if he had psychedelics, but he appeared overwhelmed. The stress has increased his hallucinations.'

Dr Ted frowned at her efforts to move the conversation sideways. 'Have you read that schizophrenic patients do better in developing countries? It's because the approach is more holistic. They're not closeted away from their community. This includes religious experiences. Do you know that the Mexicans use ayahuasca to heal and as part of their spiritual journeys? Another psychedelic.'

Maya plodded on with the normal handover structure that exists between medical colleagues. 'I've managed to catch up with everyone apart from Graham. They've all been debriefed. In fact, everyone appears to be handling the whole situation better than I expected. The only people who asked for extra medication are Steve and Lydia. Lydia likes to draw attention to herself.'

Dr Ted glared at her, sitting back down. 'Lydia has a great deal of psychic energy but Graham's a special case. He's been badly treated by our society. He was a sad man, watching pornography online. This offense was picked up by the police and he was arrested for watching child pornography. He spent a year in jail and has only recently got out. He lost his wife, his children and his work.'

Maya tensed. She had worked with enough victims of childhood sexual abuse, that she had little sympathy for Graham's troubles.

Maya could feel the tension building in the room. She knew that Dr Ted was experienced and would easily read her nonverbal signals. She disapproved of his beliefs and values. Maya's stomach was tight with the familiar sense of rising acid. God when would her gut leave her be?

Dr Ted appeared to be thriving in the tense environment, as if it empowered him. There was a darkness between them. Maya had lost any sense of her own power and was floundering. The spider analogy reoccurred to her. She was the fly, being tied up in silk thread and waiting to be disembowelled. She started to sweat.

Dr Ted said, 'It annoys me how you are taught. You're so naïve about the biases in the system. The people who come here have such bad stories about doctors, hospitals and everything. Multiple drugs, multiple admissions. At least they're willing to try something new and different.'

Maya could see his point but still carried the sense that something was wrong and distorted about the whole situation. She said, 'Why don't you work within the system? The setup allows, even encourages controlled trials. They're starting studies in Perth with psychedelics.'

Dr Ted glared at her and said, 'All the research is controlled by huge drug companies. They manipulate the data and change results. They don't publish research that doesn't suit their ends. That's why they're powerful and have made so much money. The research industry is contaminated I'd never have anything to do with it.'

Maya tensed in frustration and said, 'But when you get drugs from the Internet you really have no idea what you're buying. The people here are vulnerable, both psychologically and even physically. Aren't you worried you could cause them major damage?'

Maya knew Dr Ted was used to being adored and was likely to find Maya's questions irritating.

He said 'I can see your mind's closed to anything other than the medical model. You're young. We both know your cerebral cortex has not myelinated yet. Your opinions have no value until you have grown both biologically and emotionally.'

They stared at each other in silence. Maya put back in her box. What would be Dt Ted's next move? She was tiring.

The acid in Maya's throat burned and she longed to escape this trapped feeling. Stuck with Dr Ted's anger.

Just when she thought she was going to cry, Jack put his head around the door. 'Hi Maya could I possibly catch up with you for a moment? I've some things I want to run by you.'

Maya couldn't get out of the room fast enough. She had the image of the Titanic in her head again, and did jump onto the lifeboat as fast as possible.

As soon as she had escaped, she said 'Thank God you came in there. The atmosphere in that room was suffocating me. I felt so uncomfortable. All Dr Ted wants is for people to adore him. He's really punishing if you don't agree with him.'

'I guess you're just not used to the Guru vibe,' said Jack laughing.

'How do you stay confident when you're around him?' asked Maya.

'It helps if you don't call him Dr Ted. I try to think of him as just Ted in my own mind and say it to his face when I want to annoy him,' said Jack, speed walking down the corridor to the eating area. 'I think it humanises him. I don't buy into the myth that you have to call all doctors Dr. I would never think of calling you Dr Maya and you've passed medicine as well.

'I guess so,' said Maya entering and sitting on the broad, jarrah church pew. It grounded her. 'Was there something you wanted to talk to me about, when you came in?'

'I just wanted to get you away from Dr Ted. I don't like him and I don't trust him. He could be the murderer. I worried that you might fall under his spell. You had a dazed puppy look,' said Jack, sitting next to her. Close.

Maya said, 'I think I'm confused. I grew up in Perth and rarely saw anyone with an African background, apart from my dad. I love both my dads dearly and really respect them both. I think Dr Ted looks so much like Peter, that it confuses me.'

'I have seen murderers before,' said Jack, 'and they can be intoxicating. They radiate power and love to manipulate people.

'Yes, in psychiatry we talk about psychopaths, the smiling psychopath. Lacking empathy and remorse, but luring you in with their superficial warmth,' said Maya staring at the ceiling, frowning. 'I guess I know more about the theory than I do in real life.'

'I'm pretty sold on him being a psychopath,' said Jack, leaning towards Maya and touching her arm. 'You need to be careful around him.' Maya jumped at the touch. A sense of electricity passed through her. Damnit, what was she thinking?

'If a person doesn't feel emotionally connected to anyone, and doesn't have any guilt about hurting people, this gives them a lot of power. Do you think Dr Ted's the murderer?' said Maya.

Jack shrugged. 'He's the one who would know about the strychnine at the Station, but he doesn't have any real reason to murder Daniel. There's no payoff for him. I actually believe he loves working here and really would prefer to keep the setup under the radar,' He paused for a moment. 'When you were looking at the patient files, did you have a chance to read Daniel's?'

'Actually, I have Daniel's file in the white group room. We could go down and have a look together. I only went through it briefly,' said Maya.

'Did it give any useful information?' said Jack.

'A past psychiatrist gave Daniel the diagnosis of cluster B personality disorder, suggesting he had antisocial, borderline and narcissistic traits. It's not really a big jump to psychopathy. Perhaps there was a clash?' said Maya.

As she walked to the white room, little prickles of guilt rose along Maya's neck. She was siding with Sgt Jack over Dr Ted. Declaring her position. She worried about Dr Ted's potential fury. Was he really a murderer?

Jack appeared confident, striding forward at a rapid pace. Maya followed his lead. They opened the door to the white room and Maya stiffened in shock. Someone had forced the lock of the filing cabinet, and files were strewn all over the floor. Pages torn, private information exposed. The cover of Daniel's file was ripped and all the pages were missing.

Maya did start to cry. She was shocked, but crying like a school girl. Oh God how embarrassing.

Jack appeared calmer. He picked up Daniel's empty file and said, 'I wonder who needed to hide information from this file?'

Maya said, 'It couldn't have been Dr Ted. I was just in his office. He didn't have time to come in here. I don't think Daniel's file was hiding any special information.'

Jack said to Maya, 'Just sit down and take a breath. I'm going to ring Mitch and Dave. They're going to have to come back to help me search for the missing file. I'll talk to Dr Ted to get permission. I don't want to have to get a warrant. If we can find Daniel's file, it may give a clue as to what is happening.'

Jack rushed out of the room and Maya poured herself a drink of water. She realised that her memories of the file might be important. She gathered her thoughts and took notes.

Daniel's diagnosis of cluster B personality disorder was clear in her mind. She remembered he wasn't on any medication and did not have a history of hospital admissions. There was nothing dramatic in his past. He'd seen one psychiatrist only who had referred him to Dr Ted, at Daniel's request. Daniel seemed determined to try psychedelics as a first line option.

Lydia alleged a sexual relationship with Daniel but there was no evidence that Dr Ted noticed anything untoward. Dr Ted's notes didn't add much. He agreed with the diagnosis and seemed happy to use psychedelics to treat anything, including personality problems

When Jack returned, he said, 'Mitch and Dave haven't gone far. They'll be back in half an hour. I've told Dr Ted, who's pretty pissed off.'

He sat down and looked at her notes. 'It's a good idea to get together our recollections on Daniel. I've been told that Daniel was raised in rural Victoria by a mum and dad who owned a hardware store. He had one older sister.' Jack talked, while Maya wrote. 'I spoke to them all. They were devastated by his death but had no explanation. They aren't a close family so see each other rarely. Daniel had an arts degree, in journalism and took on casual work everywhere. A jack of all trades.'

They both sat down on the floor shifting through the scattered papers. Jack took a chaotic, haphazard approach, whereas Maya was logical and methodical. It was a mess.

7

A booming ring sounded from the veranda. Maya and Jack moved towards the sound. Maya saw Joy pounding a Chinese gong with a padded stick, like an enthusiastic Western Buddhist.

Dr Ted stood in the eating area and said to them, 'I'm calling everybody in to let them know about the search. I won't have secrecy in my Homestead.'

Lydia and Sarah arrived. Sweaty. They must've been running to answer the call. Eamon and Steve were not far behind. Graham followed, melancholy and sulky.

They sat down like obedient school children, around the long wooden dining table. The church pew benches were uncomfortable. Maya wiggled her butt and sighed. It was going to get worse if the search took time.

Jack standing, projected his voice with authority. 'We told you yesterday that the investigation has been upgraded to murder. I have to search the Homestead today. We're missing some of the patient files from the white group room. Does anyone know anything about this?'

Dr Ted frowned, glaring at Jack, and stood up to tower over him.

A testosterone power play. He said, 'I cannot stop them doing this search but we'll sit here and observe their behaviour.'

Everybody talked at once, except Graham whose face went red and sweaty. He stood to walk out of the room. Jack moved rapidly to stand in front of him and said, 'None of you can leave this area until the search's done. It must be obvious we can't have anyone interfering.'

Graham's muscles tensed and his fist balled. Maya held her breath. It looked like he wanted to hit Jack, but Jack didn't flinch. After a painful, prolonged minute staring at each other, Graham went limp and sat.

Maya was exhausted by the drama. Graham behaved as if he were guilty. Not helping his protests of innocence. He said he'd had bad experiences with the police in the past. But did this explained his aggressive behaviour?

Steve was talking to the walls and ceilings less. Perhaps the voices were easing? He appeared mystified regarding the whole situation. Maya moved to sit by him for support. She wanted to reassure him.

Joy had put away the gong and bustled in with sandwiches. 'I thought we might have an early lunch seeming as we're stuck here for a while. I've egg, ham and cheese all with salad and home-made bread. Tuck in and make yourselves a nice cup of tea. Good for shock.'

The police constables, Mitch and Dave hauled themselves round the door scowling. They'd been dragged back from Yardie Creek. Perhaps already missing Exmouth? Their precious haven of internet connection and social media. They glowered at Jack and slumped their shoulders as they set off to work. Jack had his hands full.

The situation in the eating room was equally awkward. Maya watched everyone shift around on the benches, staring at everyone else. Maybe trying to find the guilty party? Graham was dark and angry. The force field around him strong. No one seemed keen to breach it.

Dr Ted, on the other hand, was channelling Mahatma Gandhi.

He appeared unperturbed. A study in mindfulness as he ate his sandwich, focusing only on that action.

Lydia and Sarah, probably thirsting for approval, were diligently following Dr Ted's lead. Chewing their food with serious faces.

Eamon, close to tears, seemed overwhelmed by the situation. He'd told Maya he dealt well with death, but murder had to be a different stressor for someone who valued 'niceness'.

Emotions were aroused and tense. Maya was thinking hard. How to ease the tension? She jumped up, 'I'm going to put on some music with a calming vibe?' No one said anything, so she put on a yoga CD, hoping it was a soothing choice.

Everyone could hear Jack and the others moving around. They'd started in Graham's room, which was no surprise to Maya.

As impulsive as ever, Lydia poked the bear and said to Maya, 'I guess you know everything about what's happening, because you're sleeping with Sgt Jack.'

Maya gritted her jaw and glared at Lydia. She was being pushed to defend herself, in front of Dr Ted. 'Lydia, you know that accusation is untrue. I wasn't here when Daniel died so you all know more than I do.'

Dr Ted raised his head, eyebrows lifted. Maya thought he might pile on the attack, but instead he said, 'Let's get out the yoga mats and I'll lead a mindfulness session. It's the ideal time to practice this technique when we're under stress.'

Maya had to admit, for a possible psychopath, it was a great idea. The session was excellent. Hatha yoga. Even Steve managed to keep up. Perhaps his parents already taught him yoga as part of their attempts to cure him? Dr Ted's voice was calming and steady. Maya's mind settled and her thinking cleared.

In the back row, Graham struggled. He was twitchy and appeared distracted by the noises coming from the police search. It was difficult to assess his behaviour. Whether he was feeling guilty or behaving like this because of his past arrest. Had he brought pornography? The situation was complicated because she had real issues working with anyone who'd had anything to do with child sexual abuse.

The process of searching took about three hours. Jack came back to the eating area and told them they could go back to their rooms. Dr Ted left with Graham, but Maya stayed. Her butt was solid-ice already. No point moving. She wanted to know what happened.

She looked up at Jack. 'Did you find anything on Graham? His behaviour was shifty."

'We didn't find the file or any other incriminating information. Graham was upset because he had a porno magazine under his mattress,' said Jack sitting down with her. 'We checked out the magazine but it's all legal adult porn. Dr Ted implied we were going to set Graham up but we don't act like that.'

Maya said, 'But Graham was really jumpy. Does he have any links to Daniel? He hero worships Dr Ted and would probably do anything for him.'

Jack jumped to his feet. Maya startled. Her levels of adrenaline were high. He was twitchy.

Jack put his finger to his lips and gestured for them to leave the room without speaking. It was a bit cloak and dagger for Maya but she followed him. They went to the white group room. What was wrong?

The white group room remained a barren, unwelcoming place. Off putting.

Jack said, 'I thought I heard someone listening from the corridor to the men's quarters. It's hard to know who to trust. At least we're the only ones who come in here.' He was breathing faster, as if the stress was getting to him.

'I know,' said Maya, encouraging him to sit. 'I'm out of balance, off beat. I don't know what to do or think. It's stressful.' The white leather couch was sweaty and scratchy but the best option available.

Jack stared at Maya. He was pale with dark circles under his eyes. He said, 'You didn't ask directly, but we did find the file on Daniel. It was in Sarah's room, under the mattress.'

Maya's stomach gnawed into action. She took a deep breath and said, 'Sarah's been dissociated since I came here. I would've thought she was the least likely person to hurt Daniel. She's totally absorbed by trauma.'

'We have to talk to her. Would you help me interview her? I know she's vulnerable and I think I need your professional input,' said Jack.

Maya took a moment to answer. She was getting in over her head. Sharp stabbing pains began in her abdomen as she thought of Dr Ted's reaction. But Sarah needed a safe person in the interview room and Maya knew she was safer than Dr Ted. She nodded.

'Great,' said Jack, 'I need some time to prepare. Her room wasn't locked so anyone could have put the file there. Perhaps even trying to frame Sarah? But why?'

They organised for Maya to get Sarah, in one hour. Maya took time to organise the room to help Sarah focus. She moved the chairs and couch into a circle. She had some lavender oil which she sprinkled on the white cotton mat. She collected wrapped dark chocolate and made hot cups of peppermint tea for them all. Good smells. She had the lights on to avoid shadows or hazy outlines that might trigger a flashback.

Sarah had been swimming and the cooling exercise worked its charm. She was more alert and attentive.

They sat in a semicircle, with Maya on Sarah's right side.

'Sarah,' said Jack in a quiet voice, 'when we searched the rooms, we found Daniel's file under your mattress. Did you take the file?'

Sarah gasped, clasping her hands together in fists, 'No, I didn't take anything.' She twisted her body in a knot on the couch. 'Maybe I hadn't locked my door? Oh God. I'm being framed.'

Jack said, 'We know that anyone could have put the file there. We're just trying to make sense of why it was taken. Have you ever looked at anyone's file here?'

Sarah clenched and unclenched her hands in distress. 'I've never seen any of the files. If I was going to take a file it would be my own.' She blinked back tears furiously. Her anger appeared useful in holding her together.

Jack said, 'Sarah do you have any theories about how Daniel died?'

'No, I have no idea,' said Sarah. 'My guess would've been Lydia and a lover's tiff. But if that had happened, she would've stabbed him. I could've seen that on the body. I keep thinking someone made a mistake. Nothing makes sense.'

Maya noticed Sarah starting to dissociate, wide eyes, staring gaze. She pushed the peppermint tea cup to Sarah offering her a drink, 'Would you like some peppermint tea? I don't know what you usually drink, but it's very refreshing.'

Sarah turned to stare at Maya. Her face was blank. Sarah blinked, and then said, 'I'm going back to my room now. Please leave me alone.' She left, moving robotically.

Jack said to himself, 'That was really awful. I'm not sure it helped much. I still have no idea what happened.' He turned to Maya, 'Would you go through Daniel's file to see if anything is missing? I've been through it already and can't see anything.'

He gave Maya a file containing eight pages which had been ripped from the binder. The first one was typed. It was the summary page, familiar to Maya. There was a letter from the referring psychiatrist. Everything else was handwritten. Jack waited in patient silence while she looked.

Maya said, 'I can't see anything obvious that's missing. But Dr Ted's notes are chaotic and hard to follow. You have to ask him. He might remember.'

'Dr Ted's still our main suspect because of his familiarity with Omar Station. We're trying to get information from everybody else first,' said Jack.

'If anything, these notes are boring and useless,' said Maya concentrating on the papers. 'There's very little information. Nothing that would incriminate anybody. The writing is cursory and slapdash. There isn't a record of anything pertinent, or even statements directly from Daniel.'

Maya and Jack jumped as Lydia burst into the room, 'You've really upset Sarah. She's locked herself in the bathroom and won't come out.' Lydia was a jingly, jangly mess, full of gold bracelets and anklets with bells on them. 'Dr Ted sent me. He says you have to come and help.'

The corridor outside the bathroom was filled with people. Stuffed to the gills with human activity. Everyone, bar Graham, had turned up. Talking, moving around, advising.

Dr Ted glared at Jack. 'You do not have permission to meet with my patients without me present.' He turned towards Maya. 'What you did was irresponsible and foolish. You don't have the experience to manage a person who's battling dissociation without supervision.'

Maya's jaw clenched in fury. How dare he criticised her when he gave Sarah psychedelics less than a week ago. She turned away, and took a breath. Her own anger surprised her. She focused on helping Sarah. There was so much noise in the corridor, she was unlikely to settle.

Maya looked at Jack. 'Maybe we could clear the corridor. Sarah's more likely to come out if she has peace and quiet.'

Jack busied himself. Maya knocked and said, 'Sarah can I come in?'

Sarah agreed and came to unlock the door. Dr Ted reddened and glared, but moved aside for Maya.

As soon as she got in the door, Maya saw that Sarah had cut her wrists. Maya looked at the shallow cuts and slow, venous ooze. This situation was manageable without hospital resources.

Sarah said, 'I don't want to die. I was just so angry I couldn't stop myself. I feel better when I cut.'

Maya smiled at her. She pulled out iodine and bandages from the first aid kit she found in the cupboard. As she worked to dress the wounds, she said, 'Cutting and self-harm are the same for many people. They use it to control their feelings of distress. We can try to help develop healthier options. But there's nothing to be ashamed of. This is all fixable.'

Sarah smiled back. A small breakthrough for Maya.

Sarah looked at the ground and scuffed her feet. 'Do you know my secret?'

Maya's mind whirled. What secret? There were so many secrets in Sarah's background, it was hard to choose.

Maya said, 'I've read your file from Dr Ted. But it's very short and hasn't much detail. All I really know is that you had a traumatic childhood.'

The small bathroom was not going to help a psychiatric intervention. Maya was perched on the closed toilet seat and Sarah on the edge of the bath. The fittings looked as if they were bought in the 1970s, and had a yellowish tinge. The plumbing at the Homestead was dodgy and the smell of bore water was strong. This was not the place for calm.

Sarah lowered her voice. 'No, not that. It's what happened this year. They all know about it.' She gestured to the outside corridor.

Maya was drawing a blank. She bent forward on the toilet seat and said, 'I don't know what you mean. Do you want to tell me what happened?' God, the toilet was uncomfortable. The ceramic had turned her butt to ice.

Sarah's eyes filled with tears, 'I got pregnant after a one-night stand. But I lost the baby. I blamed myself and everybody blamed me.'

'Who blamed you, Sarah?' said Maya in a soft, low voice.

'I didn't even know who the boy was. I met him at a nightclub. We had sex out the back near the garbage bins. I was so ashamed. I blamed the baby,' said Sarah crying hard.

'Do you think you were really blaming yourself?' said Maya leaning towards her.

'My stepmother was a total bitch about it. She said I was a slut and a drug whore just like my mother. My dad threw me out of the house. That's the main reason I came to this retreat, I had nowhere else to go,' said Sarah, rocking backward and forwards with her arms crossed in front of her body.

'Oh Sarah, I'm so sorry you had to go through such a difficult time on your own,' Maya opened her arms and hands. She didn't dare touch such a traumatized person, but she tried to communicate a sense of connection.

'I had a 12-week ultrasound and saw the baby for the first time. It was a little girl. She had her little hand up and was waving to me. It was the first time I felt connected to anything or anyone. But then at 15 weeks I started to bleed.' Sarah was sobbing full on, tears coming out her eyes, nose and even her mouth.

Maya leaned as far forward as she could, without tipping over off the toilet. She pulled some toilet paper off the roll and passed it forward to Sarah. Maya's own eyes were wet, in response to Sarah's story. 'You've gone through so much on your own. It must be hard to trust anyone. Thank you for trying to reach out.'

Sarah looked up at Maya. She appeared to be thinking. Her crying eased.

Maya said, 'Do you have anywhere to go when they retreat ends?'

Sarah shook her head and blinked tears from her eyes, 'No one in my family will have me. My mother's dead because of the drug use. And I've worn out my welcome with all of my friends. I've no idea what I'll do after.'

Maya said, 'Have you thought about applying for public housing or any of the other services that provide accommodation? It's a practical problem, but having your own home can make an enormous difference to your feeling of safety and security.' Sarah leaned forward towards Maya, engaged in the problem. Maya continued. 'It'd take time to get a permanent home, but in the short term, you could rent a room in a group house.'

Sarah gave a half smile, 'Have you ever rented a room in a group home? It's a crappy way to live.'

'I did when I was a student. If you stick to students' accommodation it's a lot easier to find something. I could help you if you wanted me to,' said Maya.

Sarah sighed, but her muscles unclenched.

Maya said, 'Do you want to take a minute before going out there?'

'Yes,' said Sarah leaning forward on the bath edge, 'Dr Ted's going to be furious with me. I get really afraid when he's angry.'

'Do you think he's capable of harming someone?' said Maya.

'Yes, after the way he grew up, I'm sure he could kill,' said Sarah.

'It's just I can't think of a motive for hurting Daniel. He loves his place and doesn't want attention on his practice.'

Maya looked around the room and said, 'Nothing at this Homestead looks on the inside like it seems on the surface. It's all shiny on the outside but there is darkness behind the gloss.'

They both jumped, when a loud banging sounded from the door. They heard Jack say, 'Are you two okay?'

Maya said, 'Yes, we're fine.' She looked at Sarah, who nodded back. They opened the door into the corridor. Jack had managed to usher everybody away including Dr Ted. Maya respected the strength that must've taken.

'I'm going to talk to Dr Ted and let him know I'm okay,' said Sarah, paling, stressed. 'There was a suicide here the first year they opened, and he's really anxious about it happening again.'

'Will you be okay? Do you want me to come with you?' said Maya

'No, I'll be fine on my own. I want to do this by myself,' said Sarah, looking clearer, more present. She took a deep breath and left the corridor.

Jack turned to Maya, in the constricted space, and said, 'Did you know there was a suicide here, in the past?'

Maya shook her head. She did know that a patient's suicide could be very traumatic for the treating psychiatrist. It'd happened to her and she needed help working it through. Dr Ted was controlling. He wasn't likely to cope well with death.

Lydia came scurrying around the corner, jingling like a cat with a bell. 'I couldn't help overhearing what you said,' she said, puffing out her chest. 'I know all about what happened in the past. It involves Joy. She pretends to be everyone's perfect mother but she has a dark past.' Maya rolled her eyes.

Jack hushed Lydia and said, 'Let's go to the white group room. You never know who might be listening.' Maya smiled at the intended dig.

Once ensconced behind closed doors, Jack and Maya sat to listen. Lydia's facial and body movements expanded with the attention. She stood rocking forwards and backwards, telling her story with as much drama as possible.

'It happened 10 years ago when the Homestead first opened,' she said. 'There were five participants in the first group, and one of these was Joy's son, Samuel. He had a drug problem. She sent him here as a last resort, because he was really addicted.'

Maya said, 'Joy spoke to me about Sam but she said he was at university.'

'I know,' said Lydia. 'I don't think she has accepted that he's gone. She wasn't working here then. He went into this room and hung himself.'

Lydia rolled her wrists, providing a musical accompaniment to the story. 'Joy was a single mum and Sam was her only child. After Dr Ted told her he'd died, she flew straight to Exmouth, came to the Homestead and never left.'

'That poor woman,' said Maya. 'I can't think of anything worse than losing a child to suicide.'

'She's worked for Dr Ted ever since. She's the one who's been redecorating the Homestead. I think it's why she painted this room white and made it so uncomfortable. It holds the memories of her son,' said Lydia.

'How the hell did you find all of this out?' said Jack.

'I might've overheard a conversation Dr Ted had on the telephone,' said Lydia, eyes darting to the left. 'I've been really bored so I'm doing my own research on Daniel's death.'

Jack raised his eyebrows in response, and said, 'Do you think that Joy's loss, all those years ago, has anything to do with the current situation?'

'I can't see a link but it tells me people are keeping secrets in this Homestead,' said Lydia, in a hopeful whisper.

'Have you uncovered anything useful about Daniel's murder?' said Jack.

Lydia sat down with a sigh. 'No, the death of Joy's son is the only interesting information I've heard. I've been trying to spy on Dr Ted. He seems to be just as shocked by the whole situation as I am.'

'Do you have any ideas about how Daniel died?' said Jack.

'I still think it was an accidental overdose of psilocybin,' said

Lydia. 'I've watched CSI and I think the lab made a mistake. It happens. I don't think anyone killed him.'

Jack ushered Lydia out of the room, and flopped in the chair beside Maya. He said, 'I think we've alienated Dr Ted. He's so angry that I don't think he'll talk to either of us.'

Maya's stomach flapped like a large moth trapped inside her. She hated disappointing others and making them angry.

Jack's eyes bored into her. 'I want you to make sure you lock your door and window tonight. Jimmy a chair under the handle, so no one can get in your room. Make sure it's secure. There's a murderer about, despite what Lydia thinks. I want you to stay safe.'

Maya realised he was worried. Really worried. Her legs knocked sideways. She was wobbly when she stood. Maya' voice was hoarse. 'Thank you for your concern. Of course, I'll do it.'

The threat of murder felt unreal. Playing 'let's pretend'. Hard to believe the risk was genuine. But Jack's focus was so out of character, it scared her.

8

Day 5 Post Death

Kangaroo paws sat in a huge vase on the table in the eating room. The table cloth was cornflower blue. Sun shone through the large windows. Glaring to morning-time Maya. The strong colours jarred her senses.

People sat at the wooden table on the benches chattering. Jack was there and arguing with Graham. Loudly. God it was too early for that noise.

Maya sat and said, 'This muesli is amazing. Have you tried it? It's delicious.'

The two men turned to stare at her. Distraction worked. They stopped arguing and turned to eat, like a pair of toddlers.

The coffee was good. She leaned back and relaxed.

Footsteps echoed down the corridor. Everyone jumped. On edge with the unsolved murder. Dr Ted entered and said 'I've come to get you Maya.' Maya's neck crawled. 'I'm determined to teach you something. You have a closed mind that needs opening. Come to my morning session, in my office, now.' She couldn't refuse such a direct instruction, so went with him.

He was dressed in a blue robe today. Maya hoped the colour

change represented a thawing of his temper. But his expression was severe, and he walked with heavy footsteps.

Graham sat in the office waiting. Dressed in black and scowling, like an angry rain-god. His snowy-white arms folded. Maya noticed he'd grown the nail of his ring finger hideously long. Like something out of a Bond movie. She held back the urge to vomit.

Maya sat back in her observer's chair and made an effort to focus. Watching a session with another psychiatrist was a great way to learn. Even if she worried, Dr Ted was a murderer, he was unlikely to kill her in front of Graham.

Dr Ted said, 'Graham has agreed for you to learn from his session.' He leaned back with his arms spread wide, taking up space. 'Graham where would you like to start?'

Graham was pasty white. A thin line of sweat appeared on his upper lip and brow. 'I was so worried when they arrested you. It brought back the memories of my awful experiences with the police. It's so unfair.'

'Remember it is not your job to look after me,' said Dr Ted, in his slow, deep, hypnotic voice.

Graham said, 'I remember how angry I was about what happened to me. They called me a paedophile. All I did was look at pictures online. I'd no idea the girls were under 16. It was humiliating.'

'Try and focus on the experience of anger in your body. What are you feeling physically?' said Dr Ted.

'My jaw is tense, teeth gritted...... I have a headache at the base of my skull and I'm hot,' said Graham, clenching his fists.

'Do you have an image associated with that feeling?' said Dr Ted.

'Yes, the police coming to my door with the TV crews not far behind. Someone must've leaked information to the press. Because I was a school principal,' said Graham. He rocked backwards and forwards in his chair, unable to control his physical feelings of distress. 'It is so unfair. I can't let go of the injustice.'

'Talk to me about other times in your life where you experienced injustice,' said Dr Ted. Maya knew he was controlling the interview but Graham was responding well.

'The whole disgusting process ended my marriage and I no longer have contact with my teenage kids. That wasn't fair,' said Graham.

'What about further back?' said Dr Ted

Graham stopped rocking. He looked Dr Ted full in the face, absorbed in the moment, appearing to forget Maya was present.

Graham said, 'Yes, my parents treated me differently from my brothers. My mother humiliated me and told me I was useless. There was no justice in my family. Everything was my fault. I did nothing right.'

Dr Ted held the silence for a moment. Then he said, 'Feelings in the present often have strong echoes from the past. Our goal is integration of the past and present, so we can make better choices in the future.'

Graham leaned forward, eyes staring, mouth open. Dr Ted said, 'You can't change what happened but you can change your responses now, both emotionally and physically.'

Graham started to cry. 'All my life I've craved my mother's approval. She was harsh woman. Thank God she was dead by the time I went to court.'

Dr Ted said, 'What would have happened if you disappointed her. Why was her approval so important?'

'I think all children want to please their mother. It's normal. You cling to the adult who is most likely to keep you alive,' said Graham. 'But she hated me. One Christmas she gave each of my brothers a motorbike and I got a pair of sneakers. She said they ran out of money and would make it up to me, but she never did.'

Graham slumped back in his chair. 'My brothers loved my humiliation in the courts. They really drank up the shame of what happened to me. I haven't seen them since I left jail.'

'By wanting approval from these people, you give them a great deal of power,' said Dr Ted. 'If you integrate some of your fears, you can take power back for yourself. In my case, I've not given a second's thought to people's approval. I find that focusing on the here and now, and using mindfulness techniques, can really help.'

Maya wasn't sure Dr Ted was being honest. She thought he showed signs of caring more than he admitted.

Graham unconsciously mirrored Dr Ted, his full attention on his face. Dr Ted said, 'Past and present fears are strongly linked. If you can bring full understanding to your life's experience, many of your fears will fade into insignificance.'

Graham moved back in his chair and sighed. Maya thought he looked like an adoring puppy. Graham rose and left without another word.

Maya shifted in her chair. The whole interaction left her feeling unclean. Like they were both murderers. The cultish adoration of Graham and the dominance of Dr Ted. Although Maya had to admit that Dr Ted had skills and a level of excellence. He was writing up notes on the session and ignored Maya. The power plays were never ending in this dynamic.

After a drawn-out pause he addressed Maya, 'Do you see the importance of understanding the humanity behind someone convicted of paedophilia.'

Maya was not keen to get dragged into a debate on rights and wrongs, but she said, 'I've worked with many abused children. The problem with people like Graham, is they don't realise the children they're watching are real, terrified and get hurt. The government criminalised watching child abuse online, to reduce the likelihood of other kids being abused especially overseas.'

Dr Ted frowned. 'What did you learn from the interview with Graham.'

This was exactly the type of question Maya dreaded. She knew she'd only be correct if she guessed, what he was thinking. This setup was common when she was a medical student. Maya wasn't much of a guesser and usually got it wrong.

She said, 'I liked the way you linked thoughts with feelings and images. You managed to get him thinking about the past affecting the present, and I think that's very helpful.'

There was a sharp knock at the door. Both Dr Ted and Maya jumped. Lydia entered the room. She was dressed in pink and orange, with a short skirt exposing as much skin as possible. She had a real gift for sucking up all the energy in the room. Maya was curious to see how Dr Ted dealt with Lydia.

Lydia started talking, moving her arms like she was conducting an orchestra. 'Dr Ted it's my turn for a session now. I've been so looking forward to it. I find you so inspiring. I loved the way you coped since leaving prison.'

Dr Ted said nothing and stared at her. This disconcerting move appeared designed to unbalance Lydia.

Lydia sat down and the register of her voice went up an octave. 'I've been having such a bad time. I'm really suffering.' She continued, pointing at Maya. 'She was horrid to me. She was mean and refused to listen to my problems.'

Maya followed Dr Ted's lead and said nothing, staring at Lydia.

Lydia's movements became jerky and uncoordinated, like a broken puppet. She said, 'No one understands how hard it is for me. Everyone's so cruel to me.' She began weeping, as if on demand.

Maya shifted in her chair and nearly cracked. Dr Ted was made of sterner stuff and did not move. Maya kept quiet, afraid of his disapproval.

Lydia switched to anger. 'You're such a prick. You pretend to care but have no interest in helping anyone. You're so selfish. I hope you end up in jail."

Dr Ted was unmoved and sat quietly. The silence was overpowering and uncomfortable. Time went so slow, Maya thought it had gone backwards.

Maya jumped when Dr Ted leaned forward, looked at Lydia, and said, 'Lydia are you aware that in the last 10 minutes you have moved from upbeat sympathy, to anger with Maya, to sadness about lacking attention, then to anger with me. All this emotion must be exhausting for you. It certainly doesn't help you function in a healthy manner. The rapid emotional switching is part of borderline personality disorder, which is the diagnosis you're most afraid of.'

Lydia cried, but this time she seemed more grounded in reality. Acting less. She said, 'I don't know why this happens to me. It feels like standing in the middle of waves of feelings and being pushed backwards and forwards.' She swayed in all directions as she spoke. 'I don't have time to think about my feelings. They just hit me and I fall over. I don't know how to stop this.'

Dr Ted said, 'This is what we're working on in private and group sessions. I'm giving you time to process your feelings and how they affect others. Try to pay attention to your body. How you move, whether your jaw or fists are clenched, whether you feel hot or cold, your skin prickles or your hands shake. To figure out emotions it's best to pay attention to your thoughts and physical reactions.'

Maya's respect for Dr Ted grew, against her will. They did not agree on boundaries, but she liked his way of dealing with emotion.

Lydia's rocking became more pronounced. Without warning, she catapulted herself forward onto the floor and began banging her head. She vocalised her distress, moaning out loud.

Dr Ted stood and said, 'Time for lunch.' He glided out of the room, like a graceful mountain duck.

Maya knew the analogy that a duck glides because its legs are paddling furiously underneath. She had not yet learned calmness, in the face of chaos. She said, 'Lydia, we'll give you a moment to calm yourself. I look forward to seeing you at lunch today.'

Lydia's moaning increased in intensity with the attention. Maya frowned. The way Lydia clung to the center of attention worried at her. Would she kill to get noticed?

Maya tried to glide but failed miserably. She was grateful that she didn't trip over her own feet. She opened the office door and ran smack into Jack. Her spirits lightened with the sight of him and she said, 'I like that you're here at the Homestead.'

'I heard moaning,' said Jack, trying to look into the office. 'Is that Lydia? Is she okay?'

'She's okay, she's just trying to work out some issues in therapy,' said Maya.

'Thank God, my nerves are wrecked at the moment,' said Jack. 'I'm glad I'm staying here too.'

They walked, unconsciously drawn by the delicious smells

coming from the kitchen and eating area. Joy had made a roast chicken which was just out of the oven.

Maya said to Joy, 'Thank you so much. You're such a wonderful chef.' Joy beamed at her, then scurried off.

The heat was suffocating but Maya's eyes itched with the constant air-conditioning. She moved outside to sit on the veranda with Eamon. Jack followed her.

Maya said to Eamon, 'How are you managing with all the stress?' Thinking thank God the veranda was covered from the sun.

Eamon frowned. 'It's been more difficult than I thought. I feel like I'm walking on egg shells. Part of me is constantly assessing the others. Who did this terrible thing? But then I forget what happened and enjoy myself in all the nature.'

'Yes, it's like a double orientation. Part of us can see danger but the other part just gets on with it. The research on war zones confirms that ignoring danger can be a coping mechanism.' said Maya smiling at him, 'I've been surprised at myself.'

'It's a good thing to be able to forget risk and do what needs to be done,' said Jack. 'In the police force they teach us to focus on our next action. We ignore the whole picture and try to take it one step at a time.' Maya smiled at Jack. Breaking a task down into component bits was a great idea for anyone.

'Have you learnt anything that might help explain what happened to Daniel?' said Eamon. 'I've been going over and over the death in my mind. I can't make sense of it. I wish I'd paid more attention but it's not easy to concentrate when you've taken psychedelics.'

'We're working on it,' said Jack. Giving little away. Maya was glad her job didn't force her to treat everyone as a suspect.

They sat together in silence. Maya had so much to think about over the last few days. She knew she'd compartmentalised the murder. Part of her was terrified of being the murderer's next victim. While a bit of her enjoyed the challenge of solving the who-done-it.

The tall figure of Dr Ted loomed over her. Maya's stomach dropped. He said, 'I'm keen to work further with you this afternoon. Follow me back to the office. We have further interviews.'

Maya stifled a sigh, and went with him.

Sarah was waiting in the office. She hugged her knees to her chest, trying to make herself as small as possible. Maya's mind went to Lydia's accusation of a sexual relationship between Sarah and Dr Ted. She knew enough not to trust Lydia's information, but the suggestion bothered her.

Sarah appeared dissociated. Wide distant stare. Unresponsive. It was difficult to engage her in any conversation. Dr Ted did nothing except sit there and wait. Maya's mind was whirring with different options to make the conversation easier for Sarah. Sarah seemed to be in a different place altogether. Her affect was flat.

Dr Ted turned to Maya and asked, 'Has Sarah been engaging in any group or individual interactions?'

'Yes,' said Maya, 'but she's been very stressed and I've worried about her degree of dissociation. I know she's been distressed about your experiences.'

Dr Ted tried to engage Sarah. He leaned forward without touching her and said, 'Sarah can you tell us what you are experiencing at the moment?'

He waited, making a gentle humming sound. He said, 'Sarah we are both here to try and help you. Is there anything we can do to make you more comfortable?'

The silence continued. Dr Ted appeared comfortable in the quiet, but Maya was restless, wanting to fix Sarah's problem.

Dr Ted started the familiar grounding routine, using a packet of Tim Tams, he had in his drawer. This action had the unfortunate effect of making Maya crave the biscuits. Dr Ted moved into a breathing mindfulness technique. Sarah sighed as though relaxing.

Maya enjoyed the meditative process and began to relax herself. Dr Ted was excellent and confident in the area of mindfulness. His voice was hypnotic and soothing. Mindfulness was good choice as Sarah could participate as much as she was able.

They jumped when the door opened with a cursory knock, and Jack crashed into the room.

Dr Ted turned on him, furious. 'What the hell is the meaning of this? How dare you interrupted a therapy session?'

Jack shrugged and said, 'Sorry but murder takes precedence.'

Sarah had jerked back to the 'here and now', but there was something strange about her. Offbeat. Her voice pitched higher with a southern-American accent. She rolled her shoulder's back, pushing her chest forward and said, 'For God's sake doll, I am sick of the interruptions. I'm going to my room. Leave me alone. Don't follow me. I want some peace.'

Maya's eyebrows lifted. Sarah was different. Was she witnessing an alter?

Jack lowered his voice and said, 'I really am sorry for interrupting you, Sarah. I didn't mean to make the situation worse for you.'

Sarah stood and rolled her wrists. 'I don't want your apology. I just want alone time.' She left the room with an exaggerated rock to her hips.

Jack turned to Maya and said, 'Maya can you please leave us. I want to talk to Dr Ted privately.'

Dr Ted intervened. 'Maya you stay put. I've nothing to hide. I'm sure Sgt Jack will be quick and I can resume your teaching.'

Stuck between two strong willed individuals, Maya chose the path of least resistance and stayed. Part of her was curious to watch the interaction

'Suit yourself,' said Jack, turning towards Dr Ted, standing over him. 'We need to go over the sequence of events at Omar station again.'

'Great, just what we need, talking about the same thing for the 20th time,' said Dr Ted, standing up to face Jack. Again, with the power games.

Jack ignored the dig and said, 'Can you start from dinner on the third day.'

'Like I've told you over and over, Joy served us enchiladas she'd cooked in the station house and brought out to us in the four-wheel drive,' said Dr Ted. 'She left, then I mixed the psilocybin powder with lemonade in a large bowl. I handed out portions to everybody, roughly basing the amount on body size.' Dr Ted's voice and delivery were robotic. Maya realised saying the same thing over and over would get on anyone's nerves.

'Did everyone have their own glass?' said Jack interrupting.

'Yes,' said Dr Ted. 'Joy did the washing every day and brought things out to us from the station house. She gave us plastic drinking glasses before she left. No one touched Daniel's glass apart from him. Everyone drank from the same bowl. If the psilocybin powder was contaminated, we all would've died.'

'Did you see any other cars come out to the camping site after Joy had left?' said Jack.

'No. I have already answered this question,' said Dr Ted, glaring at Jack. 'There was no one except our group.'

'Did anyone in the group threaten Daniel or intend him harm in any way.'

'No. Yet again, no participants had any reason to harm him.' said Dr Ted.

Jack and Dr Ted had both gone red in the face during this exchange. They were defining their positions, opposite each other, but Maya couldn't understand the purpose of the interaction. What was Jack trying to achieve?

Jack sat down, 'Is there any way Daniel could've been suicidal?'

Dr Ted said, 'I have gone over and over this situation in my mind.' He closed his eyes and sighed. 'Daniel was full of life. He could be annoying but he was also joyful. Determined to get ahead and to make a difference. There was no evidence of suicidal thinking in this man.'

Dr Ted sat back down in his chair appearing preoccupied with his thoughts. His brow was wrinkled and he gazed upwards as if revisiting Daniel's death. Maya thought he may have been acting, trying to control their emotions in some game of his making. But if this were true, Dr Ted was a gifted actor.

The scent of elevated male testosterone faded from the room. However, two tall men sitting opposite each other, took up a lot of space. Maya skulked back in the chair, trying to remain invisible.

Jack said, 'What about the others? What were they doing that night? Do you think any of them could be our murderer?'

'I don't know. I guess I have wondered about Steve. He does have a history of violence. I was surprised by how unwell he was when he first arrived,' said Dr Ted. 'He wasn't properly vetted by his treating psychiatrist.'

Maya leaned forward in her chair. She was reluctant to interrupt them but felt she had important information. She said, 'I spoke to Steve's parents at his request the other night. His mum told me about the history of violence. It was more than 10 years ago, when he was using illicit drugs. But Daniel was part of his delusional system. Maybe that's important?'

'I'll bear that in mind, but if Steve had attacked Daniel there would've been physical evidence of injury at autopsy. Whoever killed Daniel was a planner,' said Jack, turning to Dr Ted. 'Do you think Graham's capable of killing someone?'

'Graham was a reluctant participant in group therapy throughout. He went to the psychedelic weekend with great hesitancy,' said Dr Ted. 'He did take the psilocybin, but it made him sleepy. I checked on him a couple of times during the night, but he was snoring in his swag.'

Jack nodded, encouraging Dr Ted to go on.

'I've spoken to him about his experiences. He's a very angry man because of the way the police treated him when he was first arrested,' said Dr Ted glaring at Jack. 'I think he came on retreat to please his parole officer and make it look like he was doing something. I don't think he was looking for a cure or even to change.'

'Does he have a history of violence?' said Jack.

'No not at all. There is no history of physical violence. He's far more likely to self-harm than hurt another person. He says he's angry with the police but it really is directed against himself,' said Dr Ted.

'What about Sarah?' said Jack, whipping questions at Dr Ted like a gunslinger, making the situation feel unstable and unpredictable. Maya wasn't sure if this was an interview technique or just his ADHD talking.

'I spent most of the night with Sarah. She dissociated badly and I was worried about her. I brought along some antipsychotic medication.' Dr Ted turned to Maya stretching his body upwards to dominate. 'Olanzapine wafers. I gave her 20 mg to help her settle. I'm sure she didn't move from her swag after that.'

Maya didn't reply. She was annoyed that Dr Ted gave Sarah a substance to induce psychosis and then thought it was good medical practise to treat her with high dose antipsychotics.

Jack said, 'One of the participants implied that you were sexually involved with Sarah that night.'

'That's just disgusting,' said Dr Ted tensing, fists clenched. 'I've never had a sexual relationship with any of my patients. It's against my ethical boundaries.'

'We were also told you had an argument with Daniel,' said Jack.

'That is true,' said Dr Ted. 'Daniel was a know-it-all and constantly interfered in the group process. He owed money for the psychedelic treatment weekend. I spoke to him about it, but he spent the whole time blaming others. This is not a motive for murder. In fact, now that he's gone, I'm out of pocket.'

The energy left the room like a popped balloon. Flat and deflated.

Jack said, 'What about Joy? A participant told us that she has a painful secret in her past.'

'It's complicated,' said Dr Ted, opening his clenched fists. 'She lost her child to suicide, many years ago. She's worked for me ever since.'

'We heard that her son suicided here at this Homestead,' said Jack.

'Yes, it's true. Her lovely son Samuel, hung himself in the white group room. Joy came here to make her peace with her loss. She's stayed here working ever since. I like to think it gives her a closeness to him,' said Dr Ted.

'Do you think she has any reason to murder Daniel?' said Jack.

'It's hard to imagine. She wasn't at the campsite when he died.' Dr Ted looked at the floor, staring. 'She's been here for such a long time. I consider her my second in charge. She's very dedicated to helping others get well.'

'Could she have been angry with you? Maybe she intended to cause trouble?' said Jack.

'She's maternal and caring. She loved Samuel, but Daniel's death serves no purpose for her. She's loyal to me and our treatment here. We've both seen participants improve and begin new lives away from the psychiatric system,' said Dr Ted, his voice serious and intense.

Maya moved forward. She had to stop herself from putting her hand up, like a young child. Stopping the two alpha males was difficult. 'Steve appears to be frightened of Joy. He seems to think she's dangerous. I think he has developed delusions about her as well as Daniel.'

'I didn't know that,' said Dr Ted, shutting Maya down. 'Now can you both leave me. I have a lot of work to catch up on. I need some peace and quiet.'

He turned his back on them both, facing his desk. Jack hesitated. Perhaps considering whether to push the point. But he stood and left with Maya.

9

Day 5-6 Post Death

Maya followed Jack through the Homestead to the outside. The uncertainty of who killed Daniel, frightened her. Jack was her safety line. They were clinging to a precipice and there was something about this large, disorganised, dust-covered man that reassured her.

Without a word, Maya and Jack both moved to walk to the lagoon along the gravel track. The air smelled of eucalyptus. The humidity ever present.

'What were you trying to do with Dr Ted just then?' said Maya, wrinkling her forehead.

'I wanted to catch him off guard. Everything he says is so rehearsed. I was trying to destabilise him and get to the truth,' said Jack brushing her arm, almost catching her hand. 'To tell the truth I was also worried about you.'

Maya smiled with his warmth.

'I was sorry to interrupt Sarah. She was shaken by the whole thing,' said Jack.

'It was more than that,' said Maya. 'She's so dissociated. I worry about her. I think she may be fragmenting into alters, different personalities. But it's unlikely that she's a murderer, more that she a risk to herself.' Jack nodded.

Maya enjoyed the movement of walking with Jack. Strong and powerful. The sun had softened its glare. Being outside was wonderful despite the lingering heat.

'Mitch and Dave managed to get out to Omar station. They fingerprinted the gun cabinet and the box of strychnine,' said Jack. 'It's a miracle they got that far without messing up.'

'Did they find out anything useful?' said Maya.

'Nothing so far. Workers are coming in and out of the station, all the time. There are fingerprints everywhere, so lots of people to eliminate. I don't think we're going to get much useful information out of it but it has to be done,' said Jack.

He turned to face Maya, stopping the walk. 'I'm going out to Omar station tomorrow, to interview everyone and get the lie of the land. Are you interested in coming? I'd like you to give me a hand.'

'I'm not sure Dr Ted will let me go,' said Maya. 'He's sure I'm deliberately ignorant and seems determined to educate me.'

'I'll tell him I need you for police work. I worry about you spending too much time with him,' said Jack, looking into her eyes.

'I'm scared of him. He's angry and controlling,' said Maya, pausing, thinking hard. 'I worry he's the murderer, but he's also my supervisor. It gets confusing.'.

They reached the beach and sat in the sand. The rhythm of the ocean was soothing. Maya watched the waves move in and out, and matched her breathing to its flow. She thought about her options. She needed to stand up to Dr Ted and own her decisions.

Jack appeared to relax with the peace of the scenery. Suddenly the clouds opened and it started to pour. They were soaked within minutes, like someone had drenched them with a fire hose.

They laughed. Maya said, 'Well there's no point running because we can't get any wetter. It's nice to be cold for a change.'

Jack's eyes softened and he moved closer to her, staring at her lips. Every alarm bell in Maya's mind clanged. The situation was already way too complicated. She jerked backwards before he could kiss her.

Jack jumped with her sudden movement. Maya said, 'I'd like to come with you tomorrow if you can clear it with Dr Ted. I'm nervous about being here on my own.'

They stood and start it back to the Homestead. There was an awkwardness between them. Maya was worried that she had missed an opportunity, but Jack appeared concerned that he had gone too far.

∼

DR TED GAVE his agreement for Maya to travel to Omar Station with Jack. It was like being horse traded, but Maya knew she'd got the best deal.

'Dr Ted's probably as sick of me, as I am of him,' said Maya, relaxing in the air conditioned 4WD with Jack driving. 'I just don't trust him. The cloud of murder surrounds him. It makes it difficult for me to relax and learn from him.'

Jack smiled. 'I could do with a partner. There's lots to think about, so the more observers, the better. With my ADHD I can miss stuff.'

'What about the famous Mitch and Dave?' said Maya, 'I've heard they're quite the pair.' Trying to make a weak joke.

'It was a miracle, they collected the strychnine box, and checked out the gun cabinet, without destroying any evidence. I don't want to push our luck,' said Jack laughing.

'What do we have to do?' said Maya. 'I've never collected evidence before.'

'Just follow my lead. We've already spent a whole day out here with forensics after Daniel died,' said Jack. 'But we thought we were looking at an accidental overdose. I want to go back and check things out, now we think it was murder.'

Maya relaxed back in her chair. She fiddled with the radio.

'There's no radio stations that reach this remotely,' said Jack. 'You'll find a bag of cassette tapes at your feet. It's old fashioned but works OK out here.'

Maya laughed and picked up the bag. She found a tape of AC/DC classics which looked in good condition so she plugged it in. She opened a box of homemade muffins from Joy. White chocolate, cranberries and lemon, they smelled delicious. She offered one to Jack. They had a thermos filled with piping hot coffee. Things were looking good.

The distance to the station was 120 km as the crow flies. However, it would take at least 2-3 hours, because of the condition of the gravel road.

'Geez it's bumpy,' said Maya, her mouth full of muffin.

'Yep,' said Jack. 'They won't grade the track until the end of the wet. We're lucky. The track's corrugated but it can get much worse.'

Maya adapted to the rhythm of the bumps. The bush was scrubby, flat to the ground, and full of wildlife. There were cockatoos, budgerigars, and parrots in every tree. They'd closed the windows to minimize the dust, but the chorus of birds could be heard over the raw sound of AC/DC. Announcing morning.

'Look at the joeys with their mums.' said Maya. Her face fell at her loss of 'cool', but Jack just laughed.

They were travelling along a kangaroo highway. Maya was grateful for the roo bar, on the front of the vehicle.

Given the age of the car, the air conditioner worked well. Thank God. Maya needed to protect her pale skin from the sun, so had covered up with clothing and hat. The heat was intense. 100% humidity can kill, and it felt close.

Maya got out the map to follow their path. She saw the area set aside for Dr Ted's group, 4 km north of Omar station.

Maya said, 'Why did Dr Ted organize a retreat all the way out here?'

'He said he wanted to give the participants a real, desert experience,' Jack said. 'Gary, the station owner, was thrilled to diversify his income. He fenced off an area for them, and built a donga. I know they have trouble with wild dogs.'

'Could anyone from the station come out to the campsite?' said Maya.

'Yes, but we get back to the problem of motive. No one there knew Daniel,' said Jack.

Maya mulled this over. 'You have one of the strangest jobs I know,' she said munching on a salad sandwich and offering one to Jack, as he drove. 'I'd hate dealing with the dark side of everything.'

'You can talk,' said Jack, taking a sandwich with a grin, 'you deal with madness every day.'

'That's true, but most of my clients have goodness in them. When you deal with a lot of trauma, people show surprising kindness, as well as resilience,' said Maya. 'I learn so much from everyone.'

'Why'd you become a psychiatrist,' said Jack, turning to glance at Maya.

'I like helping people. I'm a good listener,' said Maya. 'I really enjoy people's stories, and get a lot out of my work.' She took a sip of coffee and added, 'Why'd you become a policeman?'

'I struggled at school so I wanted something that didn't need more study,' said Jack. 'I didn't want to go to the big city. I like it here and wanted to stay. In the end I didn't have the imagination to think of anything other than my dad's job.'

'I guess there's a lot of psychology in your job,' said Maya.

'That's true but my focus is on the nasty stuff, not the good stuff,' said Jack. 'I know more about how bad people can be, than how good.'

Maya saw a flat green colour, on the horizon. 'What's that?'

'That's the lawn of Omar Station.' said Jack.

Maya's jaw dropped. Who would attempt to grow an English lawn in the middle of the Australian bush? They must be mad.

The process of getting to the station became complicated. There were a series of gates and Maya's job involved opening and closing them. Her hands shook as she worried the locks into place, anxious to do her bit.

The station house door opened and out tumbled a procession of kids and dogs and adults. The house was pale brick, tin roofed and had two industrial sized air conditioners perched on top. The group of welcomers, spoke at once. Maya was dazed by it all. There was laughter, shrieking, barking and yelling. Even the birds of the bush, joined in.

Gary and Jack appeared to know each other well, and shook hands. Gary introduced everyone in the group, but Maya failed to remember a single name. They were friendly and two of the children tugged at her hands, asking her to "come and see".

The mother figure ended the chaos, by sending the kids to do chores, and brought Maya into the kitchen.

She said, 'Hi I'm Julie. I don't think you heard, because of the noise. Come in and I'll make you a cup of tea. You must be exhausted after the long drive.' She wore a long green, flowery cotton dress, with a broad brimmed hat. Wide stance, with child bearing hips. An air of confidence and competence. A strong base for children to cling to.

Maya was surprised at the hot drink. She'd expected to be offered a beer. Julie made a hot pot and poured in milk with sugar. It refreshed Maya, more than she'd expected.

Julie sat with wide eyes, and flushed cheeks. 'We're dying to hear the gossip. All anyone has been talking about, is this death. What's happened?'

Maya hesitated. She wasn't sure how to handle police confidentiality. In the end she decided to give the information that was widely available at the Homestead, but leave everything else out. She said, 'We know that Daniel's death was not an accidental overdose. Did you know they were using psychedelics?'

'I thought what they were doing appeared strange. But farming's hard, and we were desperate for income,' said Julie, firming her lips in a straight line. 'If I'd realized Dr Ted was involved in illegal activities, I would've put a stop to it.'

Maya leaned forward. She was warming up to this woman. She said, 'We're left with either suicide or murder.'

'I didn't know Daniel at all. Joy stayed with us and provided food for the retreaters,' said Julie. 'I really like Joy, but she seemed to have a lot on her mind this last time. She wasn't her usual happy self.'

'Is the campsite hard to get to?' said Maya.

'It's about 4 kms from here, but it's hard going. It would take about 45 minutes to drive,' said Julie, thinking hard about Maya's questions, a good witness. 'No one could get there, without coming through this station house. That means it had to be somebody out there already.'

'We're going to the retreat site tomorrow, so I'll see for myself,' said Maya. 'Was anyone staying here apart from the family?'

'No, it's our off season. It's just me, my husband and the kids. Jimmy lives here as well, in the other house over the hill. He's our station manager. No one could go anywhere around here, without us noticing. And we've all got good alibis for each other,' said Julie smiling.

Julie stood and moved over to the long, modern, kitchen bench. It was an industrial setup, like a restaurant. Maya said, 'How many people do you cook for when you are going through a busy time?'

Julie said, 'At least 15. It's a handful. I usually get in help, because it's too much with the kids.' She turned to look at Maya. 'Do you wanna give me a hand?'

Maya smiled, stood and moved over to the bench. 'I'm pretty useless in the kitchen, so you'll have to direct me.'

They lapsed into companionable silence as they chopped and diced. Julie was a slap, dash cook. A total contrast to careful, thoughtful Joy.

Julie threw a handful of carrots in the pot. 'Where does your family come from?'

Maya had heard this question a number of times now, and associated it with country living. No one asked her what she did for a living, which would've been easier.

She sighed to herself. Her background was complicated. She was proud of her upbringing, but found it difficult to explain.

'The shorthand answer is that I was raised by my two dads, in Perth. I'm a city girl, and don't have a lot of experience with the country,' said Maya. 'It's beautiful out here. I'm sure you have a wonderful life.'

'I'm a city girl too. I came to Exmouth, as a school teacher. I fell in love with a farmer, and have been here ever since,' said Julie. 'It was one hell of a culture shock, but I've adapted to the everything now. When I go to Perth, I feel cold, even when it's over 30 degrees.'

Jack walked in, stomping boots and strong male scent. He took up a lot of space. 'What's for dinner?' he said.

'Stew,' said Julie, wrinkling up her nose. 'I always cook stew, when I have lots of people. It's a way of getting meat and vegetables into everyone. I don't have Joy's gift for cooking, but don't you dare whine about it.'

'I like stew,' said Jack. 'Nutritious and delicious.'

Maya was not surprised by the traditional male and female roles, on the station. There was so much to get done, they had to specialize. Country couples had a respect for each other's work, that wasn't always seen in the city.

They ate, and Maya went to help Julie bath the kids. Julie had six children under eight years old. She'd said, 'TV's useless out here and we have to do something with our time.'

It was a mammoth task organising that many small people. Maya laughed and joked with Julie, as they got the jobs done.

They went outside, where the menfolk tended a large fire pit.

Maya sat down, looked up and gasped. She'd never seen stars like these. So clear, like a spray of glittery paint across the heavens.

She hadn't thought about the night sky at the Homestead. The veranda was covered which blocked the view. And growing up in the city, stole any chance to immerse in nature.

Staring up at the Milky Way her spine tingled and her hair stood on end. The swirl of hundreds of millions of stars. Dusty white. The star experience must've been incredible for the participants on psychedelics. But Maya was glad she saw it sober. It was grounded and real.

It was freezing inland in station country. Hot, sweltering days turned to icy-cold nights. Julie had given Maya a cardigan. Thank God. She pulled it tight around her. Who could keep up with the weather in the Pilbara?

Beers made an appearance and the boys were drinking. Maya took one but sipped at it without enthusiasm. She didn't like the taste of beer. Strong memories of Emergency Departments and the smell of drunk accident victims, put her off.

Jack maneuvered his chair to sit next to Maya. His eyes glowed as he stared at her. Maya pulled at her cardigan. She felt awkward. She was dusty, dirty and sweaty. Yet he looked at her, as if she were beautiful.

An indigenous Australian man dressed in khaki and large hat, came up to sit on the other side of Maya. Long, lean body. Relaxed, centred. He smiled and said, 'Hi I'm Jimmy.' Self-assured, outgoing.

'Hi.' said Maya grinning back.

Gary said, 'Jimmy's our head cattle man. He knows everything about this place. He's the smartest man I know.'

Jimmy laughed. 'When the man speaks the truth, I've nothing to add.'

'Well, do you want a drink?' said Gary already passing across a beer. Jimmy took the drink and leaned back in the chair. At ease and confident in himself.

'I've been admiring the Milky Way,' said Maya. 'I grew up in the town and I've never seen stars so beautiful and clear.'

'You can really imagine the ancestors sitting, talking and telling of the Dreaming.' said Jimmy. Soft voice.

'I've heard of the Dreaming but I don't really know what it means.' said Maya.

'It means different things to different people. The stories emphasise the importance of respect for the land and for nature,' said Jimmy. 'The white man's lost his connection with Country. He needs to learn from our people.'

'It's beautiful out here. The world looks vast and infinite. It makes me feel small but in a good way,' said Maya.

Jack touched Maya's arm and leaned forward. 'Nathan's mum told me that the Dreaming is about the snake Kaljura, who travelled the land with the hill kangaroo Padjar. They started in the Kennedy Range and went north creating gorges and ranges.'

Jimmy laughed. 'It's a bit more complicated than that.'

The starlight was vivid. Maya settled back in her chair, listening to the talk flow back and forth. The gossip created a lulling noise, and her head started to droop. Weather, cattle and the neighbouring properties.

Maya jumped when Jack tapped her arm. 'Time for bed. We've got a big day tomorrow.'

Maya and Jack were sleeping in swags on the back veranda, elevated out of the dirt. A new experience for Maya. They'd set up the large canvas rolls, which contained an air mattress and sleeping bag. Zipped up, you were cocooned in your own world, until morning.

Jack said goodnight, turned over and went straight to sleep. He snored with throaty coughs and gasps. So much for romance. Maya wished she'd bought ear plugs. Gradually the cicadas lulled her to sleep.

∽

MAYA WOKE WITH A START. Small sticky fingers were pulling open the zip on her swag, giggling their heads off. 'Wake up, wake up, it's morning,' shouted the children.

Maya stuck her head out and saw Jack doing the same. He said, 'Oh God get me coffee.'

Maya giggled. 'It really does feel early. What the hell is this?'

They got up and followed the kids into the kitchen, wearing their pyjamas. Julie was busy putting out for cereals and organising drinks.

Julie said, 'Help yourself to coffee. I've a pot over there.'

'What ungodly time in the morning is at?' said Jack, groaning and massaging his forehead.

'5:30 AM. You get used to it with young kids,' said Julie. Her face was grey and her smile limp but she powered on, like a force of nature.

'Remind me to stay the hell away from them,' said Jack.

The morning routine of eating, showering, cleaning teeth and packing was constantly interrupted by small children and dogs. However, Maya and Jack were in the car and moving by 6:30 AM.

'What did you think of Omar Station?' said Jack.

'I loved it,' said Maya. 'I couldn't believe they had anything to do with Daniel's death.'

'You'd make a rotten detective. When you're in the police force, you have to suspect everybody. The team back in Perth are checking out anyone, who had opportunity. Nagging me for more details,' said Jack, his face scrunched up, straining to concentrate on the driving.

It was awful driving conditions, out to the retreat. It was like sitting on a rollercoaster, up and down, up and down. The tyre pressure was low, hub caps locked and the four-wheel-drive engaged. Jack's arms tensed, as he wrestled the 4WD along the dirt track.

Maya looked out the window charmed by the remote bush. Scrubby trees, red earth, animals moving about in the cool of the early morning.

A person could easily walk 4 kms in an hour, but it really did take 45 minutes of hard driving to get there. They arrived at a ridge on the side of the hill which had been fenced off. There were three large canvas tents. A small, square, brick building, like a shed, with a giant air conditioner stuck in the top of it. Probably to stop attendees from dying of heatstroke.

The area had been canvassed by professional, forensic technicians when Daniel's body was first found. All the belongings of the participants were in Perth. But the campsites were still evident.

'What are you hoping to get out of coming here?' said Maya

'Well, when we came here last time the participants were around and were hysterical. So many people running everywhere,' said Jack moving slowly from campsite to campsite. 'We were sure it was an accidental overdose. It would've affected my judgement. I wanted to come back and go through the setup again, in the quiet.'

Jack took Maya through the layout drawn on a mud-map, and said, 'It helps having someone else here. When I say things out loud, it makes me think and slows me down.'

'Well, my impression is anyone could've murdered him. The campsites are so close together,' said Maya, standing stretching her back. 'Have they figured out how he took the strychnine?'

'No, it's partly why we're here. I want to make sure we haven't missed any pieces of information, no matter how small,' said Jack.

For someone with ADHD, Jack was persistent and detail orientated. Maybe his training? He used a notebook, camera on his phone, plastic gloves and collection bags. He spoke out loud to himself, pushing to concentrate.

Maya became bored within 15 minutes. Not cut out for police work. She faked interest for nearly 2 hours, wanting to impress Jack. She wandered in larger circles and ended up standing on the ridge. The view was spectacular. She fancied she could see all the way to the ocean.

It was getting hotter. Maya wiggled and stretched her aching limbs. She moved into a pretend yoga flow trying to bring back feeling. At the edge of her vision, she caught something blue, foreign to the environment.

'What's that?' said Maya pointing across the ridge.

Jack jumped up and came over. 'Where do you mean?'

Maya was standing on tippy toes, stretched out as long as possible. 'Over there. It's blue. It doesn't belong in this environment.'

In his enthusiasm to see, Jack almost toppled over. He said, 'You must have x-ray vision. I can't see it. Do you think you could take me there?'

Maya was thrilled. She'd hoped to be helpful. She started down a kangaroo path alongside the ridge. She said 'It looks like someone threw something over here from the edge of the outlook.'

They twisted and turned along the path. Maya found a natural sense of direction, that she hadn't realised she possessed. They squeezed between the prickly bushes stamping their feet to warn the snakes of their approach. Red dirt flying. Dust in her mouth. Sticky, hot.

Maya stopped abruptly bent forward and pulled out a blue drinking container, grinning from ear to ear.

'Oh God, drop it in here. Don't contaminated with your fingerprints.' said Jack, almost screaming. He shoved a plastic bag in Maya's direction, hopping from foot to foot.

Maya flinched. Hurled the container in the bag.

Jack spoke in a quieter voice, 'I'm sorry, I didn't mean to yell. I just want to find the bastard who did this.'

Tears blurred her vision. The heat seared her throat with every breathe. Her sensible soul realised, they were tired and hot. But she hated the expression of anger. It made it hard to trust. And who was left if she couldn't trust Jack?

10

Day 6-7 Post Death

Maya and Jack picked their way back to the car, through the scrubby bush. Jack moved a little too close to Maya for her liking. She tensed and backed up, but noticed his eyes were wet.

Jack said, 'I'm sorry I yelled. I was so excited about the find, I lost perspective. You're more important than a bottle.'

Maya stopped and looked Jack straight in the face. 'We're both tired. I overreacted. Let's start again.'

Jack smiled at her. His jaw relaxed. He busied himself, sorting through the samples, and announced his satisfaction with the collection. The plan was to continue along the dirt track to the main highway and go into Exmouth. Jack could drop off specimens they'd collected, to send to forensics in Perth. They would complete the circle, crossing Yardie Creek to get back to the Homestead by dinner.

It was one hell of a drive. But country people are raised on long drives and could tough it out.

Maya enjoyed a road trip. The plastic bag at her feet was a container of miracles. There were tapes from all the major bands in the 1970s and 80s. They rocked to AC/DC, sang opera with Queen and jigged along to Elton John. Singing at the top of their voices. They ate sandwiches and muffins from Joy. She really was a much better cook than Julie. Maya laughed and joked. Jack's apology worked. She relaxed and enjoyed herself.

Too soon, they arrived at the Exmouth police station. A flat squat building, brick, with an iron roof. All the buildings in Exmouth looked squashed, built close to the ground, like bugs on a school child's collection tray. Practical but ugly. Maybe designed to withstand cyclones, that hit the area on a regular basis?

The police staff were warm and welcoming to Maya, while Jack organised to transfer the specimens. She was finger-printed, to exclude her prints from the drink bottle. But no one made her feel bad. She was given an appalling cup of coffee, ubiquitous to government services. Black and harsh. Not warming. She chatted to the receptionist about the weather. Weather was the safest topic of conversation available in the country. Endlessly fascinating to all. Everyone had an opinion.

Maya was happy to leave and be back on the road with Jack. She said, 'Do you want to catch up with your family? I don't mind hanging around.'

'We're not close. My dad had a drinking problem when I was a kid. I don't see them often, even when I'm in town,' said Jack, his voice tight and edgy.

Maya bit her bottom lip and said, 'I'm sorry. I didn't mean to bring up bad memories.'

Jack shifted in his chair. 'It's why I felt bad, yelling at you over the water bottle. My dad was a bully and I don't want to be like that.'

They drove past the gigantic radio towers outside Exmouth. Maya cringed. They looked like an alien net, bending over sucking up every conversation available. Spying on everybody.

Maya held her breath, trying to think how to change the discussion. Her alliance with Jack wasn't ready to get deep and meaningful.

'I loved swimming on the reef near the Homestead. Where are the best places to snorkel along here?' said Maya, keeping her voice warm and open.

Jack physically relaxed. 'Well, everyone talks about Turquoise Bay and the Oyster Stacks. But I like some of the smaller beaches in the National Park.' He turned to smile at Maya. 'I could take you one day. We could even go further in the outer reef, which is amazing.'

'Do the sharks bother you?' said Maya, hesitant.

'No, they're reef sharks and don't bother humans. The bigger sharks don't come in to the inner reef,' said Jack. 'The world under the water is so beautiful and amazing, you don't even think about sharks.'

Maya laughed.

They arrived at the Yardie Creek Crossing. Jack pulled to the side and went to talk to other travellers.

Maya gazed at the cloudy water meandering to the ocean. There was a narrow, steep sided gorge to her left, with red, layered walls, like a Tetris puzzle. The heat clouded the atmosphere, like a bad dream.

Jack appeared at her window. Maya jumped. 'Do you wanna walk the crossing? I always like to, before I drive it. That way I can see if there are any sudden drop offs or holes,' said Jack.

Maya got out. She was hot and liked the idea of wading through the sloshy sand. It was a strange feeling walking through murky water in thongs, worrying about stepping on glass. She didn't understand what she was looking for, but tried to mimic Jack's actions. Apart from the cloudy bottom, there were no obvious dips.

Jack declared himself satisfied and they set off. The bumps and roll of the car were like a ship, but the crossing went well. Maya had become used to the rolling movements of the 4-WD. She was more unsteady on the land by now. Like she'd been at sea.

'I'm having so much fun, I'll be sad to be back,' said Maya, turning to look at Jack.

'I feel the same,' said Jack. 'But there's a murderer to catch. I have to do my job.'

'Do you think anyone else is at risk?' said Maya. 'It just seems so unreal to me.'

'This has been a strange one, since the beginning,' said Jack. 'But there has to be a reason Daniel was killed. There's no way this is the action of a random murderer or serial killer.'

He paused for a moment and turned to look at Maya. 'I don't think you're at much risk. You should still take basic precautions like locking your door. But no one has any reason to hurt you. You weren't even there at the time of the murder.'

They were on the road to the Homestead and saw the flickering lights in the distance. It looked welcoming and safe. Hard to understand what had gone wrong in this place. As they drove up, Lydia's screaming voice could be heard from the paddock.

Jack rolled his eyes and said, 'Good luck with that one.'

Maya's gut clenched as she went into the house. Lydia was yelling, 'I know you took it, Graham. You're just trying to rile me up.'

Graham was in his room with the door locked. Lydia pounded outside screaming in frustration.

Maya walked up to her and said, 'Lydia if you want to talk to me, I'll be in the white group room for the next half hour. You'd be very welcome.' She walked away before becoming embroiled in an unsolvable crisis.

Maya made herself a cup of tea and went in the room to read through some academic papers on group therapy. Who knows what might help? She waited. Minutes passed and there was a tentative tap on the door. Maya opened it, to welcome Lydia in.

Lydia stood and rocked forward and back. 'The last day has just been awful. Sarah tried to kill herself again. Dr Ted's furious and won't come out of his room. Then Graham stole my notepad.'

'What notepad?' said Maya. Dumb question but she was tired.

'I've been doing my own investigations since the murder. I've written everything down in a notepad. Graham's taken it,' said Lydia.

'How do you know that Graham stole it?' said Maya. 'Is it possible you just lost it?'

'I don't know that it was him, but someone took it,' said Lydia. 'It was in the cupboard in my bedroom. I locked the door and someone broke in. Graham can pick locks, so I thought it was him.'

'What did Graham say?' said Maya. Still struggling to keep up. At least Lydia might calm down with a problem-solving approach.

'He denied it, of course. But he's the only one who could break in,' said Lydia clenching her fists. 'It had all my notes in it about the case.'

'Have you found out something about the murder that we don't know?' said Maya.

'Not really,' said Lydia looking down at the ground. 'But it had all my thoughts on the others' personalities and whether they behaved like murderers.'

Maya sat still and thought about the situation. She worried Lydia was putting herself at risk. Perhaps provoking the killer through her research? Or was Lydia trying to attract attention and place herself at the center of the investigations?

Tears appeared in Lydia's eyes. She said, 'I'm the youngest in my family. My older sisters used to gang up on me and tease me. They'd steal my stuff.'

Maya said, 'That must have been a frustrating experience for you.'

'Yes, and my mother never believed me when I told her what they did,' said Lydia, starting to cry. Tears sprung from every orifice, eyes nose and mouth. Lydia was a hurricane of emotion. Maya thought how hard it must be, living in Lydia's head.

'This's a difficult situation to know what to do. We can't force Graham or any of the others to let us search their rooms. Do you have any suggestions?' said Maya.

'I thought you would organise a search,' said Lydia, her voice rising, sounding on the verge of hysteria. 'It's so unfair They're mean to me. Graham makes fun of me and calls me small T trauma. He says I haven't suffered like the rest of them.'

Maya sighed to herself. 'You sound angry. Is that what you're feeling?' Trying to slow Lydia down, to get her to connect feelings with thoughts and behaviour.

'Of course, I'm angry. They're bastards. They don't take me seriously,' said Lydia looking up and glaring at Maya.

'No one can judge anyone else's suffering,' said Maya. 'No one can tell someone not to feel pain from a broken toe, just because they broke their hip. Everyone is entitled to feel their own pain. Physical or emotional.'

There was silence. Maya wasn't sure whether Lydia was ignoring her, planning another screaming fit or thinking about what she'd said.

Maya tried again. 'Tell me about your childhood. I'm interested in how it affected you.'

Lydia sat up throwing her arms and legs all over the place. Maya almost toppled off the chair.

Lydia said, 'I was the youngest of three girls. My mother was overwhelmed and couldn't cope. She never gave me the attention I needed. My father was a pharmacist. We moved from town to town because of his job. I went to seven different schools.'

'That sounds difficult. How did you cope with all that change?' said Maya.

'I guess I coped with drugs. A bit like my dad coped with alcohol. I started on marijuana by the age of 11. I was using ecstasy, cocaine and LSD by 14,' said Lydia looking down at the floor. 'It really helped at first, but then I was always chasing the first high. I can tell you it's no way to live. Nothing was ever enough.'

'All that moving as a child must've been hard. You were very young when you first used marijuana,' said Maya.

'I worry that I've permanently damaged my brain with the drugs,' said Lydia pulling at a thread on the bedsheet. 'That's why my family sent me on retreat. They want me fixed as soon as possible.'

'I've never heard of people taking psychedelic drugs to cure addiction. I'd worry that it would make everything much worse,' said Maya.

'Dr Ted says there are case reports of alcoholics using LSD to stop from drinking,' said Lydia

'That may be true, but there's a risk of swapping one addiction for the next. Have you ever tried AA?' said Maya. 'They're big on abstinence. And they work from lived experience.'

'I'm not keen on AA. Too many rules to follow. And I don't identify as an addict. I use mostly on weekends,' said Lydia. 'But I do worry that drugs have hurt my brain.'

'There's so much more that they don't know about your mind. You're right the drugs do affect the brain chemistry. Just don't ever assume you can't change it back to its normal healthy state. It's a lot more malleable than you realize,' said Maya.

'To be honest with you, I think the drugs made my emotions unstable. I'm getting more impulsive,' said Lydia.

Maya looked at Lydia's eyes. She was beautiful, but so sad. Her drug use had taken something precious from her. Lydia was out of touch with her feelings. But had it pushed her further? Could her anger and impulsivity be lethal?

Lydia said, 'What would you do if you were in my situation?'

'I'm with the Buddhists on this issue. They believe that life involves suffering and teach acceptance. They'd tell you to focus on others and their problems rather than your own. Sometimes if you can help another person, it can empower you to help yourself,' said Maya.

'But who could I help around here?' said Lydia.

'Why don't you start with practical help. Joy really needs a hand. She's overwhelmed. Or you could help Sarah. I've seen you being kind to her,' said Maya. 'The idea is to take the focus away from your own problems.

Lydia sighed. For once silent.

'Why don't we go look for your journal? Writing's a good way to figure out your problems,' said Maya.

They went through to the female wing. Lydia opened the door to her bedroom and startled. There was the notebook, on the bed.

Lydia startled. 'I didn't do this. I didn't put it there. I've been framed.'

Maya said, 'It really does look like it was stolen and put back. I don't believe you would've missed it. We need to go and talk to Jack. You might know more than you think you do.'

Lydia picked up the notebook and said, 'Jack should have involved me from the start. I lived in Exmouth when I was younger so I know a lot.'

Jack was surprised by Lydia's story but listened.

Lydia thrived on the attention, becoming louder and more expansive. 'I think the murderer's Graham.'

'Why?' said Jack.

'He's gone to jail for paedophilia and pornography. Then he stole my book,' said Lydia, using her own logic and a total lack of evidence.

'Do you have any evidence that Graham stole your journal?' said Jack

'No, not really. But it looks bad for him if he did,' said Lydia.

'What about the others?' said Jack.

'I don't think Dr Ted stole my notebook. He doesn't know I'm doing this work. Sarah's preoccupied with the past. She isn't interested in the present. Steve's sick and not on planet Earth. But he's really sweet and doesn't have a mean bone in his body. And Eamon is just Eamon. He wouldn't hurt a fly,' said Lydia.

Jack's eyebrows rose. 'It's not enough to hold up in court.'

Maya gritted her jaw. Lydia really didn't know any more than they did.

Jack said, 'Do you mind if I keep your journal and go through it. You may have discovered something but not realise its importance.'

Lydia puffed out her chest. 'Of course. But I want to be more involved in the investigation.'

'Noted.' said Jack and then dismissed her.

Maya's head throbbed and she frowned. 'I'm going to bed. I've done a lot and need a good night's sleep.'

She was so tired that her eyes closed as her head rested on the pillow. The day had been eventful but they still didn't know what had happened the night Daniel died.

∽

It was a worried huddle of guests that met in the eating area the next morning. No one had gone to the lagoon to swim on the reef. They were subdued. Even Joy was distracted. The food was slapdash. Bread, cold meats, fruit and yogurt. Adequate food, but nothing like the previous meals.

'Are you okay Joy?' said Maya.

'Yes, dear I'm fine. I think the worries of what happened and the police investigation are getting to me,' said Joy. Her usual bustle into the kitchen was edged with agitation.

Eamon turned to Maya and whispered, 'I heard her arguing with Dr Ted last night. I couldn't hear what they were saying but it sounded heated.'

'I guess a police investigation would take it out of anyone,' said Maya. 'I'm feeling nervy myself.'

Sarah came stumbling along the corridor into the eating area. She was a grey colour and looked drained. She fixed her gaze on Maya, and mumbled, 'Can I see you this morning? As soon as possible.'

'Of course,' said Maya. 'Go to the white group room and I'll meet you in there'

Maya sipped her cup of tea, while she planned an approach to Sarah. Dr Ted was correct when he accused her of lacking experience. But she was a damn good psychiatry trainee. She knew her worth. Abused female clients found it much easier talking to females. She wanted to help Sarah.

She walked to the group room, taking long, deep breaths. Keen to radiate calm when she met with Sarah.

Sarah sat curled in a ball on top of the couch. Maya sat on a separate chair, to the right of her eyeline. She waited.

Sarah turned her head to look at Maya. Maya smiled. Good, a connection, hard to achieve with dissociation.

Sarah said, 'I took an overdose of sleeping tablets. while you were away. The night you left. Dr Ted's furious with me.' Her eyes glowed with tears.

Maya shifted forward in her chair and handed Sarah a tissue. 'I'm sorry to hear the suicidal thoughts got worse. It can be very hard fighting them.'

'You don't understand,' said Sarah, rocking up and down. 'It's all my fault.'

Maya sat for a moment thinking, and then said, 'I'm not sure I do understand. What's your fault?'

Sarah bit her lip and chewed on the inside of her cheek. 'Do you know what dissociative identity disorder means?'

'Yes. It's part of our training and I've looked after people with that diagnosis,' said Maya leaning forward. Trying to project calm concern.

'Well, one of my past psychologists gave me that diagnosis,' said Sarah, gritting her jaw. 'I have memory lapses... Blackouts... I do things that I can't control and don't remember, like that overdose. Who knows what I might have done when dissociated?'

'Are you worried that you are responsible for Daniel's death?' said Maya, closing her eyes, thinking hard.

'Of course,' said Sarah. 'Dr Ted yelled at me, but I don't have any memory of taking the overdose. It's impossible for me to know what I've done.'

'Do you have a sense of any alters?' said Maya. 'Have you worked on developing co-consciousness with them?'

'No, I'm pretty much in the dark about any of it,' said Sarah curling tighter on the couch.

'I think I might've seen a switch when Jack interrupted your session. Do you know long do the periods of memory loss last?'

'Maybe 15-20 minutes, not longer than that. But I've never hurt anyone before only myself,' said Sarah.

'Sarah, the murder was well planned and organised. It seems unlikely to be the action of a confused, dissociated person,' said Maya in a gentle voice.

'But it's possible, isn't it? Even if it's doubtful.' Tears flowing down Sarah's face.

'People in a dissociative state are far more likely to harm themselves than others. The Hollywood version of Multiple Personality Disorder is made up to sell movies. But DID is a confusing diagnosis at the best of times,' said Maya, touching Sarah's arm. 'Does anything help the dissociation?'

'Not really. It's all so unconscious. It just happens,' said Sarah.

'I'll keep a close eye on you and try and help with grounding and reorientation techniques.'

'What about Dr Ted? He's so angry with me. I don't know what to do,' said Sarah, her eyes welling.

'If it makes you feel any better, Dr Ted's furious with me too,' said Maya smiling. Wanting to give Sarah a sense of confidence. 'Remember he has a lot more to worry about, apart from us. Are the suicidal thoughts still there for you?'

'No, it's strange,' said Sarah, unfurling herself and sitting steadier. 'As soon as I do something to hurt myself, the impulse for suicide goes away. I don't understand it.'

'When you get back to Perth, try to find a good psychotherapist, who will work with you on these issues. It takes time but it works way better than psychedelics,' said Maya. She liked Sarah and wanted her to find peace.

Maya stood and moved to the door saying, 'Let's go and find Jack now. We need to let him know about your worries. He's a good man and will listen.'

She pulled the door open and Lydia fell into the room. Bright green lycra clothing. Hardly undercover detective wear. Maya turned on her and said, 'Stop playing these stupid games. Someone has died. Show some respect.'

Lydia ignored Maya, moving forward towards Sarah, speaking at the top of her voice. 'I have been diagnosed with DID myself. I can tell you all about it.'

I bet you can, thought Maya.

Sarah's face fell. Maya put her hand on Sarah's forearm to guide her around Lydia. She said, 'Lydia leave Sarah alone. Let her figure out her troubles on her own.'

Maya and Sarah found Jack sitting alone outside on the veranda. Maya was adjusting to the northern summer. The heat felt less fierce, less demonic in intensity.

Sarah sat opposite Jack and curled herself back into a ball. Maya positioned herself next to Sarah to provide emotional support.

No one spoke. Everyone in the group had a high tolerance for silence.

After several uncomfortable minutes, Maya said, 'Sarah and I have been talking. She has a history of dissociation which causes her memory loss at times.' She shifted on the chair trying to get comfortable. 'She's worried she might have hurt Daniel, in a dissociative state. I've told Sarah that I think this is unlikely from a psychiatric viewpoint, given the circumstances of the murder.'

Jack looked from face-to-face, trying to find his bearings. 'Okay. That sounds believable. We are looking for a planner anyway. The murder was not impulsive.'

'Sarah describes short lived episodes of amnesia associated with self-harm. She may have alters, but we are still trying to figure it out,' said Maya. 'It's unlikely it was her.'

'Okay Sarah, just try not to worry about it too much,' said Jack

Sarah sighed in relief and stood to leave. She said, 'I'm going to have a nap. I'm exhausted.'

'Remember you can always come and find me if you feel suicidal or start to dissociate,' said Maya smiling at her.

Maya and Jack twisted to stare at each other. The sweaty, prickly iron chairs were uncomfortable. Like trying to think leaning back on a sticky plastic raincoat. But Maya liked the closeness. Damnit this attraction was distracting.

Jack said, 'Are you sure it wasn't Sarah? I don't know anything about dissociation.'

Maya leaned forward. 'It's doubtful but not impossible. I'm going to keep an eye on Sarah because of her risk of suicide, but it would help if you watch out for her too.'

'Ok. I wanted to show you Lydia's pictures to see what you thought from a psychiatric point of view. She's quite the artist.'

He opened the notebook to show a picture of Graham's face drawn as a satyr, a wicked grin, eyes wide with debauch depravity. And Dr Ted's face in the shadows reflecting the sense of evil.

'Good God,' said Maya, paling. 'That's appalling. They look awful.'

'The smart art people in Perth tell me it's an adaptation of Reuben's Two Satyrs from the 1600s. They say it's really good artistically,' said Jack. 'I wouldn't have a clue.'

'Me neither,' said Maya.

'Yep. She's managed to make it look wicked and horrifying,' said Jack.

'Have you asked Lydia what she meant by this picture?'

'I have and she gave me a long lecture on Graham killing Daniel on behalf of Dr Ted. She thinks I'm too dumb to see it. But she has no evidence.'

'It could even implicate her. A sort of elaborate double bluff to through the blame on someone else. She's unstable, angry and might kill just to see what happens.'

'What do you think about Graham?' said Jack, moving around, trying to get comfortable.

Maya sighed, remembering the single long fingernail. 'The drawing only really proves that Lydia suspects him. Graham's hard to read. He's so closed down. I get that he's angry with the police, though he does have a sense of darkness about him.'

'Yes, he could kill.' Jack sat up straighter.

'Maybe, but we are back to the old problem of no motive,' said Maya. 'Graham physically shudders every time he talks about prison. He gives the impression he'd do anything to avoid going back.'

'I'm going to interview him again. Would you like to come?' said Jack standing up. 'He's done everything he can to avoid giving me much detail so far. It might help to have a second interviewer present.'

They stood together, almost touching shoulders. Maya felt the energy between them. Those horrifying pictures made her move towards him, to a sense of protection. And she liked it.

11

Jack and Maya wandered over to the main eating area, looking for Graham. 'He's probably run off again to avoid me. I had an appointment with him but it makes no difference,' said Jack.

Joy came past on her way to the kitchen. She was mumbling to herself.

Jack said, 'Hi Joy do you know where Graham is?'

Joy said, 'He went off to the lagoon hours ago. He loves swimming on the reef. He goes several times a day.'

There were grey circles under Joy's eyes and she was dishevelled. A very different appearance to three days ago. Maya worried. 'Are you okay Joy? You look like you're carrying the troubles of the world on your shoulders.'

Joy looked up at Maya's face and said, 'I'm fine dear. It's just a lot has happened and I'm trying to catch up.'

'Are you worried about Dr Ted?' said Maya, trying to engage her.

'Well dear, he's been behaving like an infant, sulking in his room and avoiding work. So yes, I'm annoyed with him,' said Joy, hustling out of the room.

Jack said in a low voice, 'Good catch Maya. I didn't notice, but she looks strung out. She must be really stressed.'

'I'm worried about her. We all have our breaking point and she works so hard to keep this place running. It's superhuman,' said Maya.

'Shall we walk to the lagoon to find Graham?' said Jack, 'The worst heat of the day hasn't come yet.'

Maya agreed but had little faith in Jack's concept of hot weather. She strode off to her room and mummified herself in cotton.

Jack grinned at her, like she was beautiful, rather than an entombed caterpillar. They started walking and he reached out to hold her hand. Maya stiffened. It was humid with a wild ferocious sun, and thick, sweaty clouds across the skyline. God was confused about the weather in this part of the world.

Her sweat combined with a light breeze, that did feel cooler. Neither of them spoke. The ocean was dark green, churning with undercurrents. The wind-chop waves made snorkelling impossible. Graham was sitting on his own staring out at the horizon.

Jack went up and stood over him. He said, 'We had an appointment to speak this morning. Why weren't you there?'

Graham stood up and faced Jack square on. 'The police are always trying to nail someone. They don't care whether you're guilty or not. I don't want to be your stooge.'

Jack pushed out his chest, 'I'm not interested in arresting an innocent man. I really do want to know who murdered Daniel.' He crinkled his brow, 'Aren't you worried, you're living with a murderer?'

'I don't believe you'll ever work out who did it.' said Graham, 'But I'm determined that you won't set me up.'

Maya intervened. 'Graham why don't you just talk about the others that night. That way you can't incriminate yourself.' Some of the energy drained out of the two men. Maya smiled to herself. She was good at her job.

Graham still glared at Jack, but he said, 'I have no idea what bloody happened that night. I wanted to try psychedelics for my depression. But that sure as hell, didn't work.'

'I noticed that your swag site was right next to Daniel's. You must've seen him even if you didn't spend time together.' Jack had lowered his voice and unfolded his arms.

'Daniel was carrying on as per usual, big noting himself. The man who knows everything about the psychedelic experience. Lydia was drinking up his bullshit as per usual. That ended when they had a fight,' said Graham.

'Did you notice Daniel argue with Dr Ted?' said Jack.

'They were always arguing. Daniel had a hostile force field around him. He fought with everyone,' said Graham. Maya's eyebrows raised. Maybe he was unaware that he'd described himself?

'Who do you think killed Daniel?' said Jack.

'I don't know and I don't care. I'm just determined you don't pin it on me.' Graham stood and marched off down the track. Something was off about him. Creepy.

Big fat raindrops started to fall. Plop, plop. They were sharp and strange against the skin. Too large for normal rain.

Maya said, 'It's going to pour. We'd better make a run for it.'

They started back along the bush track, pounding through the mud, in sloshy leaps. Maya was a strong runner. She ran well with Jack. He may have been chubby, but he was fit and paced her. They passed Graham. His face like thunder. Plodding through the red ooze, slamming his footsteps.

Jack grabbed Maya's hand and pulled her towards the old white gum tree, on the left side of the house. She went with him, laughing at the rain. The tree provided some shelter. Its limbs and leaves stretching towards the angry clouds. Long strips of bark peeled back to reveal the pale green limbs underneath. The fragrant, distinctive smell grounded Maya.

Jack placed his hand either side of Maya's face and moved forward. Maya closed her eyes and felt his lips on hers. A rush of electricity ran through her body, lighting her up like a thunderbolt. His scent was musky and manlike. His lips soft, but pushing with strength and purpose.

As fast as it happened, he pulled back. Jack laughed. 'We'd better keep it professional, as long as possible.' Then he ran back to the Homestead.

Maya was shocked, but felt a real physical tingling. Her unconscious, chatty mind stunned into silence. It was confusing, but wonderful. So much for planning. Being kissed spontaneously was liberating. She ran to the house and went straight to the showers. Covered in mud. She needed to clean up.

Everyone turned up for lunch at 12:30 PM. Nothing was on the table. Maya went through to the kitchen, and found Joy crying.

Maya moved forward to put her arm on her shoulder. 'Joy are you okay? What's happened? What are you upset about?'

'I think I'm just exhausted,' said Joy, through sobs.

'Why don't you go through to your room and have a rest?' said Maya. 'We can organise lunch for ourselves.'

Joy looked up tears running down her face. She nodded and left without a word.

Maya went out to the waiting crowd and said, 'Joy's worn out. She's going to rest. I've said we'll manage the meal on our own.'

Faces dropped around her. 'Err, does anyone have cooking experience? I have no idea what to do,' Maya said.

'I was a pastry chef in my younger years and I'm sure I can throw together an omelette,' Eamon said. An excellent group rescuer, when the need arose.

'I'm an enthusiastic chopper, so I'll be your sous chef,' said Maya. 'Can the rest of you find cutlery and glasses?'

Graham's face was red, after the run in the rain. He went to the couches, put a towel over his face and lay down. Not much help there.

Steve came into the kitchen with Eamon and Maya. He found the biscuit barrel and started munching his way through it, 'helping'. They heard Sarah, Lydia and Jack clomping around, opening drawers and cupboards, looking for utensils.

Eamon found red capsicum, chillies, some ham and abundant eggs. Like all farm houses, they had plenty of chooks. He hummed to himself, as he started a Spanish omelette.

Maya chopped with reckless abandon. Typical of inexperienced cooks. Ingredients flying everywhere, as she tried to anticipate Eamon's needs and wishes.

Eamon said, 'Do you know if the police are any closer to finding the murderer?'

'No, I don't really know,' said Maya. 'I don't think there've been any good clues.'

'Don't you think it's bizarre, that it could've been one of us?' said Eamon, his voice rising. Maybe he was anxious?

'I guess so. It's just no one had any reason to kill him, and it wasn't an act of impulsive violence,' said Maya. 'I don't know what to think.'

'I remember when my parents died, after that, it seemed like everyone else kept on dying around me,' said Eamon.

'Who else has died around you?' said Maya, her voice tight and short.

'Oh God, you're probably going to think I'm the murderer now,' said Eamon. He bit his lip, turned away from Maya, and stopped talking.

Maya realised she'd been clumsy. She was a psychiatry trainee not the police. She didn't need to interrogate him. But she couldn't see how to fix the situation, so she went out to call the others to the meal.

Lydia and Sarah had worked together, for once, making the table beautiful. They'd found a tablecloth and put flowers down the middle. It was welcoming and calming.

The omelette was delicious and everyone called out their thanks to Eamon. He appeared calmer, unclenching his muscles. He said, 'I'm going for a nap. This weather is exhausting me.'

The remaining group stayed, sprawling over the benches. The shiny heat was at full force. Harsh on the eyes. Maya turned on the lazy fans, three of them, standing like inattentive soldiers. Soft whirring sounds.

Maya's eyes grew heavy. The hot world lulling her to sleep, despite the awkward chair.

'When you think about it, Joy's behaving in a really guilty

manner,' said Lydia, drawing attention with controversy. 'Do you think she's the murderer?'

Groans rose up from all directions. Jack said, 'For God sakes, Lydia. She wasn't even there when he died. How the hell could she have been responsible?'

'I think it's you, Lydia,' said Graham, glaring. 'Isn't that the television trope? Look for the person who gets overinvolved, in the investigation.'

Lydia blinked and said, 'I never thought anyone would think it was me.' She appeared torn between wanting the attention, and wanting to protest her innocence.

Maya said, 'I don't think we should talk about the investigation. I think we need a break.'

'Well, it's hanging over our heads, whether you like it or not,' said Graham.

'Yes,' said Sarah. 'I never thought I'd say this, but I'm longing to go home.'

'I'm glad the police are here. It makes me feel protected,' said Steve, smiling at Jack. 'I think Daniel was a secret agent and has been murdered by the FBI. They probably set us up.'

'Anything's possible,' said Jack, nodding at Steve.

'It could be any of us,' said Sarah.

'It could be Eamon,' said Lydia, picking on the absent group member, not there to defend himself. 'Isn't that another television thing? The grey man. Hidden in the background, but going around killing people.'

All this 'he said, she said' business was exhausting to Maya. It was too steamy hot to get involved. She excused herself to do some work.

Maya sat in the white room and looked at the wall. Time passed slowly. Tick, tick, tick. Her mind was blank. No concentration and no idea what to do to help. She went back to the eating area to make herbal tea. Drinking fluids just to pass the time. At least dehydration was unlikely.

Nathan, tall and relaxed, was standing outside on the veranda with Graham, dark and black, holding binoculars. Maya saw Graham as an evil Satyr, as soon as she looked at him. Her heart rate increased. Bloody Lydia had her starting at shadows. But there was something about his awful fingernail.

Maya came outside, 'Is everything ok? Is there a fire?'

'Not likely in the wet,' said Nathan, a laugh in his voice.

'We're birdwatching,' said Graham. That possibility was the furthest thing from Maya's mind. It was so unlikely.

Nathan put down the binoculars and turned to Maya. He said, 'We're both twitchers. I love birdwatching and so does Graham.'

Maya was astounded. Graham appeared relaxed and engrossed in the activity. So different from his normal mask of dark anger.

Nathan said, 'We're watching the hawk over in the south east. I think there's a wedge tailed eagle flying around as well.'

'You're right,' said Graham, scanning the horizon. 'You can see the fingers on the ends of the wings.'

Maya laughed. 'Birds don't have fingers.'

'Yes, but when you're watching from a distance, the eagle feathers at the end of the wingspan, separate to look like fingers. That doesn't happen with peregrines,' said Nathan. 'Look through my binoculars and you'll see what I mean.'

Maya looked. He was right. The feathers did separate like fingers. The eagles had a clear wedge shape in their tail as well. No need to ask about their name.

Eyes shining, Maya put the binoculars down. 'Where the hell did you learn about birds? Is it part of tribal law?'

'No, like I said, I grew up in the town. My dad was a truckie,' said Nathan smiling. 'It was a normal middle-class upbringing. The bird watching comes from my mum, who loved animals of all kinds. I've only gotten closer to my mob since coming here to work on Country.'

'There're some mudlarks worrying the wedgies,' said Graham.

'The wedgies will eat baby birds, so the mother birds try and drive them out of the canyons,' said Nathan.

It was true. Maya saw the tiny brave birds swooping around, to frustrate the giant birds of prey. The breadth of the horizon amazed her. Like standing on a mountain, viewing the edge of the world.

Stark contrasts of red earth, blue sky and olive-green trees. Distant shapes of birds acting out life and death drama.

'How did you get into birdwatching?' said Maya turning towards Graham. As the words left her mouth, her heart dropped. He might think she was accusing him of watching women.

But he put down the binoculars, and turned to Maya. 'I've have always loved nature. After prison, I turned more towards the animal world. Animals and birds don't judge like humans. I'm thinking of retiring and moving to Exmouth, on a permanent basis.'

Maya's mind whirled. Thoughts of protecting children from potential abusers. She'd seen too much to switch it off.

'I'm not a really bad man, you know,' said Graham looking down at his feet. 'I've never directly abused a child. I was stupid and wrong. I watched stuff online that I shouldn't have. I've paid my debt and want to start over.'

Nathan was alert, listening to their conversation. He said, 'This area attracts a lot of rejected people from the city. But if you move here Jack will watch you like a hawk.'

'I'm thinking of living remotely, away from everyone, especially children,' said Graham scuffing his shoes. 'I'm never going back to prison and I don't want to give anyone any reason to accuse me.'

The heat was getting to Maya. The sky changed. Clouds came through. The air heavy with water and the sun glaring at them. It was like the ancient gods were planning to strike. Thor's hammer poised to shatter through the clouds at the earth.

Maya went back to her room and lay on her bed. She reached for her phone, in her empty pocket, but nothing was there. The isolation hit her in the guts. She took out her worry doll and rubbed her hair.

She closed her eyes and went through the participants. Lydia with her jingly nervous energy. Sarah curled up in camouflage. Eamon the archetypal grey man. Steve clunking around like an aged hippie. Even Graham dressed in black, but playing with puppies. It really did seem impossible that any of them were the killer. It had to be Dr Ted. She didn't know why he did it, but it had to be him.

12

Day 8 Post Death

A booming gong sounded throughout the Homestead. Dong, dong, dong. Maya jerked upright. Where the hell was she? The bed sheet tightened across her chest. Her eyes clenched against the brutal sunlight. Oh God it was morning. Her muscles tightened and her breath quickened. What had happened now?

The corridor filled with rapid footsteps and anxious voices. Maya peered out her door and saw everyone emerging from their rooms.

Sarah turned to Joy and said, 'What's going on?' Joy shrugged in response, still bleary eyed.

They moved towards the veranda following the source of the sound.

Dr Ted was dressed in white and gold. Tall and thin, he was using his wiry muscles to pound the gong hard.

They went outside, mouths agape and eyes wide. Dr Ted, sweating and breathless, turned to face them. He projected his voice, louder than was necessary. 'This group has lost discipline. Starting today we are following a Buddhist training program. Move in silence. Yoga starts in 15 minutes.'

Maya's heart sank. Her stomach joined the conversation,

complaining about the lack of food. She wasn't good in the morning. Downward dog on an empty stomach was a nightmare.

But the power of the Guru persisted. They hustled back to their rooms and changed. All in silence.

Maya's small bedroom clock told her the horrible truth. It really was 5 AM. She stared at her suitcase. She'd brought clothes for work. Mostly simple cotton dresses, shirts and trousers. She hadn't planned for hours of yoga. In the end she resorted to bathers and shorts.

Maya was late. Steve hadn't changed. He'd stayed in pyjamas, which was a sensible plan now that Maya thought of it. Graham and Eamon were a pigeon pair in black and grey. Sarah remained in camouflage colours, but Lydia hurt Maya's eyes. Bright purple with clashing green active wear. It was going to be a long day.

The yoga session was unpleasant. Maya had seen Dr Ted lead a gentle meditative flow. This morning he was angry and willing to take it out on everyone.

Up, down. Up, down. Maya's arms wobbled with exhaustion. Dr Ted shouted, 'Plank and downward dog are rest positions. Flow, flow.' So much for spiritual awakenings.

Maya's unconscious was sending her messages. Why are we doing this? The power of a loud male presence, and everybody folded. It felt foolish to argue.

Finally, it came to an end. They looked at each other in dismay, sweat dripping from their elbows.

Joy flung open the door and said, 'Come for breakfast.'

Smells of coffee, buttered toast and scrambled eggs filled the air. Maya's body was in shock, but her stomach knew its way around the Homestead. It followed the lure of the good food.

Joy's eyes were heavy and her face lined. But she'd pulled herself together over night. The table was simply laid, but the food was excellent. As she passed Joy, Maya said, 'Are you feeling better today?'

Joy gritted her jaw as she said, 'I am dear. I just needed a little more sleep.'

No one spoke as they ate. Dr Ted radiated fury. No one wanted to put their head above the parapet. The whole scene re-enacted the trauma of an abusive father figure. And the participants knew their role of passive puppets, only too well.

Dr Ted stood and said, 'Sessions begin at 8 AM. I expect you all to be prompt.' He turned and left.

Jack wandered into the room, bleary eyed. 'What are you doing up at this time?'

Maya smiled in spite of herself. 'Didn't you hear the gong? It was loud enough to wake the dead.'

'I guess I did,' said Jack blinking. 'I just assumed someone would come and get me if it were important. The late nights are killing me.' He sat down and started shovelling food onto his plate at an alarming rate.

Maya bent forward and whispered in his ear, 'Dr Ted is on the war path.'

Jack replied at a normal volume, 'So what? Everybody's grumpy at the moment. You should talk to my bosses in Perth.'

Maya paused and thought about his point. Saying no to Dr Ted hadn't seemed a real option but she could change her perspective if she wanted.

They arrived early to the group session and sat in silence. The stark, white group room with sticky couches. Everyone stared at their feet.

Maya worried about Dr Ted further traumatising the participants, but just couldn't see how to stop it. Like a slow-motion train crash. She'd deal with the wounded afterwards.

Dr Ted slammed open the door, then slammed it shut. He sat down, glaring at everyone.

Dr Ted said, 'Graham we will start with you.' Graham cringed and looked down at the floor.

'We know your history of jail time for watching paedophilic pornography. What do you have to say for yourself?' said Dr Ted.

This was a change of heart. Dr Ted had been begging Maya to understand Graham's position. Now he was on the attack. A head spinning reversal.

'Children in the Philippines are forced to make these videos. Have you thought about their predicament?' said Dr Ted.

Graham blinked and swallowed hard. 'It was always late at night when I'd been drinking. I just never thought about it.'

Every muscle in Dr Ted's body tensed. He appeared to hold himself back from hitting Graham. The participants gasped.

Graham's voice rose in pitch to an irritating whine. 'I was in a bad state. Drinking every night. My wife and children wanted nothing to do with me. I was just trying to make myself feel better.'

'What about now? Do you regret your actions?' said Dr Ted.

'Yes, of course I do. But it was hard on me too. I've really suffered,' said Graham, face red, staring straight ahead.

Dr Ted stopped talking and glowered at the floor. Maya looked around the room. Sarah appeared dissociated and Steve was chatting to his voices. Eamon's facial expression was one of horror and Lydia's was fascinated, as if watching her favourite reality TV program.

Dr Ted re-started his line of attack. 'You Westerners are so spoiled. You know nothing of true suffering. You're always whining about your childhoods.' He turned to look directly at Graham and said, 'Real children were being abused in real places.'

Graham tensed. 'I didn't think. I'd never want to hurt a child. It's not in me.'

'And yet you did,' said Dr Ted, articulating every word with biting precision.

Maya rescued. She couldn't help it. It was her nature. She said, 'Graham, I think it's great, if you can recognise the terrible pain and damage for children, involved in the pornography.'

Tears came to Graham's eyes. 'It's hard accepting how wrong I was. I didn't mean any harm. It all seemed so unreal at the time. I don't want to think of myself as an abuser. But I can see the harm I caused, even though I try to hide it most of the time.'

Maya said, 'I've admired your love for the dogs. There's something really kind about the way you take care of them.

'Kindness to animals is all very well, but abuse of children is unforgivable,' said Dr Ted turning on Maya.

'Look I agree with you,' said Maya, meeting Dr Ted's gaze eye to eye. 'But if a person only sees badness in themselves, they'll feel hopeless and give up.'

'How dare you try and teach me psychiatry,' said Dr Ted rearing up. Maya reddened and looked at the floor. She'd tried to help Graham, and calm the situation, but had failed.

Lydia chimed in. She had an instinct for poking the bear. 'Maybe it's in Graham's past. I know he had issues with his mother. Maybe that affected his sexual interests.'

Maya sighed. Just what they needed. Talking about sexual drives was not going to help this situation. Like a flashback to Freud. Thank God, Steve and Sarah were distracted by their own illnesses.

Graham clenched both his jaw and fists. 'My issues with my mother are none of your fucking business.'

Maya closed her eyes to focus her thoughts. This approach was not helpful, but she couldn't see how to change direction. And Dr Ted appeared to want to fuel the flames.

Eamon had gone grey, the colour of his clothes. But he was just as addicted to rescuing as Maya. He said, 'Didn't Freud say that issues with your mother are at the basis of all psychiatric problems.' He had the group's attention but shifted in his squeaky chair. 'I know mine are. My stuff stems from my mother's death.'

'Your issues are based in Bowlby, and his theories of attachment.' said Dr Ted in a tight, restricted tone. Everyone paused, holding their breath.

Dr Ted's face darkened and he turned to Maya, 'Tell us about your mother.'

Maya's gut spasmed and acid rose in her throat. She didn't want to talk about her problems, especially her mother. Apart from boundary issues with her patients, the group itself felt unsafe.

She fell back on the old 'half-truth' strategy, and said, 'She was a lovely woman who was very kind.' Or so her dads had always told her.

Dr Ted harrumphed but Maya kept her eyes down. Dr Ted assumed a shark like approach to the group, moving his eyes steadily side to side, looking for his next victim. Maya was determined not to draw attention by splashing.

'Lydia, tell us about your family and your childhood,' said Dr Ted.

Lydia seemed to miss the menace in his tone and said, 'I was the youngest of three girls which was really hard. We were two and a half years apart. My mum was worn out by the time she had me and didn't give me enough attention.' She moved in her chair, re-arranging her bright purple skirt.

'Why do you think you deserved her attention,' said Dr Ted, lowering the timbre of his voice. Perhaps a warning?

'All children deserve their mothers' attention. It helps them grow right,' said Lydia. Her narcissistic view of the world worked to protect her from Dr Ted's attack. Maya smiled to herself. Sometimes being oblivious can be helpful.

'Let's ask the group whether they believe you need more attention, or you've had too much, and are really spoiled.' said Dr Ted, glaring at everyone.

Maya was ready this time. She said, 'The Buddhists say the best way to help yourself is to help others. I've noticed that Lydia, you seem the happiest when you are helping others.'

Lydia glowed. Maybe she was right and she did need more attention, just the right kind.

'I think so too,' said Eamon looking up. 'You've helped me a few times with the group process. You've had a lot more experience in these situations, than most of us. I agree with Maya. You're happier when you're thinking of others.'

The mood in the white room lifted a little. The couches were sticky, like fly paper, but more of the participants looked up.

Graham's face was dark. He said, 'It's hard to think of others when you are drowning in your own emotional pain.'

'That's true, but you can try just a bit. It's a hell of a lot better than taking your pain out on those around you,' said Maya. An indirect stab at Dr Ted. It might miss, but was worth a shot.

'I'm calling this session to an end. We can meet again after lunch.' Dr Ted had tightened his facial features, masking the micro movements that could tell his emotions. Maya mirrored him. She intended to play her cards close to her chest. She didn't trust Dr Ted. The session was directed at causing pain, rather than relieving it.

As she stood, she noticed Lydia taking Sarah by the hand and murmuring to her. They moved out of the room together with Lydia's steady, reassuring footsteps leading the way. Lydia really could help others when motivated to do so.

A wave of utter exhaustion spread over Maya. Heavy feet, thudding back to her room for sleep.

Jack stopped her in the corridor and said, 'Are you okay? You look like death. You've gone white.'

'It's getting up so early. I'm a night owl. Useless in the mornings. The sessions today have taken it out of me,' said Maya.

'Everyone seems upset. They're in the eating area, debriefing each other. I'm going to try to help but I think I need your backup,' said Jack.

Maya sighed but turned around and moved towards the smell of coffee. 'I was never much good at early morning duty but I've learned to fake it.'

She poured the strong, black coffee into a mug, and felt better, before she'd taken a sip. Being suggestible, worked in her favour.

She sat at the back of the group and watched. They were grilling Jack.

Graham said, loud and hostile, 'You said we'd be out of here within a couple of days. It's been that already. When are you going to let us go?' Maya gritted her teeth. He could be offensive at times. And his long fingernail made her feel nauseated.

'Yeah, I'm so sick of waiting. I demand to leave now,' said Sarah, who'd shifted out of dissociation, into frank anger.

'Where are you going to go Sarah?' said Maya, in a soft voice. 'You're all meant to be here another week. As far as I know, no one, except Steve, has accommodation arranged in Perth.'

Faces turned to stare at Maya, red and sweaty. Hostile but hesitant. She was right, no one had a simple option. The rental market was a nightmare in the city. Their lives needed arranging, but with no Internet connection, it was going to be complicated.

'Can we go into Exmouth to get things worked out?' said Eamon.

Jack said, 'Of course. I'm going in this afternoon to talk to the others. We can take the four-wheel-drive Troop carrier. It seats eight, so anyone who wants to go, can come.'

Voices rose from all directions. Everyone was keen for a change of scenery. And to avoid Dr Ted's fury

'What about Dr Ted?' said Eamon paling. 'He'll be so angry with us, if we aren't around for the afternoon's session.'

'Not a problem,' said Jack with a wide grin. 'I'll leave a note that I took you into Exmouth for police business. I don't care if he's mad with me or not.'

'It must be so freeing not caring what anyone thinks,' said Maya. 'I'm such a yes-person, that sometimes I annoy myself.'

'I worry more about some people, like my bosses. But there really is nothing Dr Ted can do, if I say it's police business.' said Jack.

Maya noticed Steve staring at the floor. She moved closer to him and said, 'Do you want to go with Jack?'

Steve said, 'I'm really tired. I just want to sleep.'

'No worries. You go off to your room and I'll let the others know. We had a very early start this morning,' said Maya.

Maya hummed, as she went to get her purse. She hadn't recognised how trapped she felt, until the chance of escape arose. She glanced at her mobile phone but decided not to take it. Her secret shame lurked in the background. At the Homestead she didn't have to think about it, but she didn't want to know what was out there on social media. She dreaded exposure. Her dads were both at work and a hurried chat would unsettle her more than no contact.

It was a much chirpier group that gathered around the transport, ready for escape. The vehicle was huge, a troop carrier from the 1990s. Gray-green. Box-like. It was top-heavy, and looked like it could roll, at any moment. These four-wheel-drives had been called widow makers in the past. Maya could see why.

Jack was cheerful and smiled broadly. He jumped in the driver's seat and said, 'Maya you're upfront with me. Don't whine Lydia, its driver's choice.'

Maya was embarrassed to be singled out, but was grateful to control the air-conditioner.

Jack drove with confidence. His experience was obvious. They had no trouble traversing the now familiar Yardie Creek. Everyone got out and waded across. Enjoying the cool, red muddy water, and stiff breezes coming across the ocean.

Loud, happy voices melded together, giving a sense of excitement to the group. Jack dropped them off near the shopping arcade at Lydia's suggestion.

Lydia said, 'You guys, have to come to the bakery. They do the best iced coffees in Australia.'

It was a culture shock being back in shops. The noise, colours and smells assaulted Maya from all directions. Pressured with choice. Urgency. Shop, shop, shop.

Maya passed on the iced coffee and went for a chocolate milk-shake instead. Not everyone had Lydia's tolerance for caffeine. The group made their way to the library to use the free internet and start planning their futures.

Maya sat outside and watched the world pass. Her secret, perhaps exposed on the Internet, worried at her. She didn't want to think or talk about it. And she really didn't want to know if the world knew. Stabbing pains rose from her stomach and she bent forward on the chair.

Even with the unbearable heat, Exmouth was a tourist town. She missed the quiet of the bush. Too many options. Ads everywhere. Swim with the whale sharks. Snorkel on the reef. Buy an ice cream. Drink a coke. It made her sick.

Maya distracted herself by smiling at the passers-by, and was rewarded with nods and waves. People were friendlier in the North.

The participants emerged from the library looking glum. Eamon said, 'The rental market is a disaster in Perth. There's nowhere to stay.'

Maya nodded her agreement. 'It's been bad for the last year. Most people I've worked with, have made do renting a room, until they've found their feet.'

'But even rooms are so expensive. They're up to $200,' said Lydia, shoulders slumped.

'At least we've caught up with social media,' said Sarah.

'But after all this time, it seems pointless and uninteresting,' said Lydia. Maya grinned. Amazing insight from such a social butterfly.

Graham said, 'I'm still thinking of staying in the country. I like animals. I've been looking for a job. I've had an online chat with the local vet who might take a look at me. It's difficult with a criminal record.'

'Maybe you could ask Jack to do a reference for you once this murder is resolved,' said Eamon. 'That'd help.'

'You want my help with what?' Jack appeared from the side of the building, as if he'd been shadowing them.

Graham scuffed his thongs and said, 'Nothing mate.'

'Do you lot want to go to Wobiri beach for a bit? There's a surfing break where they teach the young grommets. It's fun watching them We could go for a swim as well,' said Jack.

'I think that's a great idea,' said Maya standing up. 'Everyone's feeling flat. It'd cheer us up.'

The beach was bloated with people. Perfect, curved waves. Just the right size for small humans to learn the ancient craft of surfing. Mums and dads swimming, shouting and grinning with pride. Noise from every direction, wind, waves, birds and people. The scent of saltwater, fresh and invigorating.

The group from the Homestead were chattering and laughing, even before opening the doors. No one had brought their bathers, apart from Maya, who'd started the day wearing them to yoga. They slathered themselves in sun cream and jumped in the water wearing T-shirts and shorts.

Jack and Maya bobbed about together in the ocean. It was refreshing, after the sticky heat of the day. Maya laughed out loud from the sheer pleasure of the fresh, cool water on her limbs.

Jack said, 'Why do you worry so much about what people think?'

'I don't really know,' said Maya, playing with her buoyancy in the water. 'I guess it's a girl thing. But being adopted makes you feel like you don't quite belong. I think I learned to please when I was very young.'

'Dr Ted can't really do anything to hurt you,' said Jack, following her, in a clunky fashion.

'He could make life much more unpleasant for me. I'm still learning and he's one of my assessors,' said Maya. 'Don't you worry about people judging you?'

'I don't care about it as much as you do,' said Jack. 'I'm going to make mistakes whether I like it or not. If the boss can put up with Mitch and Dave, he should have no problems with me.'

'Are they really as bad as you say they are?' said Maya.

Jack rolled his eyes and said, 'They've managed to break two four-wheel-drives in the last two months. They don't know how to change the car's oil or top up the water or even fix a punctured tyre. It's just unheard of in the country. The local mechanic thinks he's died and gone to heaven. So much more work.'

'I guess even I know how to do some of that,' said Maya laughing again.

'Well, you're unlikely to put petrol in a diesel engine and drive off in it. That takes a special degree of incompetence,' said Jack.

'How did they get the nozzle in the hole?' said Maya.

'It's easier than you think,' said Jack coming closer to Maya. 'They filled the whole tank, before they realised. Then they drove it and wrecked the engine. Everyone's furious.'

The group participants started to leave the waves and were standing on the beach, air drying their clothes. No towels. Jack and Maya went in to join them.

The atmosphere was joyous. Getting cold and wet in the humid heat, was a wonderful feeling. Even if it left your clothes, salty and scratchy.

'We'd better start going back. We'll be driving in the dark.' said Jack to the group.

Groans and moans rose all round.

'I think we want to avoid Dr Ted. Everyone's worried that he's going to be furious,' said Maya, raising her voice to be heard over the wind. 'But we can't sleep on the beach, and facing your fears can be a good thing.'

'You can go in first then,' said Lydia glaring at Maya. 'You can be the sacrifice, like Daniel to the lions.'

Maya laughed. 'Okay. I'll wear my hair shirt.'

They climbed aboard the troop carrier and Jack turned the key. The engine choked and gasped, dying, then nothing. Silence.

'Shit.' said Jack. It was the first time Maya heard him swear.

13

No one said anything, as they got off the bus and lined up like school children.

Jack popped the car bonnet and started belting the engine with a wrench.

'What the hell is he doing?' said Eamon, gritting his teeth. 'There's no point beating the car to death.'

'He thinks it's the starter motor and he's trying to jig the bristles,' said Graham. 'I know my way around an engine, so I'm going to go and help him.' He was handy for a school teacher.

Maya looked around. Everyone had left the car park. It was isolated. Her anxiety rose. At least they weren't on a bush track. She guessed they could spend the night here, if necessary. She thought of food rations. The four-wheel-drive was full of water containers.

A bus came round the sand dune. An actual bus. It honked, arms waving out the windows, and came to a stop next to the Troopie.

The doors swung open and out poured a remarkable number of humans. Maya counted them. There appeared to be a mum, dad and four little kids, probably all under 5. Dressed in rainbow dyed hemp clothes, loose and baggy. Charm bracelets, anklets with bells and braided lengths of hair. It was chaotic. Warm and cheerful, but crazy.

The mum figure made her way to their little group, waddling with a strange, wide legged gate. She said, 'Hello, hello, hello. We always stop for breakdowns. It's karma. Makes people more likely to stop for us.'

Kids around her, were jumping up and down, 'Mum, mum, mum can we go to the beach?'

She grinned and said, 'I'm Dayna. I'll get my cushion and take the kids down. I've got the worst haemorrhoids, so I'm trying to sit on frozen peas. If anyone has a better solution let me know.' She spoke rapidly, in a breathless, high-pitched voice. 'Do any of you want to come with us to the beach?'

The faces in the group were stunned. Shocked speechless by the energy and easy oversharing from Dayna.

Maya pulled herself together first and said, 'I'll just let Jack know.' The husband had joined the others, round the open bonnet. Three men, staring into the engine bay. 'I think they're going to be a while.'

Dayna chatted away, as they walked. She waved her henna painted hands, as though weaving the story in front of them. 'We're travelling around Australia. We started in Queensland and have been on the road for six months. Where are you from?'

Lydia hesitated then said, 'Most of us are originally from Perth, but we've been on a retreat at a local Homestead for four weeks.'

Dayna and Lydia had the same restless energy. But in Dayna, there appeared more sweetness of temper. Lydia's temperament was somehow twisted. Maybe it could straighten out? Maya hoped that Lydia could see her own positive traits in Dayna.

'Cool,' said Dayna. 'I'm always up for a retreat. I'm a wiccan. We go on lots of weekend retreats. Worshipping the moon and the goddess. What's your retreat for?'

'I guess, mental health,' said Lydia, appearing subdued when facing this level of inquiry.

Hands waving with enthusiasm, Dayna said 'That's great. I think that it's really important to own your own journey. Even if it involves haemorrhoids.'

Maya laughed out loud and said, 'I admire your honesty. Haemorrhoids are literally a pain in the arse. It happened to me once. You can get some cream from the pharmacy if you're desperate.'

'I'm not into modern medicine. I prefer to find the natural way of healing. But thank you for trying to help me,' said Dayna.

Maya smiled, 'I agree that we all have our own path to follow. The body's great at healing itself.'

The three men were walking down the beach, faces glum.

When in earshot, Jack said, 'We agree it's the starter motor. I've contacted Nathan. He's got one in the shed at the Homestead, he thought it was dying. He's bringing it out to us but it's going to take hours.'

'That's great,' said Dayna with defiant optimism. 'Brad and I are going to build a bonfire on the beach for the kids, and eat vegan sausages. We make our own sausages and I've just done a bunch so there's plenty for everyone.'

Her husband puffed out his chest. 'You're welcome to share with us.'

The children came running up the beach, carrying pieces of wood. Maya thought it must be a wiccan-psychic communication thing. They knew it was time for the bonfire.

A delightful, tingling spread over Maya's chest. She found herself grinning and laughing. Growing up a single child, meant she hadn't experienced the fun of a big family. The kids were hopping up and down, full of energy, to begin the bonfire. They piled up the branches, and went to get more, with the adults now helping. They soon had a pile about 6 foot high.

Brad got a container from the bus filled with 'magic' lighting fuel, poured it on the branches, lit the match and off it went. God knows what it contained.

The kids danced in a circle, around the flames, like tiny, pigmy warriors. Stamping their feet, shaking their booties and shouting at the top of their voices. Their mum joined in, waving her hands at the other adults, encouraging them to come into the circle.

Maya forced herself to move forwards, and start to dance. She was naturally shy, but wanted the kids to continue to celebrate their joy with the adults. Once she started, it got easier. Lydia cranked up the cassette player to provide music. Eamon's movements were awkward, but well-meaning and enthusiastic. Even Sarah and Graham swayed in time to the beat.

Brad was an excellent dancer, and Jack followed his lead, watching carefully, like a chubby, apprentice ballerina. The sky was clear of cloud cover, and the moon rising. The fresh, salty air filled the lungs and the whisper-fine sand squeaked under their feet. The shouts of the children rose in the night air and disappeared. The universe was a big place.

As everyone's energy started to wane, Dayna left the party, to walk to the bus. Maya followed and helped her carry back the sausages and homemade rolls. Jack and Brad manoeuvred a flat metal plate on top of the flames, securing it with bricks. They threw on the sausages and delicious smells rose in the air.

'This reminds me of the Bunning's sausage sizzles. My dads used to take me every Saturday,' said Maya.

'Were they handymen?' said Brad.

'No. They hoped to get good at DIY one day but they were bloody hopeless,' said Maya laughing.

'My dad was a great handyman. He built his whole house from scratch,' said Brad thrusting his chest forward.

'I'm not surprised at all. You seem to be the same yourself,' said Maya.

'I did do the bus up myself. We sleep six of us in it, and we have room for a toilet and kitchen,' said Brad.

'The kitchen is pretty squeezy but it's a godsend when it's raining,' said Dayna, grinning at Brad. 'We're taking the kids everywhere.'

'It looks like they have an amazing childhood,' said Maya, watching these small people dance with joy.

'That's true. So many people overvalue schooling and academic achievement. We're way more interested in personal growth and common-sense,' said Dayna.

'You're doing a fantastic job. They're great kids,' said Maya looking at Dayna and Brad, standing there with their arms around each other.

Down the beach came a torchlight. As it got closer, there was Nathan smiling.

Jack shouted out, 'Nathan, thanks so much for coming mate. I owe you big time.'

The kids ran to hide behind their parents. Dayna said, 'Do you want a sausage?' And one of the children edged out of the pack with a bun held extended forward.

Nathan said, 'Thanks, looks great.' And sat on the beach to watch the show.

Maya slumped down next to him and said, 'I'm out of breath. These kids've got spades of energy.'

'It's a beautiful night. Less humid than it's been,' said Nathan.

Jack came over and said, 'Do you want to get working on the car? I'll come over and give you a hand.'

'No rush. I'm enjoying my sausage,' said Nathan.

Maya chewed her sausage, cautious at first. But it really did taste good.

There was such a sense of warmth and laughter in the group. Dayna approached Maya and started talking to her about Wicca. Being in nature, Maya felt the power of the concept of mother Earth. But she'd make a rotten wiccan though. Too concerned about what others thought of her, to dance naked with the moon.

Maya liked the concept of a bigger world than that which was taught in the academic sciences. A dreamy, relaxed feeling came over her, as she listened to the ebb and flow of Dayna's voice.

Maya said, 'At times I really miss my mother. She died when I was very small. I've two wonderful dads but they don't provide the connection that you talk about with the mother Earth.'

'I love being a woman. Your connection to nature and the rhythms of life will increase when you have your own children. It's great if you could learn mothering from your own mother but it's a power that exists in all women,' said Dayna.

Maya wondered if she were drunk, as this made perfect sense to her. By now, both Sarah and Lydia were lapping it up. There was something about the stillness of the night, the waves of the ocean and the moon, that did bring forward the image of the mother goddess. Maya wanted that sense of womanhood. She did fear that she lacked mothering skills because of her childhood. But the experience of connection with something larger than herself, was strong on that beach.

Maya heard Jack calling out, over the wildness of the sea breeze. The car was fixed and it was time to return to the Homestead. Dayna, Brad and the kids realised the group was leaving. They cried, hugged and swore lifelong devotion. It was like being an invited guest on Oprah Winfrey.

'I look forward to seeing you again and hearing about your journey,' said Dayna as she hugged Maya, after staring deep into her eyes.

Anything Maya said in reply was going to be inadequate. She wasn't wild about being hugged and kissed. She pushed herself to make an effort and said, 'Thanks for the sausage and the dancing. I had a great time.' Inadequate but, at least she was honest.

Everyone went silent in the Troopie. Bone tired and anxious. The group had nothing left.

'I'm worried Dr Ted will be mad with us,' said Sarah. No one replied, but a quiet dread over Dr Ted's potential wrath, spread over Maya.

Time appeared to slow down as they drove. Maya's thoughts did the opposite, racing from disaster to disaster.

Approaching the Homestead, every light was blazing. There was yelling and crashing. What were they returning to?

Dark and angry, Dr Ted stood outside with his arms crossed, and a glare on his face. 'How dare you leave to go to Exmouth, without discussing it with me.' His voice was tight and tense.

Everyone looked at the ground, except for Jack who said, 'Sorry Dr Ted we had to go to town for police business. I left a note.'

'Whatever you think I'm in charge of this retreat,' said Dr Ted, overemphasising every word, his tone threatening.

'Unfortunately, murder comes first no matter what or who's in charge,' said Jack, turning his back on Dr Ted.

Dr Ted grabbed Maya's arm and said, 'At this rate I'll have to fail you for this placement. You don't have the experience to manage the group without my supervision.'

Given his uncontrolled fury, Maya thought that most of the participants were way better off under her care. But she said, 'I'm so sorry. It won't happen again.'

'I know your secret and I won't hesitate to share it with the group if you provoke me again,' said Dr Ted, projecting his voice to be heard by everyone.

Maya's stomach dropped and her heart cringed. Tears welled in her eyes. Oh God, she was going to vomit. All of the groups' faces stared at her. Questioning, curious. Her head spun. She felt she would faint.

Dr Ted said, 'I'll see you all, 8 am tomorrow for group.' He turned heel, and marched back to the house.

Jack moved towards Maya and helped her sit down in the gravel. 'You look as white as a ghost. Put your head between your knees before you faint.'

Eamon said, 'Are you okay? He didn't need to be so cruel. It's not your fault we went into town.'

Lydia moved forward, jangling with curiosity. 'What's your secret?'

'Yes. You know ours. What are you hiding?' said Graham, moving towards Maya.

Help came from an unexpected direction. Sarah said, 'Leave her alone. The first rule of psychotherapy is that you don't have to share until you're ready.' She directed her attention towards Maya, touching her on the shoulder, 'You don't have to say anything. It's nobody's business.'

Everyone gathered their belongings and went into the house, leaving Jack and Maya in the gravel. Sprawled out like puppies.

Maya said, 'It's really late and we should try and get some sleep. God knows what Dr Ted has in store for me tomorrow.'

'You still look white. What are you so worried about?' Jack's brow furrowed. 'Why don't you put in a bullying claim against Dr Ted. I'll be your witness and I bet the other participants would support you.'

Maya stared up at the moon, the goddess mother according to Dayna. Representing feminine power and intuition. Perhaps womanly wisdom as well? Maybe it would be alright? 'It was a medical mistake at my last job,' she said, voice cracking.

'What happened?' said Jack putting his arm around her shoulder.

'Someone died. It was a man with severe schizophrenia. He was treated with a medicine called clozapine,' said Maya stumbling over her words. 'He'd stopped smoking, but didn't tell me. Nicotine pushes down the levels of this medication, which meant that the blood levels of his medication went toxic. He had a heart attack and died.' Tears coming to her eyes.

'Oh Maya, that sounds so painful,' said Jack rubbing her back.

'My boss blamed me, because I didn't check if he stopped smoking. I just didn't think. I felt so guilty,' said Maya.

'You're not God and you can't think of everything,' said Jack.

'The worst thing is there is going to be a coronial inquiry. My boss says he's going to write that it was my fault,' said Maya, hiccupping in her distress.

'Your boss sounds like a total bastard. They're meant to have your back when you're learning,' said Jack in a low voice.

'That's true. Lots of psychiatrists are supportive, but the bad apples make life difficult when you're at my level,' said Maya, clearer now that the weeping started to settle. 'I think he's worried they'll blame him, because there were no processes in place, to monitor these vulnerable patients.'

She turned to look at Jack straight on. 'Do you think I should tell the others what happened.'

'Well, Lydia will probably drive you crazy until you do,' said Jack smiling.

'I do feel better now I've said it out loud,' said Maya shifting her hips on the gritty gravel surface. 'It sounds so much worse going round and round my head.'

'You have to be able to make mistakes. It doesn't make sense to try and be perfect, especially when you're in training,' said Jack rubbing her shoulders. 'We have the same problem in the police force. Mistakes can mean that people die.'

'I just feel awful. When I think about it, I feel like vomiting,' said Maya. 'My brain keeps saying should've, would've, could've.'

'You'll just go round in circles if you keep that up,' said Jack. He continued lowering his voice. 'The worst thing I ever did, was when I was called out for a domestic violence situation. I spoke to the husband and then the wife. It all seemed fine so I left. But an hour later he killed her.'

'Oh Jack, that sounds terrible. What a horrible thing to happen,' said Maya turning to look at him.

'Yes, it was. But my boss was fantastic. He made me see a psychologist. And he constantly told me that I'm not God and I can't fix everything,' said Jack. 'We both have difficult jobs. We aren't going to get everything right.'

Maya said, 'If someone had reassured me it would've made all the difference.'

They rose together, arm in arm. Not hiding their bonding anymore.

Maya's small bedroom was sticky and hot. Her chattering mind reviewed the day's activities, over and over. She worked to slow her breathing. The alarm clock next to her bed worked against her. Tick, tick, tick. Wake up, wake up, wake up.

Her hand kept reaching for her mobile. Like it had a mind of its own. God, she would've given a lot for that mindless distraction.

Her joints ached, as she tossed and turned. Despite the early morning wakening, she couldn't sleep. She slammed her pillow, trying to shape it to her neck. In the end, she accepted that sleep wasn't coming and got up to distract herself.

Maya was well-trained in insomnia focused CBT and sleep hygiene strategies. All the rules. The basic principle is to stop lying in bed worrying. Get up, distract yourself and wait for the wave of sleep.

She liked to read Les Miserables when restless. She brought the book everywhere with her, like a talisman. She'd read the damn thing more than 17 times, throughout her studies. But she found it soothing, and it helped her calm.

Maya padded into the kitchen looking for chamomile tea. Eamon was already there, sipping his cup. He'd propped the door to the kitchen open with his slipper, so that the ghostly moonlight drifted in. He stood next to the kettle staring at nothing. The silence was unnatural for this area. She could smell the open box of tea leaves. Reassured, she moved forward.

'Can't you sleep either?' said Maya, putting on the kettle and rustling through the cupboards.

Eamon said, 'No, I just can't. It's bloody annoying.' He moved to mirror her actions. Camomile tea for all.

Maya smiled at him and said, 'Insomnia can drive you crazy. I remember being taught how 'not to sleep' in insomnia courses. It seemed stupid.'

Eamon softened his jaw line, and said, 'I've felt like smacking my psychologist in the head, if she shows me another breathing technique.'

'In the USA, one of the hospitals treats insomnia with sleep deprivation. They have people running round the hospital until midnight, and then get them up at 5 AM to walk around again,' said Maya. 'They say the treatment's effective, but I think everyone lies and says they're better, so they can go home.'

'I've been worrying about what I said to you the other day.' said Eamon, staring at the floor. The square white tiles, looked iridescent in the moonglow.

'What on earth was that?' said Maya moving towards him. 'I don't remember you saying anything wrong.'

'It was when I said that everyone around me dies,' said Eamon. 'I worried you'd think I was the murderer. But then it brought up all the memories of grief.'

Maya sat down at the kitchen bench leaning her arms on the natural wood surface, thick and solid. This was going to take a bit of time.

Eamon took the space next to her. He said, 'One of the kids in foster care suicided. I found him. He'd hung himself. Then my girlfriend overdosed five years later. I keep seeing their faces.'

He stole a look at Maya, and hesitated. She took in his tiredness. Fading into the background.

'I'm so sorry to hear of your suffering. That's an awful lot of pain,' said Maya running her fingers over the smooth wood, mimicking the movements Eamon was making. 'I found a patient who'd hung themselves at the hospital once. It's something you never forget. And it sounds like you were very young.'

'The main problem's that I blamed myself,' said Eamon staring out the window at the dark world. 'I still do. That's why I worry that you all think, I'm the murderer.'

'Two other participants have told me that they're worried everyone thinks that they are the murderer. I think this makes it highly likely that they're not to blame,' said Maya. 'I'm not a police woman but I never thought it was you. You're a people pleaser like me, not a cold-hearted killer.'

Lydia poked her head around the door, notebook in hand. 'I agree. In all my research I never thought it was you.'

Maya jumped up and turned on Lydia. 'Lydia, stop sneaking around and listening to other people's private conversations. You're going to get yourself into trouble.'

Lydia stood in the doorway blocking the moonlight, hands on hips, jaw jutted. She glared at Maya and Eamon. 'Jack's spending all his time arguing with his bosses in Perth. Who's going to find who did it, if not me?'

'You'd better be careful or Sgt Jack will decide it's you, and that you're just trying to deflect attention with your detective work,' said Maya, turning to the hot kettle and pouring out her tea.

The moment with Eamon was lost, but his face appeared lighter. Maya took her book to the dining table in the meals room and sat concentrating on the words. The familiar rhythm of the story took over. Poor Jean's troubles made hers fade into the background. Sure enough, the wave of sleep started rising through her body. Like surfing on the ocean. You just had to trust the wave would come.

Maya wished Eamon and Lydia a good night and made her way to bed.

14

Day 9 Post Death

The next morning, Maya's footsteps echoed on the lino floor as she walked into the glaring, white group room. The participants lifted their heads in unison to stare at her. The condemned man.

Dr Ted was yet to arrive. No one spoke. They breathed in the silence. The room felt hostile, like it had an independent energy, intent on doing harm. The fluorescent tube light buzzed as if linked to an electric chair. Maya sat perched on the edge of the white leather couch and sweated. Every time she moved the chair squeaked.

Maya jumped as the door slammed open and Dr Ted entered. Channelling a dark god of retribution. Every muscle in Maya's body tensed, and her face flushed. Her chattering mind went quiet. Awaiting the execution.

Dr Ted threw his body into the largest chair and gritted his jaw. 'We were talking about secrets.' He turned his head to stare at Maya, 'Does anyone here have something to disclose to the group?'

Maya sighed. She knew he was bullying, but decided to take control of the narrative. 'Yes. I was involved in the death of a patient.

It was a medication error. There's going to be a coronal inquiry and this has caused me a lot of anxiety.'

She waited. Then nothing. No one spoke. Dr Ted stared at the ceiling. Maybe planning his counter-attack? Perhaps trying to make her even more uncomfortable?

Steve leaned forward and said, 'Are you okay?'

Maya was stunned. Steve lived in his own psychotic world but was reaching out to her. While Dr Ted sat with tensed muscles. Ready to attack?

She said in a hoarse voice, 'Yes. I've had trouble accepting that I made a mistake but I'll survive it.'

Sarah unfurled from her coiled position, and leaned forward into the circle. 'We all make mistakes and have trouble accepting them.' The two most vulnerable participants were moving forward to protect Maya.

Dr Ted swept in. 'The problem for Maya is that people die, when doctors make errors. Sometimes a sense of shame can be appropriate.' Maya blushed. Hot, flustered.

Graham looked up from the floor. 'The problem with shame is that it's paralysing. It stops you from trying to get on with your life.'

Maya's mind was blank. Everyone was moving forward to try and protect her. She leaned into the group, chair squealing in protest and said, 'I agree with you, Graham. Shame doesn't help. I have to find a way to forgive myself and keep going. It's just hard.'

Dr Ted looked as if he were at sea. The participants had shifted their alliances. Hesitant in their comments, but circling the wagons around Maya. He changed tracks. 'The privileged, white culture doesn't think about anyone other than themselves. A sense of shame might help. So many wrongs against so many other people. As a black man, I can tell, you should all feel ashamed.'

'You're right about our country. The stolen generation, the massacres, taking of the land. It's very wrong,' said Graham leaning into the group. 'But I tried to protect you from the police. I argued with them that it was wrong to arrest a man on the basis of his skin colour.'

Maya said, without thinking, 'But Jack said it wasn't due to skin colour. It was based on Dr Ted's knowledge of the environment.' Her breathing quickened. Not wise to challenge Dr Ted in this hostile situation.

Dr Ted glared at her. 'We've discussed the inadequacies of the mental health system in this country. I believe in psychedelic treatments. I've been targeted for trying to make a difference.'

Maya scowled back then turned to the group. 'Did anyone here find the psychedelic treatment helpful?' She was angry. Fed up with being a yes-man.

Lydia said, 'I've used psilocybin and LSD in the past. I thought it helped me. It lifted my mood but drugs brought their own problems.'

'I think the psychedelics open the boundary between the conscious and the unconscious. You become really suggestible and open,' said Sarah.

'Yes,' said Eamon, 'it can be good or bad, depending on what you allow into your deep unconscious. The problem with this retreat is that Daniel's death clouded any good.'

Maya nodded to them both and said, 'That's interesting. You're both saying that it might help, but the environment needs to be controlled.'

'I've 10 years' experience, and I've seen it work,' said Dr Ted through tight lips.

Maya sat rocking back and forth, thinking. Squeak, squeak, squeak. 'I'm still learning. But I've grasped two main things here. Firstly, we need better research into psychedelics and the environment where they are taken, but maybe they might really help people. And secondly, people are not just bags of chemicals. You can't ignore the psychological.'

Eamon smiled. 'And I guess, murder's a powerful stressor.' Maya smiled back.

The tenseness in the room softened. Dr Ted glowered at them but said nothing. The Homestead gong rang out. No one jumped.

Steve grinned. 'Food, great, I'm starving.'

Everyone followed his lead and walked out of the room. Maya was the last to leave and saw Dr Ted seated, staring at the ground. Surrounded by the blinding white walls. Like an inverted form of hell. In some ways she was grateful to him. Relieved to let go of the secret keeping and touched by the group's support for her.

The table was laid with a red cloth and green plates. Joy brought out platters of salad vegetables and fruits. There were stacks of cheeses and nuts. The bread was from the freezer, not freshly baked. Joy bustled around but there was an air of fragility to her.

'Joy why don't you eat with us?' said Maya, touching her on the elbow as she flittered past.

Joy hesitated, and then sat down. Neat and prim. Dressed in a simple cotton frock. Like a church parishioner taking her place on the pew.

Maya said, 'I'll make you a cup of tea. It's good for the nerves. And we'll all help you clean up.'

There was almost no talking while they ate. Out of character for this group.

'I'm tired,' said Lydia, lifting her head.

'We're exhausted. It's living in an unsolved murder mystery,' said Eamon yawning.

'Our busy minds are saying what happened, am I at risk, who was it?' said Maya, 'It's a wonder we haven't gone mad.'

'We should institute an afternoon siesta,' said Eamon, stretching his arms over his head.

Maya took the cup of tea to Joy who sipped in silence. Maya had made the typical country cuppa, she'd learned from Julie. Strong tea, loads of milk and two sugars. Guaranteed to raise the dead. Joy looked spent.

Maya imagined how hard it would be to have lost a child to suicide, and then find yourself in the middle of a murder inquiry. She'd heard Joy arguing with Dr Ted. Joy was angered by his withdrawal and avoidance. But now she wasn't saying anything which was worse.

Boots down the hallway and Jack appeared. He looked just as

exhausted as Joy. He said, 'Maya can I talk to you in the white group room? Police business.'

'Of course,' said Maya getting to her feet to follow him. Eamon moved into her position next to Joy, trying to help.

The white room had the severe, sterile sense of a judge's chambers. Closing the door, Jack sat down and said, 'I wanted to check that you're okay after Dr Ted's morning session.'

Maya grinned. 'It was fine. All the others supported me. Steve was the first one to step in and back me. I was stunned. He's unwell, but he reached out.'

'That's great. People can surprise you,' said Jack, touching Maya's hand.

Maya said, 'My dads always told me I was too ready to feel judged. They said I should talk about the incident and get more support.'

Jack smiled at Maya and leaned towards her, 'I've just heard from the techs in Perth. The water bottle you found had strychnine in it. There were partial fingerprints, somewhat degraded.'

'Wow,' said Maya. 'That sounds like a breakthrough. Who was it?'

'The fingerprints suggest that the water bottle was handled by Daniel, Joy, Lydia, Dr Ted and Graham. I guess that makes Sarah and Steve less likely.' Frustration showed in his clenched jaw. 'But the actual murderer may've worn gloves, so it doesn't prove anything. At least we know how he was poisoned.'

Maya shuffled back in her chair. 'The standout suspect has to be Dr Ted. The participants had opportunity, but would've acted impulsively. The planning suggests someone who's been there before.'

'I guess I've come to the same conclusion. Gary up the station, reckons Ted would've known about the powder, but they never spoke about it.' Jack stood and started to pace the room. He thought better when he moved. 'I just can't see any benefit to Dr Ted in the murder.'

Maya adjusted her chair to keep Jack in her eye line, 'I'd ask Dr Ted about it, but he's not talking to me. He only yells at me, when something goes wrong.'

'He won't talk to me without a lawyer present. I'm not getting anything out of him. How do you get someone to confess to murder?' said Jack.

Jack stared into Maya's face, 'Have you considered the possibility that Joy's the murderer?'

'Only in passing. She's so motherly, and she wasn't even at the campsite when he died,' said Maya.

'My bosses think that her relationship with Dr Ted is weird,' said Jack.

'Her attachment to him makes sense psychologically. She was a single mum who lost her only son to suicide. I think she displaced her positive attachment for Sam, onto Dr Ted when she came here after Sam's death. She would've been highly motivated to protect him,' said Maya. 'Dr Ted can be helpful. It gave Joy a cause to join. It's why she had so much trouble with his avoidance now. It's a complete change of his character.'

'Doesn't that mean she would do anything to protect him? Even murder?' said Jack.

'No. This isn't a cult. Dr Ted shows no sign of controlling her in that way. Murder's a step too far. She wouldn't act against her own morals. And Daniel wasn't a threat to Joy or Dr Ted,' said Maya. 'Dr Ted is far more likely to kill someone.'

'Why?' said Jack, rocking backwards and forwards on the chair.

'Well, he's a man and has testosterone, which makes murder more likely. I don't know about his background, but it can't have been easy growing up in the Congo. He must've seen killings,' said Maya.

'We know he was the much-adored son of a single mum, who protected him. But he did see murders. It was a rough upbringing. It would've numbed him to death. But it doesn't mean he's the killer,' said Jack.

'I've spoken to Joy. She had a wonderful upbringing on a farm. Good mum and five siblings. I doubt she's numb to murder,' said Maya.

There was silence in the room as they both thought.

'When we arrived at the retreat after Daniel's death, the whole place was in chaos. Everyone had come up from the station house.

There were people running everywhere. It was a nightmare of a crime scene,' said Jack.

Maya bit her lip, then said, 'I guess the fingerprints also turn our attention to Lydia and Graham.'

'Yes, I've discussed those two with the bosses. What do you think?' said Jack frowning and moving closer to Maya.

'Lydia has had every diagnosis under the sun, but she shows clear evidence of borderline traits. She is high functioning but she struggles with boredom, impulsivity and rapid emotional change,' said Maya.

'I guess she's the only other one who might know of strychnine powder, as she lived in Exmouth as a teenager,' said Jack.

'Clients with borderline personality have problems with anger. But she'd be more likely to lash out. Stab him, or something,' said Maya. 'There's good in Lydia. I often see her sweetness in the way she helps the other participants. I'm not sure she has enough darkness in her, to plan a murder.'

'I know what you mean. Cold-hearted, planned poisoning just doesn't seem like her,' said Jack.

'But it's true that she's inserted herself into the investigation, and is loving all the excitement,' said Maya.

'Yes, maybe you could imagine her murdering someone just to see what happened?' said Jack.

'She chops and changes her mind about Daniel,' said Maya. 'One moment she hates him and thinks he's a narcissist. The next she goes on and on about them being lovers.'

Jack laughed and said, 'I suppose those two things are not mutually exclusive. I've fallen in love with a number of narcissists in my time.'

'And we've discussed Graham. The caricature Lydia drew of him kind of said it all,' said Maya.

'Yes,' said Jack. 'He's one to watch. There's a darkness in him for sure.'

'How are you going?' said Maya. 'You look dead on your feet.'

'The bosses in Perth keep pushing to get a resolution to this case.

They're frustrated. We're lacking strong evidence,' said Jack, shoulders slumped.

Maya said, 'What were you doing in town yesterday? Was it about some evidence on the case.'

Jack gave a short tense laugh and said, 'God no, I was rescuing my dumb brother from custody.' He stopped walking and sat down to face Maya. 'My older brothers were so thick, they played throwing stones at each other when we were growing up. The game was over when someone bled too much.'

Maya raised her eyebrows but made no comment.

Jack said, 'Phil was arrested for DUI. He's a real menace and is going to end up in prison, if he's not careful. I bailed him.'

'That sounds hard. I'd no idea you were under this extra pressure,' said Maya.

Jack said, 'Family's family. My dad's useless. He's turned to more alcohol since his retirement. Pickled his brain. If I don't rescue my useless brother, no one will.'

There was a knock at the door. Nathan entered. He was dressed in his trademark broad brimmed hat, dusty jeans and shirt. Tall, dark and poised, like an athlete, connected to nature. He said, 'Are you two interested in coming to watch a turtle hatching tonight. I'm only taking five of us. Steve's on-board and excited. It should be pretty special.'

'You bet,' said Jack, turning towards Maya. 'It's something really special.' Maya nodded. She was following Jack no matter what. He was her sense of security.

Maya was thrilled. She'd never been this close to the natural world. Watching turtles hatch. She stopped herself from jigging up and down, and said, 'Oh yes, I love to.'

The sudden change of focus from murder was jarring. Like she'd caught ADHD. But it was fun living life without much planning. Exciting to be impulsive.

Maya set her alarm for the midnight hours and woke to it shrilling. She slammed it off. No need to wake anyone else. She dressed and went to the kitchen in search of coffee. Steve arrived in his pyjamas. Maybe he'd decided that his pyjamas were all purpose clothing? He looked like a walking zombie so she made a cup for him.

Nathan popped his head around the door as Jack, Lydia and Graham dragged themselves into the kitchen. Nathan said, 'They're already starting to hatch. The scientists from Jurabi are already down on the beach. Hop in the four-wheel-drive and we'll get going.'

Maya's heart beat faster. She gulped. The others had shiny eyes and smiling faces. A real adventure.

The full moon shone on the track. The car's windows open, exposing the constant buzz of cicadas. Kangaroos gathered in groups, like mothers chatting at school drop-off. Having a gossip. The world smelled fresh and clean. The peppermint trees gave off their characteristics smell. Like they'd just clean their teeth. It was magical.

When they arrived at the sand dunes, Nathan turned to them and said, 'You can't interfere with the turtle hatchings no matter what happens. It's tempting to help them get to the water but it's forbidden. We teach the kids to stop, drop, act like a rock, stay low, no glow. That means no light at all. It confuses the hatchlings.'

'Why?' said Lydia, 'Why can't we help them?'

'When they are born, the turtles need to get oxygen into their lungs before getting in the water. That's why the mothers bury the eggs so far away from the ocean,' said Nathan to the group. 'If you pick them up and put them in water before they're breathing, they'll drown.'

As they mounted the sand dune, they saw a hive of activity on the beach. There were two scientists with clipboards counting and recording numbers. The nest was 200 m from the shore, buried in the sand.

The large circular eggs were jiggling and cracking. Pale-white, like dinosaur eggs. Tiny black turtles no longer than Maya's palm were climbing over the edge of the sandpile and furiously pushing themselves towards the ocean, using their flippers. Their single-minded determination was remarkable. No risk, no danger was going to stop them finding the water.

Ghost crabs had gathered up the beach and watched the proceedings. Scrawny, scrappy beasts with alien eyes and curved claws. Like hungry diners waiting for a restaurant table. They appeared intimidated by the human presence, but edged closer. One broke ranks and swooped up a hatchling. Soon they were gorging on the turtles.

Maya was horrified. She understood the advice to stop, drop and act like a rock, because every fibre in her being yearned to rescue the turtle hatchings. Nathan came and laid down beside her. He said, 'It's hard but you can't interfere with nature. If you rescue them, they won't develop the strength to cope in the ocean. Only one in a thousand survives to adulthood.'

The scientist moved next to Nathan and said, 'It was a good hatching. We counted 54. Thanks for the tip.' They shook hands lying on their stomachs in the sand and the scientists left.

The action at the nest had slowed. A few stragglers, looking lost. Unlikely to survive.

Nathan stuck his head up to call the others. Maya rolled onto her back feeling the cool sand, wriggling to create a head support. Everyone followed her lead. Staring up at the stars and the moon.

Steve said, 'I didn't like it when the crabs ate the baby turtles.'

Maya agreed with him. Her chest was tight and her heart pounded. It had been awful to watch them die.

'Me neither,' said Jack rolling towards him, 'but that's Mother Nature. You can't interfere.'

'I remember the first time Nathan and I came out to watch the turtles hatch,' said Jack between yawns, 'We went with Nathan's mum. She was a fantastic teacher of nature. She took us on amazing adventures.'

'Yeah, it was when you came to stay with us, after your dad beat the crap out of your mum,' said Nathan.

Maya jumped. This was too personal. She felt like an intruder. Jack said nothing. No one moved.

'If anyone interested in some hot chocolate with a nip of brandy.' said Nathan sitting up, 'I've made a thermos. In your mum's memory, Jack.'

Maya flushed. Too much information. Her mind whirred. Nathan spoke as if Jack's mother had died.

Jack just said, 'Thanks mate.'

The thermos made the rounds. Welcomed by all.

The night sky held them in place. Maya felt small compared to the breadth of the universe. But there was an insidious weight in the pit of her stomach, an unsettling feeling of being both exhausted and on edge.

'We'd better get going or we'll not get any more sleep tonight,' said Nathan yawning. Yawns were contagious and everyone started.

'Thanks Nathan,' said Maya, on the way back to the car.

'I'm not sure I liked it. I worry too much about the baby turtles. But it made me think,' said Steve frowning.

'I think it was wonderful. Mother Nature can be cruel but also magnificent. Not many people will have the privilege of seeing what we saw,' said Graham.

Maya stared at Graham. The death of the tiny turtles horrified her. He was cavalier, just as she'd imagine a killer. Icy fingers poked her stomach.

Maya sat next to Jack on the way back in the car. She squirmed in her seat. Not getting comfortable. She didn't know how to ask what happened to his mum. Was she dead? It was so confusing. She was hyperaware of his movements but the air was heavy.

Jack sat still, staring out the window. Lost in thought.

Everyone has secrets. Psychiatry taught you that. Sometimes you had to let them come to you.

15

Day 10 Post Death

Jack entered into Maya's domain. The white office had become her home away from home. The room and Maya had made peace with each other. It was a symbol of Joy's sadness and Maya accepted that.

Jack's face hung. 'The papers have got hold of this story. It'll be out tomorrow. It's too intoxicating for them to hold off. Bad psychiatrist, taking liberties with drugs and a death.' Maya sensed him lingering near her. Tall but awkward. Not knowing where to put his limbs. Perhaps hoping to touch?

'Will it affect your work?' said Maya, trying to push professional, but longing for physical contact.

'There's always push from your superiors to clear cases. Usually, they don't care much about the country,' said Jack sitting opposite her. 'But this time they're likely to pressure me because of the press interest.'

'Are you any closer to figuring out what happened?' Maya leaned back and sighed. The lack of knowing resulted in a leaden weariness in her limbs. No wonder they were exhausted.

'I'm getting some more forensic support from Perth. They found a second sat phone in one of the locked boxes from the shed, which caused excitement. But everyone's had the flu, which is slowing them down,' said Jack.

Maya watched Jack moving around on the couch, squeaking.

The memory of the turtle hatching came to her mind. Clear details of what Nathan implied, but didn't say. She wanted to reach out, but not to pry where she wasn't wanted.

Jack was bustling on the couch, moving her notes around. Making a mess of them. He stopped and looked at her. 'What? What do you want to ask me?' His jaw tensed.

'I don't want you to feel I am psychoanalysing you,' said Maya looking down. 'I was just worried about what Nathan said to you last night.'

'About my mum you mean?' said Jack, his voice cracked.

Maya nodded. 'He spoke like something bad had happened to her. You don't have to tell me. I just wanted you to know that I've got your back. We're partners after all.'

Jack held his breath and bit his lip. Tears flooded the corners of his eyes.

Maya leaned forwards, her eyes welling in sympathy. 'I'm so sorry.' She touched his arm.

Jack sighed. 'Yes, she's dead. She died five years ago. They said it was a car accident. But I've always wondered if my father beat her to death and covered it up. He was the senior police officer in Exmouth.' Creak, creak, creak went the couch, as he rocked.

Maya didn't know how to respond. What do you say to someone who's been through the death of a loved one? Her mind darted to alternatives, but they sounded false and stupid.

'Was it the anniversary of her passing last night?' she said, in the end.

'Yes. We lost her five years ago. Sometimes it feels like it was only yesterday,' said Jack. 'But you know what it's like. You've lost your mum yourself.' He bit his lip and leaned forward to hold Maya's hand.

'It was different for me. I never knew her. She died in childbirth and my dads never wanted to talk about it. I think they worried I'd blame myself,' said Maya.

'My mum was a terrific lady,' said Jack. 'You would've loved her. I take after her, not my dad, thank God.'

'She sounds great. I would've loved to meet her,' said Maya.

'I can't block out the anger I feel towards my father. It's like a stabbing, bright red colour in the corner of my vision. It never goes away,' said Jack, gritting his teeth.

Jack's sat phone rang. They both jumped. Loud, insistent. 'It's a damn nuisance trying to talk to anyone out here.' He left the room.

Maya closed her eyes to think of Jack. She visualised him before her. Tall, chubby but strong. Impulsive and disorganised. Like a little boy in so many ways. He'd had to grow up too fast. It'd damaged him.

She was making her way through the participants' files. Trying to put the information together in a useful format. Daniel's papers were torn and the hardest to fix. The coroner would need them. The others had useful information and were easier to put together.

Maya's tendency to obsession had got her through medicine. It was helpful to her now in piecing together the past. When her time at the Homestead was over, she hoped the information in the files would help the clients to move on with another psychiatrist.

Jack came back in the room, triumphant. He glowed with enthusiasm. 'I think we have our smoking gun.'

'Was that the forensic unit? What did they say?' said Maya.

'Yes, it was. Dr Ted was suspicious of Daniel. So much so he'd hired a private detective from Perth. The day before they went to Omar Station, the detective emailed Dr Ted saying that Daniel working undercover as a journalist on. Dr Ted opened the email when he was in Exmouth. Daniel was sent in by a newspaper to expose what was happening on these retreats,' said Jack.

'Oh my God,' said Maya swallowing hard, 'Dr Ted's so protective of his program here. I can see how angry he would've been. He's so narcissistic he couldn't tolerate anyone crossing him like that.'

'Yes, I agree,' said Jack fiddling with the files on the desk. 'I knew

Daniel was a journalist but I hadn't thought that he was spying on Dr Ted. This gives me a clear shot at motive. He has opportunity to murder because of the isolation of the station. He's also good friends with the station owner, so he's more likely to know about strychnine than any of the participants. And his fingerprints are on the blue water bottle.'

'It all comes together,' said Maya smiling up at Jack. 'Are you going to arrest him?'

'I have to run it by my superiors but I think they will approve it,' said Jack still standing and rocking. 'The main problem is that the evidence is circumstantial but there's a lot of it.'

'When will the arrest happen?' said Maya.

'Mitch and Dave are already here from Exmouth. I'd called them in. I need to clear it with the bosses and then brief Mitch and Dave, so they can arrest Dr Ted and take him back. I have to get some statements signed off, then I'll follow,' said Jack. He bustled out, channelling his alpha male. He was really suited to his job.

Maya left the room to hustle the troops and check on everyone. Her task was simple. Joy had pulled herself together to make a maple syrup and cashew loaf which smelled amazing. All participants, bar Graham, had come and were sitting around the dining room table, gorging on fresh warm cake and coffee.

They sprawled out over the church pews. Like stranded whales on the beach. Looking exhausted but their irritability sinking in the sea of sugar.

Maya joined them and said, 'How's everyone going? I know it can feel a little claustrophobic not being able to leave. The police are hoping to get you all home as soon as possible.'

Eamon sprung to her aid. 'We all understand how difficult the situation is. We know that Jack is doing the best for us.'

'Speak for yourself Eamon. I'm sick to death of all this crap,' said Lydia rolling her eyes.

'You're such a bitch,' said Sarah. 'You pretend to have loved Daniel just to get attention. You don't care who killed him.'

The experiences on this retreat were giving Maya a perfect, yet unwanted, masterclass in dealing with anger. First up, distraction techniques.

'Have all of you been out snorkelling today?' said Maya 'There's strong evidence that exercise in a wild environment is good for our mental health. Maybe we could organise a group snorkel this afternoon?' She paused. Her voice sounded grating, even to her.

Lydia and Sarah sighed in unison. They were more alike, than either of them would want to admit.

Maya would love to encourage any outside activity to reduce the terrible sense of waiting in the Homestead. But no one took her seriously.

Eamon sprung to his feet and said, 'I'm going off to help Joy. This is a stressful time and she has her hands full.' Maybe he was fed up too?

'I'll join you,' said Maya.' I like to keep busy and I'm pretty good at housework.'

Joy sent them down to the bedroom wings to clean the bathrooms and toilets. She couldn't have chosen a better option for Maya. Maya loved the smell and feel of rubber gloves, disinfectant and scrubbing. She took great pleasure in cleaning. Eamon was less keen but followed Maya's lead

Eamon talked as he cleaned. He focused on his childhood and chatted with energy, while working in parallel with Maya. 'I was seven when my parents died in the car crash. The hardest thing was everybody feeling sorry for me. I could tell what they were thinking by the look on their faces. It was awful.'

He moved faster, scrubbing the shower now. 'I was so angry. I was angry with my parents for leaving me. I was angry with the police and ambulance for not saving them. I was angry with my grandparents who refused to look after me.'

He moved on to the toilet. The smell of bleach was everywhere. Maya followed behind to complete the jobs he started but failed to finish.

Eamon said, 'I ended up in the foster care system. I wouldn't wish this on my worst enemy. A family took me in but there were eight children and I never got any attention. And then when I finally did get someone's attention, it was worse than ever.'

It was a tsunami of emotion. Maya gritted her teeth to hold on.

Eamon stopped and turned to look her full in the face. 'The problem in this place is I have no idea what anyone's thinking. I'm usually good at reading people. But there's this creepy sense of dread here. I hate not knowing and sitting around worrying.'

Maya took a moment wiping down the toilets, to think about how to respond. She said, 'I'm in the same position. I usually have a strong sense of intuition, but I can't read the non-verbal cues in this situation. I'm drawing a blank.'

Eamon said, 'I don't even know how he was killed. I saw the body and we tried to resuscitate him. He hadn't been stabbed, shot or beaten in any way. It's hard to know how he could have died. His muscles were tense and he looked like he'd just stopped breathing.'

Maya said, 'I'm not sure whether knowing how he died would help any of us.' She would deny knowing cause of death if she had to, she could see the importance of keeping that information secret.

'It's made worse by all this hanging around,' said Eamon. 'When I was a foster kid, we had to go to the court twice a year for a review with a judge. This situation reminds me of sitting around waiting at the court. Just a horrible sense of boredom and helplessness.'

They heard a commotion in the eating area and followed the noise. The sunlight was pouring in through the long windows heating the area. It was crowded with irritable, over cooked human bodies, many of them screaming.

Mitch and Dave, dressed in their neat green uniforms, were in front of Dr Ted, trying to arrest him. Looking like sulky teenagers, arguing with their principal. Dr Ted was making a tremendous noise. Yelling in fury. At 6 foot 5, he was physically intimidating.

Steve had wandered off and Maya was grateful he wasn't witnessing the scene. Both Lydia and Sarah were there and added to the chaos by screaming.

Dr Ted said, 'This is racial profiling. This is immoral and wrong. I'll sue both of you and everyone in your department.'

Constables Mitch and Dave were red in the face as they struggled to get Dr Ted's hands in cuffs. Their eyes were wide and sweat poured down their faces. They kept glancing at Jack who was leaning against the wall, in a position of nonchalance.

Graham shouted at Jack, 'You're arresting the only black person in the group twice. He's right. This is racial profiling. Stop this. It's wrong.'

Jack said, 'If you all stop making such a fuss there's no need for us to cuff you, Dr Ted. You just have to come outside and hop in the back of the car. When you get to Exmouth you can ring your lawyer and discuss the situation with him. I'm sure it can be resolved.'

Despite the wall of noise, Dr Ted heard Jack. 'I'll go but under protest. What's happening here is wrong.'

'I'm protesting too. It's all wrong.' said Graham. Dr Ted's echo.

Jack said, 'I'm not going back with the constables. I have some paperwork to get together here but I'll be back in Exmouth in a couple of hours.'

Dr Ted lost some of his fight and went out to the car. Joy passed through on her way to the kitchen, carrying a bunch of spinach. She mumbled to herself, 'What a terrible lot of fuss. The police are bumbling about, as per usual. Of course, Dr Ted had nothing to do with any of this murder. It's a crime to suggest differently.'

As Joy left the room, Eamon turned to Maya and said 'That woman seems to live on a completely separate planet to all of us. She's insanely cheery at times. But depressed and overwhelmed at others.'

'Yes, everyone has their breaking point and I worry about Joy. She's worked for Dr Ted for years and seems to adore him. This whole situation must be so distressing for her,' said Maya.

Sarah followed Maya and Eamon as they went back to their work in the bathrooms. She was a picture of misery. Small, thin, gaze turned inward.

Maya said, alert and concerned, 'Sarah are you okay? Do you want to help us finish the cleaning? We're giving the bathrooms a good scrub.'

Sarah stared at them blankly.

Eamon joined in. 'Yes, it would be great to have some help. You start on the bath.' He sprinkled around copious amounts of lavender smelling cleaner. He put a cloth in Sarah's hand and she began moving the cleaning solution backwards and forwards.

Maya got stuck into the next set of toilets, splashing around the wonderful smelling products that she loved. Eamon moved on to the shower screen. It was really satisfying watching the room transform into sparkling white.

In a small voice Sarah said, 'Do you think Dr Ted will be okay?'

'I do,' said Maya. 'He grew up in the Congo, which was a war zone when he was a kid. He's handled so much more than any of us. He's been a consultant psychiatrist for years. And he has the financial backing to hire a good lawyer.'

'I agree,' said Eamon, 'Dr Ted hasn't shown any real fear since he was first arrested by the police. He's been calm and collected the whole time. He has consistently said he's innocent.'

'I think he's really angry this time,' said Sarah moving her cleaning rag to and fro over the surfaces but making little difference. 'It's so unfair.'

Lydia came careening down the corridor. Bright and jangling, she made a real racket. She said, 'Sgt Jack sent me to ask you if anyone has seen Joy?'

Maya wrinkled her brow in confusion. 'She walked through the room where Dr Ted was arrested about twenty minutes ago.'

Lydia said, 'She seems to have disappeared. We've looked everywhere.' Lydia rocked her body in a jerky motion ready to take off at a moment's notice. 'One of the four-wheel drives has gone missing. Did she say anything to any of you about going into town?'

All three shook their head dumbly. A gong struck up, echoing down the corridors. They ran to the veranda expecting to see Joy in her usual position calling them in for a meal. But it was Jack.

Maya's sense of nausea and sickness, struck up again. The torrid weather was incandescent with heat.

Eamon walked up to Jack and said, 'What the hell's happening?

Where's Joy. You've only just arrested Dr Ted,' Eamon was more assertive, than when Maya had first met him.

Jack spoke in a hyped-up manner, like wound up doll with too many batteries. 'I'm sure she's okay. But given there's been a murder, I like to know where everyone is at all times. I've explained this to Joy. She'd agreed to meet me to review and sign her second statement regarding Daniel's death.'

Lydia behaved as if promoted to Jack's de facto assistant. She had too much adrenaline, hopping from one foot to another. 'I'll go and find Graham. He's probably swimming at the lagoon. Maybe he's heard from Joy. She might have told him where she was going.'

'I'd like to keep everybody together,' said Jack. 'I can't afford to lose any more of you.' He swung his arms, just avoiding slapping the sides of his body. Looking strung out on high tension.

Graham came into view riding a bicycle. Still in the same damn, black clothes. Jack shouted out, unable to wait for him to fully arrive, 'Have you seen Joy?'

Graham heard and shook his head. 'Not since lunch.'

Steve turned up on a bike. He was sweaty too, but appeared distracted and confused.

Jack said,' Steve have you seen Joy around?'

'No, I haven't. I don't like that woman,' said Steve frowning.

'I'm going to try and reach the constables on the sat phone,' said Jack, 'You all stay here so I know where you are.'

Jack left the veranda to a din of protest. Maya went back inside and the others followed her. Thank God it was cooler. Maya could barely think in the heat.

Lydia was the loudest. 'It's not fair. I'm sick of being told what to do. As soon as I can, I'm leaving here. I have rights.'

Graham stood frowning. 'I agree Lydia. We do have rights. I'm leaving too. This is bullshit.'

Eamon physically flapped his hands, in an effort to calm the others. 'We have to do what Sgt Jack tells us.' He rocked forwards and back. 'He's investigating a murder.'

Sarah involuted into herself, and curled up in the corner. Maya went and sat by her, to give her a sense of support. Where the hell was Jack? He'd left her in an impossible situation. There was no way of controlling this chaos.

Everyone was busy shouting about their plans for escape, when Jack returned. His mouth was grim and severe. His brow wrinkled. Maya's stomach dropped to hit her bladder. Oh God, now she needed to go to the toilet.

Jack said, 'The constables have seen Joy. Their car broke down about 5 km south of the Homestead crossing on the bush track. Joy turned up in another four-wheel-drive. She said she was going into town.'

Graham said, 'Well that explains it. You've got us all wound up for nothing.'

'Let me finish. She got out of the vehicle to help the constables who were working under the hood. The boys were distracted by the car problems. They heard a noise and looked up to see the other four-wheel-drive race off, heading north/east along a different track,' said Jack

'That's strange,' said Eamon, 'Joy has no business in that direction. It goes off to Cape Range National Park.'

'The story gets worse,' said Jack. 'When the car broke down, they let Dr Ted out of the vehicle because of the heat. He wasn't cuffed. I'd told them not to. They think he abducted Joy and the vehicle. So now we are missing both Dr Ted and Joy.'

'Oh my God,' said Lydia, 'can't you lot do anything right? This is such a mess.' Lydia had changed her allegiance from Jack in a heartbeat.

'Could they see who was driving?' said Maya. 'Joy adores Dr Ted and may've gone willingly to help him.'

'They couldn't see the driver because of the angle of the track,' said Jack. 'They said it happened too quickly.'

'So much for trained police observers,' said Graham, clenching his jaw.

Maya grimaced and took a deep breath. 'Do we have a car here?'

Jack said, 'Yes, we have two. Nathan, our station manager is using one to go and rescue Mitch and Dave. I'm going to use the sat phone to call the State Emergency Service. We need the SES up here to help us organise a search.'

Sarah stood up and raised her hand. 'I volunteer to help in any way I can.' A startling change in her mental state.

'I volunteer as well,' said Lydia, scrambling to get ahead of the attention.

Graham and Eamon nodded their willingness to participate.

Steve said, 'I don't like that woman, but I don't want her getting murdered. I'll help too.' Distracted, but wanting to help in his own way.

'Yes, we will probably need you all, but the most important thing at the moment is to not wander off,' said Jack, heading out the door. 'I don't want to lose anyone else. We need to focus and concentrate on our current problem of finding Dr Ted and Joy.'

The Homestead itself appeared to take a breath and the world exploded into chaos.

16

Maya's head pounded as the dining room filled with shrill voices, shouting to be heard. Humid heat streamed in through the windows. She was squashed in the remaining space, smelling the hot, sweaty bodies around her, trying to control her nausea.

Loud voices, waving hands. Everyone had an opinion. They wanted to organise a search. Or just do something, that wasn't sitting around. Maya empathised. She was fed up with the whole situation.

'Why don't we go through the kitchen and living quarters of both Dr Ted and Joy?' said Graham. 'I'm a bit of a locksmith and can get us in just about anywhere. We might find some clues about where they've gone.'

Maya's muscles tensed. Graham was proving rather canny. Maybe a bit too handy with locks for someone with his history? Where would a school teacher learn this skill? The group shouted their enthusiasm, wanting to do anything.

Maya tried to get them to stay put. It was what Jack wanted. But their momentum was strong, so she gave in. At least a search would keep everybody together.

'Let's start with the kitchen,' said Eamon. 'I feel a bit awkward about going into someone's private bedroom.'

The kitchen and food stores were as neat as a pin. Surfaces shiny. Containers labelled. Smelling of Spray and Wipe. Maya was jealous. Joy was an excellent manager. They found her calendar and notepad. Nothing out of the ordinary.

Sarah had changed in the crisis. Her focus and attention to detail was helpful in the search.

Steve was not helpful. He looked for food and ate, as everybody worked around him. But his kind nature calmed the group and was good in its own way.

Graham showed a real skill at cracking locks and got them into Dr Ted's room. It was sparse and monastic. The walls were white, as if in homage to the sterile group room. Maybe they had leftover paint? He was reading "Memories, Dreams and Reflections" by Carl Jung. Maya loved that book. The perfect choice for a guru. There were no notes or maps. His wardrobe contained a rainbow of kaftans. He had a jewellery box of gold chains. Costume jewellery. Nothing incriminating.

Graham broke into Joy's room, even more quickly. Great thought Maya. Practice made perfect.

Joy's room was overflowing. Trinkets, objects, embroidered doilies covered every surface. There was a home-made, crocheted rug on the single bed. A knitting bag was propped up on the bedside table. Papers were everywhere.

The whole wall at the foot of the bed was a shrine to Samuel. There were photos, certificates, letters, even school sports day ribbons, pinned to a giant cork board propped up on a small desk.

'That poor woman,' said Eamon. 'She's suffered so much loss but keeps on caring for everyone.'

'I agree with Steve. I think she's over the top. It gives me the creeps,' said Lydia.

'God Lydia, you could show some empathy,' said Eamon. 'Joy could be already dead.'

There were so many people crowded into the small room, that

Maya worried someone would break something precious. She could barely breathe.

'I think it's ridiculous that everyone thinks Dr Ted is capable of murder,' said Graham. 'I bet he's going into hiding and Joy's helping him. I don't blame them. The justice system sucks.'

'Sgt Jack is right. It doesn't matter why they ran. We still have to find them. In this heat, they could both die without water,' said Eamon.

'The 4-wheel-drives have five 20L containers of water in them at all times,' said Lydia, puffing her chest out as everyone turned to look at her. 'They'll be fine for days.'

Maya watched Lydia going through the drawers of the small table, where the shrine for Samuel was balanced. One was locked, so she asked Graham to open it using his talents. He found it tricky, jiggling the lock. Multiple attempts. But it slid open and inside was a single sheet of paper.

Graham grabbed it and said, 'It looks like a copy of Dr Ted's emails. I wonder why Joy had it.'

Maya snatched it out of his hands. 'It might be private. I don't think we should read it.'

'But how are we going to investigate if we don't look at everything,' said Lydia trying to get a grip on the paper in Maya's hands.

'I agree,' said Graham. 'We have to consider all the evidence available.'

'He's right,' said Eamon, succeeding at grabbing the paper. 'I know it's important to respect privacy but we need to know everything. We must find them before it gets hot tomorrow, whether they have water or not.'

Eamon opened the paper. 'It looks like an email.' He read it to the group.

"Hi Ted, Just to let you know that my search for information has been successful. You are right to suspect Daniel Comstock. He is a freelance journalist who is working off books for the Sydney Herald. They are looking into your business with the intent to write an expose and discredit you. They think it could be a story of national interest. Be careful of him. Yours John Holmes, Private Detective."

Lydia gasped. Sarah said, 'You pretended to have an intimate relationship with Daniel. How come you didn't know he was a journalist?'

'My question is why did Joy have a copy of this email and why did she keep it in a locked drawer?' said Eamon. Appearing to enjoy his role as a junior Sherlock Holmes.

'I bloody hate journalists. They're the scum of the earth,' said Graham. 'He deserved to die, sneaky little bastard.'

The group was interrupted by Jack opening the door, 'What the hell are you lot doing? I told you to stay put.'

'We are looking for clues,' said Lydia. 'Graham's a real whiz at getting behind locked doors. He used to be a locksmith.'

Jack went red and the artery in his temple pulsed. 'You can't go around breaking into locked rooms. It's illegal. There are privacy laws.'

'We didn't mean any harm,' said Eamon in a firm, strong voice. 'We're just trying to help.'

'Will everyone go back to the eating area? I've found some sandwiches and we're going to wait for police reinforcements,' said Jack. 'The Perth office is sending searchers, dogs and even a helicopter. They're getting in touch with the local SES and asking them to coordinate.'

The group shuffled out and moved to the eating area. Maya was really hungry, so grabbed a couple of sandwiches. She took one to Jack who sat glaring at the group from the furthest corner of the room.

'I'm sorry we upset you. It was the only way to keep the group together. They all got behind the idea of searching for clues,' said Maya. 'I think we might've found something. Joy had this email, but I'm not sure if it's useful.' She leaned forward and passed the paper to Jack.

Jack scanned the email. His eyebrows raised and his eyes widened. 'You found this in Joy's room?'

'Yes, but I'm not sure what it means. It was in a locked drawer,' said Maya. 'I can't understand why she had this.'

'Bloody Mitch and Dave searched that room. I can't trust them to make a cup of coffee,' said Jack.

Maya smiled.

Jack wrinkled his brow. 'Maybe Joy was doing her own investigation of Daniel's murder? That could've been what got her kidnapped. Lydia's doing the same thing and it worries me.'

'Did you get to interview Joy?' said Maya.

'Yes, I got a full statement from her and just needed to get her to sign it,' said Jack.

Sarah had shuffled closer to Jack and Maya, listening to their conversation. Her face was alert. She said, 'If Dr Ted found out that Daniel was spying on him, is that why you think he might've killed Daniel?'

Jack sighed. Everyone was listening in by now, even if they pretended not to be. He said, 'Did any of you know that Daniel was a journalist spying on Dr Ted? He wanted to unmask the illegal activities happening here.'

'No, no, no, no.' Answers came from all round. No one admitted to knowing this information.

Jack stopped and stared at Graham. He said, 'I didn't hear you say no.' The room went whisper quiet.

Maya stared at Graham. He shrugged, shuffled his feet and looked at the floor. Time stretched on and on, Maya held her breath.

Graham said, 'I did know that Daniel was a journalist and planning a story about Dr Ted. He told me about it, after arguing with Dr Ted on the retreat.' Maya's stomach muscles tightened. Like she'd been punched in the guts. Was Graham the murderer?

'So why didn't you tell us?' said Jack, riled up with muscles tensed.

'Because I don't trust you. I was too trusting of police before I went to jail. My lawyer told me never to speak with a policeman unless a lawyer is present,' said Graham, gritting his teeth.

Jack paused, rubbing his hand over the broad, wooden dining

table. 'It can look worse if you don't tell. Fill me in now. What happened?'

Maya sat down to rub her hand on the wood like Jack. She liked touching the jarrah too. It grounded her.

'Daniel told me about the argument. Lydia only heard part of it. Dr Ted accused Daniel of spying on him. Daniel was furious,' said Graham, looking directly at Jack.

'Was he a spy? Was he writing an article?' said Jack.

'I think Daniel was confused about what to do,' said Graham. 'He originally came as a freelance journalist, but he found the therapy helpful and didn't want to destroy this place or Dr Ted.'

Lydia butted in. 'I think Daniel didn't tell me about the article because he was trying to protect me. We were lovers you know.'

'Yes, we do know,' said Eamon with a sigh. 'But that doesn't get us closer to why Daniel was killed.'

'I think my story suggests Dr Ted's the murderer,' said Graham. 'He was such a private person, any thought of media exposure would've driven him insane.' Maya noticed he was willing to throw Dr Ted under the bus, when threatened. Not much of an acolyte.

'Well, he abducted Joy for a reason,' said Sarah. 'Maybe he's trying to run from the law?'

The door opened and everyone jumped. Constables Mitch and Dave skulked in, clenched jaws. Keeping their eyes down as if determined not to look at Jack. Nathan followed relaxed but serious. Jack tensed to strike, but Nathan interrupted him. 'I really don't think that this one was Mitch and Dave's fault.'

Jack gritted his teeth and said, 'Every other time it has been. What makes this one different?'

'Well, I couldn't get their car going. I had to tow it back. And there's sugar around the fuel cap.' Everyone turned to stare at Nathan who scuffed at the floor tiles, 'I think someone put sugar in the fuel tank so it would drive for a while and then break down. I'm going out to have a better look at it now.'

'Who the hell would've done that?' said Jack.

'Maybe Joy really was working for Dr Ted, to help him escape?

She has dedicated her life to his work. Maybe they cooked up a plan for escape together?' said Eamon.

'It seems a long shot,' said Lydia, glaring at Eamon who had the group's attention. 'Dr Ted might've had time when the constables rocked up before they came in search of him.'

'But how would he have known, he was about to be arrested?' said Sarah, frowning as well.

'At least it wasn't our fault. That's the main thing,' said Dave, moving out of the background. 'I'm sick of everything being our fault.'

'Me too,' said Jack, glaring at him. 'You two break everything you touch and you're not off the hook yet.'

Jack's sat phone rang. Everybody jumped, with their hands searching for their phones. The ringing and buzzing of daily life was foreign in their disconnected world. Nerves were raw.

Jack went outside and the investigating group decided to move into the kitchen to refuel with caffeine.

Maya filled the kettle to boil. Eamon found the biscuit barrel and a date slice in the fridge. Stressful situations require a great deal of sugar. The routine of coffee and cake was settling. Steve was enthusiastic about more food and went from person to person, getting in the way by helping.

There were multiple voices talking at once. The conversation sounded like the roaring wind at the beach. They all had a theory about what had taken place.

Graham and Lydia were sure that Joy helped Dr Ted escape whereas Eamon and Sarah believed Joy had been abducted by him. The only thing that Mitch and Dave knew for sure, was that they were innocent of any wrongdoing.

Jack came back in, flushed in the face and sweating. He said, 'Things have just got more complicated. Police admin checked the weather. Turns out there's a cyclone warning for Exmouth over the next 12 hours. No one can get in or out.'

Maya's focus turned outside, listening for the wind. There was a ferocious howl out there. She'd been so distracted that she hadn't noticed the wind pick up.

Maya looked at Lydia, who was white.

Jack said, 'Lydia and I remember Cyclone Vance that went through Exmouth in 1999. It was the strongest cyclone to ever hit mainland Australia. It was really frightening.'

Lydia spoke in a shaky voice, 'We're so near the coast. What about the storm surge?'

Anxiety rose in the room. Questions started. Graham said, 'What about Dr Ted and Joy? They may have water but they aren't set up to survive a cyclone.' Maya flushed. She hadn't even thought of their predicament.

'Look they were heading north east towards Cape Range several hours ago,' said Jack. 'There are caves and higher ground in that area. They'll find shelter. We have to look after ourselves.'

'Can we get to Omar Station in time?' said Maya. Her hands clammy and heart racing. She'd never had to deal with such extremes of weather. She hoped the others didn't notice how scared she was.

'Actually, we don't have to go that far,' said Jack chest thrust forward. 'I've been talking to the local authorities. This Homestead's equipped with a cyclone proof building. Nathan will know about it. He was probably building it. It's a 15-minute drive south east on the higher ground.'

Everyone was paused until Lydia said, 'Thank God we can be safe.'

'Yes,' said Jack. 'It was the first thing Joy built when she started renovations a decade ago. She did a great job. It's steel reinforced concrete, on solid ground, above any likely storm surge.'

'I can't believe that Joy is going to save us and she might've been abducted,' said Lydia, pale.

'It's going to slow the search by about a day. But we'll find her,' said Jack. 'Now Steve, you come with me and we'll load up the water and portable generator. I need a strong bloke. And we'll find Nathan. He knows this place like the back of his hand. Can the rest of you pack provisions? We'll have to do 2 trips to the shelter. We've only got one four-wheel-drive and the troop carrier. There're loads of us.'

Steve grinned from ear to ear, thrilled to have been singled out. He was a big lad and likely to be useful. Mitch and Dave glared at Jack, being dumped in with the others. Perhaps Jack was trying to save them from being strangled?

Lydia returned to her usual bossy self and said, 'Given that I've been through cyclones, I'm in charge.' No one argued. Just moved around her, organising stuff.

Mitch and Dave wondered off together, heads close, gossiping.

Maya went into the pantry looking for canned goods. Sarah was bustling around looking for torches. Maya said, 'I've noticed you're not dissociating as much anymore.'

'That's true,' said Sarah. 'It feels good to have a real enemy rather than fighting all the ghosts in my head. It helps me focus.'

Graham said, 'I'm going off to pack clothes for everyone.' He was followed closely by Eamon. Maybe worried about Graham's ability to break and enter? God that man was creepy.

It was good to have something to do. Maya felt useful. Lydia, bossing her around, said, 'Don't forget a can opener. It's a real newbie mistake.'

Joy's gifts of organisation were evident everywhere. There were stackable plastic boxes for food and supplies. They found stored raincoats and Wellington boots in a closet. There was a portable gas burner. They even found dehydrated food.

'Just add water. She's thought of everything,' said Sarah.

They packed their mobile phones into their pockets, by force of habit. No real hope of getting connections out here. But who knew what might help in an emergency?

Sarah found a portable radio, which she put in one of the boxes. 'Who knows? It might help.'

Jack came back with a beaming Steve and a concerned-looking Nathan. He said, 'We've got everything ready. Maya and Sarah, you're up for the first trip.'

Maya had slipped some medication into her pocket. It was impossible to know whether it would be needed or not.

The rain was poured from the skies as Maya made her way to the four-wheel-drive. Drenched in seconds. A squally wind came from the north west. The clouds dark and threatening, with the occasional shock of lightning. Maya's heart raced but she tried to hide her fear from everyone.

'The storm is approaching from the north west. The cyclone is rated category four, not the worst but certainly not the best situation,' said Jack, like an anxious meteorologist. 'I'll leave Steve with you while I go to get the others. Nathan's bringing Mitch and Dave in the Troopie.'

Nobody said anything. The wind was wild. It rocked the four-wheel-drive as they drove along the bush track. Maya had never heard such a howling noise, like the souls of a thousand angry, dead men had risen up against them. She was terrified, despite Jack's calm confidence.

The track gradually rose to the south east. Maya stared out the car window. The land was empty. The wildlife, usually seen in the bush, had disappeared. Its inhabitants hidden, or gone to higher ground.

Without warning, the cyclone shelter appeared to their right on a rise. It was a flat square building made out of cement and steel. Maya got out of the four-wheel-drive and brought the bags inside, so Jack could go and get the others. Nathan arrived in the Troopie with Mitch and Dave, 5 minutes behind them.

The walls of the building were thick, like an ancient castle. Roughly painted white. Cement and steel showed throughout. Practical and solid

Steve whistled as he entered. Maya said, 'You're remarkably cheerful for a man facing a cyclone.'

Steve puffed out his chest, grinning from ear to ear. 'I can't talk now. I've got secret men's business. We have to protect the women.' He followed Nathan, as they organised the supplies.

The inside of the building was basic. The floor space was covered with four mattresses with scattered cushions. It smelled stale. Like it'd been closed up for years. The roof was flat and square, latched on with heavier steel bolts than Maya had ever seen.

Maya helped the others unpack and set up. There were hooks on the wall to hang the lanterns. Nathan said, 'The batteries in these things can last a thousand hours. Pretty impressive.' Maya laughed to herself. Men can be easy to excite.

Although it was day time, the storm darkened their world. There were no windows in the building. Less glass to break. There were vents on the wall to allow air to circulate. They had brought their own water but the refuge contained two 500 L containers already filled.

Jack returned with the rest of the group. Eamon looked pale, carrying a large pile of clothing. Graham came in with Lucy on a lead and the puppies in a cardboard box, scraping and woofing to get out. Maya was mortified that she'd forgotten about the dogs in the drama.

Jack said, 'I know that some of us don't like dogs. But we're going to have to put up with them. There's no way I'm leaving animals on their own in this storm.'

Graham said, 'We need volunteers to hold the puppies throughout the storm. I'll manage Lucy. You might have to do put up with a dog weeing on you.'

Maya and Sarah put their hands up. Lydia looked the other way.

Jack said, 'This place is brilliant. I can't think of a safer place to wait out the storm. Joy's thought of everything. Behind that door in the corner's a composting toilet. We'll be right no matter what.'

Nathan and Jack wrestled the main door closed and bolted it. They sat on the mattresses and everyone stared at each other. There was silence, uncomfortable silence.

Mitch and Dave took the grey plastic container they'd transported and moved to the back corner of the room, whispering.

The wildness of the wind outside echoed around the bare room. The wind smelled salty, like the door was being pelted with raw fish. The lantern light added to the feeling of menace.

Maya stretched and said, 'How long does it take for the cyclone to pass?'

'Well, Jack, Nathan and I've been through cyclone Vance, so we're the experts,' said Lydia fidgeting. 'I can't remember exactly but it's hours. Maybe six or seven?'

Nathan, calm and solid, said, 'She's bang on. It was that long. But this one's a lower rating so maybe it'll be quicker?'

'What the hell are we going to do for all that time?' said Sarah, her face pale.

'The priority is to save lives first and worry about entertainment second,' said Jack, frowning.

'But it's not going to help if someone loses it,' said Eamon, glancing sideways at the puppies.

'I remembered to bring a tape deck to distract us,' said Lydia sitting up straighter. 'Last time the silence drove me mad.'

She fiddled in the supplies, withdrew the player and put on Madonna. Maya held in her laughter. Cassette tapes were always going to force an 80's reunion.

The music helped. It gave a background to the wailing wind and warmed the space.

'Our contribution is this,' said Steve, drawing a bottle of brandy out of his bag like a proud magician. 'Nathan and I found it when we first got here. It'll give everyone a bit of warmth and courage.' Steve had blossomed under Nathan's kind direction.

'I found a stash of Tim Tams in Dr Ted's office,' said Graham producing five biscuit packets like an alchemist focussed on creating chocolate. Maya's eyes widened and her mouth watered. Who knew Dr Ted could be so practical and useful?

The situation appeared less bleak. Everyone took a sip of the brandy, wiped the opening on their sleeve and passed it round.

'Liquid courage helps warm the chest, but I really want to get my hands on the chocolate biscuits,' said Jack, smiling for the first time since the cyclone warning came. Around went the chocolate.

'Let's play a game,' said Lydia. 'Truth or Dare.'

There were groans from all sides.

'We have to do something to pass the time and no one's going to get drunk on that small bottle,' said Lydia.

Eamon leaned forward and backed her. 'I agree it'll distract us and keep everyone calm.'

'We really are going to be fine,' said Jack, increasing the volume of his voice. 'This building is one of the safest places in Exmouth in a cyclone.'

'I'll go first,' said Maya. A number of the participants were very sensitive to stress and a game would help to distract them. 'I choose Truth.'

'Are you in love with Jack?' shouted Lydia.

'Lydia that's an inappropriate question. But I will answer it this time. I've known all of you less than three days. That's not adequate time to fall in love with anybody.' Maya was proud of how she handled this. 'Your turn's next Lydia.'

'I choose Dare,' said Lydia.

'That's a tricky one while we're locked in here,' said Jack, rolling his eyes.

'You're a yoga teacher,' said Sarah,' I dare you to do a handstand for longer than a minute.'

Lydia laughed. She tucked her short, pink skirt into her underwear and tipped upside down. Eamon timed it and they counted her down. Everyone clapped. This game was working.

'Sarah's next,' said Jack.

'I choose Truth,' said Sarah smiling. 'You all know everything about me anyway.'

'Have you ever had a boyfriend?' blurted out Steve. Maya blinked. Who would've thought that Steve might like Sarah?

'No, I haven't and I'm not looking to start now,' said Sarah. Power to you thought Maya.

'My turn,' said Steve. 'I choose a Dare.'

Graham said, 'I dare you to hold one of the puppies for a minute.'

'No worries. That's easy,' said Steve. He'd really got his confidence. Maya handed over the sleeping puppy. It nestled onto Steve's lap and then dropped its head back down. It was an easy minute and everyone cheered Steve at the end.

'I'll go next,' said Jack. 'I choose a Dare.'

'I dare you to do a handstand for one minute, like Lydia,' said Eamon laughing.

To Maya's surprise, Jack kicked his legs up and stood there for the full time. Pretty damn impressive for a well-covered person. The man had hidden talents.

'I guess it's me now,' said Eamon. 'I can't stand on my hands at all, so I choose Truth.'

Graham said, 'Why don't you like dogs?'

Eamon paled and his face fell. He looked at the ground while everyone was cheering him on. Maya saw that the question went too far, but couldn't understand why. She projected her voice loudly. 'No one has to answer anything that makes them uncomfortable.' There was a sudden silence.

Eamon bit his lip and said, 'Pass me the brandy and I'll tell you.' Steve handed it over.

Eamon took a swing then looked down to avoid eye contact. 'I was sexually abused as a child in foster care by a man who had lots of dogs.'

Maya bit her lip. How do you stop an avalanche?

Nathan moved first. He put his arm around Eamon's shoulders and said, 'People can be bastards to children. But you're a good man. You've moved beyond it.'

Eamon looked up at the group and sighed. 'I've blamed myself for such a long time. I didn't want to carry the secret on my own anymore.'

Nathan said, 'Well you decided to tell us and we will carry it with you.' Nathan's generous respect and simple kindness, did a much better job of managing the situation than Maya could have.

The room quietened. Everyone looked at the floor. How do you move through a disclosure in these circumstances?

17

Day 11 Post Death

Lydia's flounced her shoulders and said, 'I'm bored of this game. Does anyone have something better to suggest?'

Maya raised her eyebrows. It was going to be a long night. She leaned back against the cold, concrete wall. The soft, warm puppy in her arms hiccupped, as it slept. Unimpressed by the roaring winds outside. The air bracing. Strange to feel cold after so much stifling heat.

'When I went camping as a child, we used to play the Best and the Worst,' said Jack grinning. 'You have to do say what your Best and Worst experiences were over the last week. Would that work for everybody?'

Maya groaned inwardly. Exactly the type of awkward game she dreaded. But Jack was so enthusiastic, that she stepped up to the plate. 'My Best is that Joy built this shelter so we're safe in the cyclone. My Worst's that I'm worried about her safety with Dr Ted.'

'I still don't think that Dr Ted's the murderer. I think that Joy realises this and is helping him escape. The system's rigged,' said Graham, up on his soap box. 'I've already made my point that you arrested the only black individual twice.'

Maya sighed. Graham was like a broken record.

'That's true,' said Jack, voice tight and tense. 'But I made my point that it has nothing to do with the colour of his skin. Daniel was planning to expose Dr Ted not any of you.'

The situation was getting hostile. Maya tried to move the conversation sideways. 'I bet that Lydia's Best is Madonna's music. I can't believe you've found so many songs from her. Hours and hours' worth. That woman's a singing machine.' Lydia grinned, loving the spotlight.

Eamon said, 'I have already told you all my Worst. But my Best is working together to try and solve the case today. It's cool being detectives.'

'That's my Best as well,' said Sarah. 'It gave me something to focus on other than my past.'

'I liked it Best when Nathan and I were getting ready to come here,' said Steve. He turned towards Nathan and said, 'You make me feel good about myself.'

'My Best has always, and will always, be Lucy and the puppies,' said Graham. 'Animals are never judgemental and always accepting. I'm going to get a dog when I go back to civilisation.'

'They're using a lot of therapy dogs in the US and the UK. We're just trying to get them going in Australia. A well-trained dog can make such a difference to a person's life,' said Maya.

Maya sensed a real warmth, present in the group. Now that Dr Ted was assumed the murderer, the tension in the group had evaporated. It was very dark outside, and the wind howled. However, the space within the 'castle' walls felt safe.

But what if they were wrong about Dr Ted? She looked at Graham, remembering Lydia's picture. Her stomach spasmed. God, why did she have thoughts like that?

'What time is it?' said Lydia.

'It's 6:30 PM,' said Jack, wearing a complicated watch like all good policeman. 'Too early for bed but maybe a good time to eat something.'

A muffled giggle came from the back corner. Jack turned to stare in Mitch and Dave's direction. 'What are you two doing over there?'

Mitch and Dave glared back and said, 'Nothing.' In unison, like guilty teenagers.

Steve perked up. 'They're looking at the nudie magazines, they found in the garage.'

Maya's jaw dropped, that was different.

Jack said, 'How the hell do you know that, Steve?'

'Because I found them first and I've already had a look,' said Steve.

Mitch and Dave reddened. Dave said, 'These are good quality Black Label Penthouse magazines from the 1980s. We're reading the articles.'

'Yeah,' said Mitch. 'The articles are excellent.'

'Leave them alone,' said Maya. 'It keeps them quiet. Who cares what they do to pass the time.'

Lydia started shuffling around in the supplies. She got out the camping stove and found the butane cannisters to get it going. Soon she had a kettle of water boiling.

'There's enough for everyone to eat a freeze-dried meal and have a cup of tea or coffee,' said Lydia. 'If you want tinned food you need to find the saucepans.'

Everyone oohed and aahed at the dried food. So many combinations. Eating gave mixed reviews, some enthusiastic but most negative.

Maya was unimpressed. She ate a few mouthfuls of dried chicken satay, but gave the rest to Steve. He was one of the eager ones. She sat back with her cup of tea and sucked on a Tim Tam. Not half bad.

The men were impressed by the variety of food. They played like child scientists inventing bizarre and even frightening combinations. It passed the time.

'I vote we leave the lights on for the girls, when we go to sleep,' said Steve.

Maya smiled. Good on him for speaking up. She said, 'I second that idea.' There were too many abused people in the group to be in total darkness.

They lay down two apiece on the mattresses on the floor, covering themselves with rugs. The building was snug. Nothing was leaking.

Maya's eyes went heavy and closed.

She woke when Sarah kneed her in the head. God damn, Sarah was a restless sleeper. Maya saw Jack's light on near the radio.

'What are you doing?' she said.

'I'm trying to get some news from anywhere,' said Jack. 'The wind's died down this last half hour but I think we're in the eye of the storm.'

Maya listened. It was true. The howls and whines of wind had lessened.

'Have you had some sleep?' said Maya.

'No, I haven't,' said Jack. 'I'm on alert until the danger has passed. I bet Nathan's awake. He's just not saying anything.'

In the dim light Maya saw Nathan grin. 'Too right mate. I find it strange that anyone else's sleeping.' He shuffled to his side. 'Mitch and Dave are totally out to it. Doesn't speak too highly of your police force.'

'They're hopeless. I don't know how to fix them,' said Jack, leaning over towards Nathan. 'How bad do you think the damage will be with this cyclone?'

'I don't know. We're protected in here. It's hard to tell what's happening out there.' said Nathan.

'When's the storm surge at its worst?' said Maya.

'It's after the cyclone has passed,' said Jack. 'If we could get a radio station, it'd give us some idea.'

Maya lay there listening to the howling outside. The wind was picking up again. Good. More than halfway through.

She continued her restless night. Sarah fought her demons, kicking and moaning. Lydia snored, but was outclassed by Steve, who shook the building with his noise.

Jack and Nathan whispered together, protecting their flock. Graham slept with Lucy by his side, and the puppies in his lap, with their warm tummies in the palm of each hand. Eamon was on the other side of the room but appeared to be getting some sleep. Mitch and Dave were to the right, far away from Jack's wrath.

As time passed, trips to the composting bathroom increased. The dark lightened and the wind stopped. There were groans and moans on all sides. Someone called out, 'What's the time?'

Jack said, 'It's 5:30 AM. The worst is passed. Nathan and I are going to look around. We're trying to get the radio working so we can pick up the local messages about the storm front.

Lydia sat up and groaned, and fell straight back down with her eyes clenched.

'I'm going to try to get the kettle going,' said Eamon. 'It can't be that hard.'

Maya helped him and soon the whistle of a hot kettle rang out. A cup of coffee would go down nicely.

Mitch and Dave slept, showing an inhuman ability to ignore noise or movement.

Steve and Eamon found the dried food and started going through the options.

'Oh my God. You two can't possibly be considering sweet and sour chicken for breakfast,' said Maya.

'I'm hungry. I'll eat anything,' said Steve.

'I have no trouble believing that,' said Maya smiling at him, 'At least you'd do well in a famine.'

Lydia and Sarah were curled up on the mattress with rugs wrapped around their heads. 'It's too early.' said Sarah moaning.

Maya was happy with her coffee. She rustled through the supplies and found dried apricots. She moved away from Steve and Eamon, who were back to performing science experiments with the food.

The puppies had weed all over Graham's rugs. A fact that'd made them very happy. They were rolling around in all their muck, yelping with joy. Their mother, Lucy laid to their side. She looked as if she'd roll her eyes if it were possible. Despite the smell Graham kept sleeping, but it was hard to tell if he was faking.

Eamon said, 'I slept okay last night. I'm surprised that I wasn't more disturbed.'

'I slept good too,' said Steve. Groans sounded around the room.

Lydia said, 'Yes, we know Steve. Your snoring was so loud it sounded like an earthquake.'

'Well mate, you didn't disturb me. I had a good night and I was right next to you,' said Eamon.

'I wonder where Jack and Nathan have got to?' said Maya.

The door rustled and Jack and Nathan entered. They were flushed and wet, but grinning.

'We managed to get some reception after walking up one of the hills,' said Jack. 'The cyclone has passed. It was a category four but there's been very little storm surge. It's going to be wet but we can start packing up and plan to go back to the Homestead.'

'Thank God,' said Sarah. 'I couldn't stand the thought of eating more dried food.'

'Try the apricots,' said Maya. 'They're not bad at all.'

'I need a coffee first,' said Sarah.

Jack and Nathan took off their wet gear and huddled in the corner with maps. Discussing important details in whispers.

'We really are lucky that Joy built this place,' said Eamon.

Nathan said, nodding, 'She got expert help and it really shows. The only thing I hate is the God damn, composting toilet. They're a bugger to clean.'

Maya worked with Eamon to give everyone in the group a steaming cup of coffee and muesli bar. Jack kicked Mitch and Dave awake with his wet boots, but they welcomed the coffee.

Lydia said, 'More coffee please.' Shovelling in at least another tablespoon.

'I'm not sure you need more stimulants,' said Maya smiling at Lydia. 'You already jingle, jangle enough.'

'Lydia is the world's champion coffee drinker,' said Sarah. 'She out drinks anyone I've met.'

Jack organised the group into two for the return journey. Graham was in the first group with the dogs, Steve and Lydia. Jack said, 'We need you Steve to help Nathan depending how the Homestead fared in the storm.' Steve stood taller. Nathan was to follow with Mitch and Dave.

Maya said, 'Sarah, Eamon and I can spend our time packing and cleaning up.'

'I volunteer to have a go at the composting toilet,' said Eamon. 'I've seen one cleaned before and I'm willing to try.'

'Well, I'll try and clean the rugs the puppies were on. I'll go outside to find a puddle of clean water,' said Maya.

'Good luck with that,' said Nathan with a smile.

They worked well together. Packed up the supplies and cleaned up the rubbish. With her OCD tendencies, Maya was in her element. Everywhere was dirty, crying out for a good clean.

'I hate Madonna but I do have to admit that the music helped,' said Sarah packing up the tapes and deck.

'I didn't remember there were that many Madonna songs in the world,' said Maya. 'That woman must work 24 hours a day.'

Eamon came in smiling. 'I managed to sort out the toilet. Thankfully no one did a number two, so it was pretty easy.'

The snorts, shrieks and whines of a hard working four-wheel-drive sounded. They rushed outside. The car was covered in red sticky mud. Jack and Nathan jumped out grinning.

'It's a God damn mess out there so I've tagged along to help Jack in case you get stuck,' said Nathan, a smile plastered all over his face.

'You look pretty happy about it,' said Sarah laughing.

'It's no great secret, we're having tremendous fun rolling around in the mud,' said Jack.

They packed the car and bundled in. Trees and branches had fallen all over the property. A colossal wind had pushed them flat. But the wildlife was back. There were kangaroos and wallabies out surveying the damage. Birds everywhere were chirping and singing, like housewives gossiping amid the drama.

The track was much more rutted than the day before, with red puddles of mud. As Nathan drove red cloudy clods splashed all over. A child's dream adventure.

'I thought Jack was the designated driver,' said Eamon.

'It's so much fun, we have to share it. I'm not a selfish hog,' said Jack.

Back at the Homestead, the building was still intact. But the veranda was decimated. Furniture thrown all over. The gable roof torn and split by the cyclone.

Maya got out of the four-wheel-drive and sunk up to her ankles in thick red mud. Jack laughed and said, 'You'd better get used to it, there's mud and water all through the Homestead.'

Maya and Sarah sloshed their way through the warm, sticky mud to the inside. Jack had said there wasn't much of a reactive storm surge following the cyclone, but the Homestead was flooded with red cloudy water.

'You can see why Joy brought so many Wellington boots,' said Sarah, opening the cupboard to find them. Maya chose a red pair that were a bit big but looked funky. Sarah went with practical black.

The place was starting to heat up already. Graham marched out of the kitchen carrying a toolbox. He said, 'We're going to try and restart the generators. Nathan's working on one and I'll do the other. We need some power.' He rushed off, busy and purposeful.

'That man has hidden talents for a headmaster. I was shocked when he got into the locked bedrooms so easily,' said Sarah.

'Yeah, me too. It seemed too easy. I worry because of his history,' said Maya.

Jack marched past and said, 'I've got the two satellite phones and am going to try to reorganise the search parties. I know we've all been worried about Joy. And Dr Ted, I guess.'

Eamon came in and said, 'Do you two want to help me start cleaning up.'

'You betcha,' said Maya. 'You know I'm a cleaning freak. I'd love to get into this mess.'

There was so much mud, it was difficult to know where to start. They managed to find three mops, tied towels around the base and started pushing the muddy water out the doors. It was marginally successful, but they were contributing.

The heat made Maya sweat, but she was determined not to be a wuss. Lydia sloshed in through the front door and Sarah yelled, 'Mind the floor.' Maya bit her lip to stop from joining in.

'I'm in charge of the drinks. You have to keep your fluids up if you are working in this heat,' said Lydia. She gave everyone a drink bottle and dragged in a 20 L container of water to fill up more when necessary.

Eamon's face was drawn and his eyes duller. Maya said, 'Are you okay? That was a pretty eventful night.'

Sarah followed Maya's lead, saying, 'I remember when I first talked about some of my childhood experiences, I felt pretty wobbly for a while.'

Eamon smiled. 'I'm okay, just tired. I've been working towards telling everyone for a while. It's probably helped me feel a bit better. I'm glad I did it. If nothing else, Graham has stopped pushing those bloody dogs onto me.'

'Yes, he's a strange man. When he said he knew Daniel was a journalist, I thought it gave him good reason for murder,' said Sarah. 'He had as much reason to fear disclosure as Dr Ted.'

'I've thought that too. When he says it can't be Dr Ted, I wonder if that's a guilty conscience,' said Eamon.

Maya kept quiet but they were making good points.

There was a distant roar of a machine coming to life. The smell of diesel pooled into the room. Lydia entered with mangoes picked from the trees.

'You're a miracle worker,' said Eamon. 'A mango would go down just right.'

Graham and Nathan wandered in, looking proud of themselves. Nathan said, 'Graham here is a talented man around an engine. Power's going to make everything easier.'

Everyone in the group took a mango. Biting into the sweet warm flesh. Liquid nectar running down their faces. Getting back to nature, and having a terrific time.

'Let's pair off into couples and tackle the mud. We have three more mops and buckets. It'll be much easier now we have water,' said Nathan.

'I want to go with you Nathan,' said Lydia moving forward. 'You've got all the experience round here.' She appeared attracted to whoever held the power.

'I'll go with Maya,' said Sarah, leaving Graham and Eamon together.

It was damn hard work. But accessing fresh tank water made all the difference. The red, muddy film over the floor began to shift.

Mitch and Dave were nowhere to be seen.

'I've always loved cleaning. It feels so great when you can see the difference,' said Maya. 'I'm a bit obsessive but that's not the worst problem in the world.'

'I think you have to be OCD to do medicine. If it comes out in cleaning skills, who cares?' said Sarah.

Jack rushed in the front door. 'Not over the clean floor,' said everyone in unison.

He backed out, took off his Wellington boots and came in.

'I've spoken to Perth. It's all a bit of a mess up here because of the cyclone. No buildings were lost in Exmouth, but trees are down everywhere. The police searchers are coming up and the SES will help as much as they can. They have to come the long way round through Omar Station. They'll try and send a helicopter as well,' said Jack.

'We'll help you,' said Steve, who'd just wandered in carrying the biscuit barrel from the kitchen.

'That barrel seems to be never ending. Can we all have one too?' said Jack.

Steve handed around the biscuits while everyone drank more water.

An inhuman, shrieking howl reached Maya's ears first. Like the devil himself had unleashed the demons from hell. She moved to run in that direction, before Jack reacted. Heart thumping, legs pumping. Oh God, not another murder.

The sound came from the dog yard. She rounded the corner.

Graham was on his knees sobbing, staring up at the heavens. Surely no one would kill a mother dog or her puppies.

Maya blinked and gulped. There, in front of Graham, lay Lucy seizing. A 6-foot snake with a broken neck next to her. Brown, with a shiny diamond pattern to its scales. A demon in the safe home.

Graham sobbed. 'Help her Maya.'

Maya dropped to her knees, gravel spiking through her trousers. She would've done anything to help but couldn't see where to start. 'She must've been bitten while protecting her pups.'

'That's a mulga. A king brown. It's deadly,' said Jack. His voice choked up.

Jack moved forward to put his hand on Graham's shoulder. 'Lucy needs anti-venom but it's a 3-hour drive. We can't cross Yardie Creek. We'd have to go the long way round. It's too far away to get to the vet in time.' Graham shook him off and bawled.

Maya's eyes were full of tears. They'd grown to love Lucy in such a short time. Animals were just easier than humans.

Maya moved forward to stroke Lucy's back as she fitted. She murmured, 'You're such a brave dog. You fought so hard to protect your babies.' Keeping her voice low and lyrical. Like a gentle lullaby.

Jack picked up the puppies and moved them away from their mum. Cuddling them.

Nathan arrived, pounding round the side of the house. 'I heard yelling. are you lot, okay?' He gasped as he saw Lucy in the red dirt. 'Oh God no, not Lucy.'

Graham's face was red and streaming. Contorted in grief. There was nothing they could do to fix the situation.

Slimy red mud covered everything. Surreal, like they'd been wrestling. Lucy took one more shuddering breath and stopped.

No one said a word. In the silence Maya felt for a heartbeat. There was none. she looked into Graham's eyes and shook her head.

He looked at the sky and screamed. Everyone backed away except Maya. She stayed. A silent witness to his emotions. She knew that grief needed presence. No matter how painful. Someone needed to stand with you.

She didn't touch Graham. Jack had tried and it didn't help. She focused on slowing her breathing and staying calm. Graham stopped wailing. No more breath. His movements slowed. Less agitated.

Maya rustled through her pockets to find a clean tissue, trained by her dads to always have one on hand. She passed it to him. A way to connect. He blew hard to clear his sinuses. She waited.

'Lucy was the first thing I dared to love after leaving prison,' said Graham.

Maya stayed still. 'She was a wonderful dog. You had a very special relationship with her.'

'I think it brings up all the other losses I've experienced,' said Graham.

'Yes. That's my experience of it. Grief is like an onion. You'll never get rid of the layers but you can survive,' said Maya.

'Can I carry her into the house? I'd like to wash her and put her in her special rug before we bury her.' said Graham.

'Of course,' said Maya. 'I'd like to make it special for her. Have a bit of a ceremony. Maybe we could all say something about her?'

Graham gave a half smile. Not with his eyes but he was trying. He scooped Lucy into his arms and disappeared around the corner of the house.

Everyone gathered in the kitchen. They watched Maya enter. Silently. She followed Graham carrying Lucy in his arms.

Maya's tongue was thick and coated. 'Lucy has died. She was bitten by a snake, fighting to protect her puppies.' Her mouth dry, hard to swallow.

Tears in her eyes, Lydia said, 'But we loved her so much.'

'Yes, I know,' said Maya welling up herself. 'Graham wants to wash her and then have a funeral when we bury her.'

'I'll go and dig a hole to prepare a grave for her,' said Jack, ignoring his busy phone. 'I'll find somewhere beautiful, where she can watch the puppies.'

'All the men should help. It's a job for menfolk,' said Steve. Eamon nodded, flushed face and wet eyes.

The puppies were rooting around on Nathan's lap. Maya had an overwhelming need to cuddle them. Sarah was faster. She picked them up and said, 'Lydia and I'll look after the puppies. We can find some things that Lucy loved to play with, to bury with her.'

An hour later they gathered under a surviving white gum tree, which overlooked the puppy play area. The mysterious, olive-white trunk reaching into the deep blue sky. Shimmering from the oils. The tangy smell of eucalyptus. An idyllic resting place.

The men were hot and sweaty from digging. Nathan placed a cross he had fashioned from wood at the base of the gum tree. He'd chiselled Lucy's name in the wood and the words "much loved". Sarah brought a bunch of wildflowers, scraggy after the winds. Beautiful in their own way.

The group turned to look at Maya, like she'd been voted minister. Maya brought a sprig of rosemary for everyone.

She handed these twigs around, saying, 'Rosemary is for remembrance. We've come together to remember Lucy. If anyone has a special memory or a wish for Lucy, please say it now.'

Graham held Lucy, washed and cleaned, in a soft blue rug. She had a blue ribbon tied to her collar. Graham's tears flowed as he said, 'Lucy, you were my best friend up here. I felt loved and accepted by you. I wish I could've saved you.' He moved forward and gently placed her in the gravesite.

Steve brought a ball with him. He put it next to her and said, 'Lucy I hope this is useful to you in heaven and you have lots of fun playing catch. '

Sarah came forward and laid the flowers next to Lucy. 'I hope the heavens are full of wildflowers and grasses for you to run through.'

'But don't get grass seeds in your paws,' said Jack, to teary smiles all round.

Lydia was holding one of the struggling puppies. They'd both been washed and groomed. She'd tied a ribbon around their necks. Iridescent purple of course.

Lydia said, 'Lucy, we promise to look after your babies and to make sure they find a good home.'

'About that,' said Nathan. 'I believe Dr Ted told you that Lucy was his dog. That wasn't true. She's mine. I breed working dogs in my spare time.'

'Oh Nathan,' said Maya, 'that's such a loss for you.'

'I think it's harder on Graham. He's been looking after the dogs for the last month,' said Nathan. He turned to look Graham full in the face, 'Graham I want to give you the female pup. She has a weak back leg and will never cope with the working life. You're great with animals and I trust you to care for her.'

Everyone held their breathe. Graham lunged forward and hugged Nathan hard.

'But what about us?' said Lydia. 'I want a new dog too.'

'It's going to be hard enough to find accommodation in Perth, without including a dog,' said Jack glaring at her.

Maya took back control and said, 'Is there anything else about Lucy that someone wants to share?'

'I remember swimming with whale shark on Tuesday. Nathan told us about the grandmother spirits they carry,' said Eamon. 'Lucy loved swimming in the ocean, so I'd like to ask the grandmother spirits to take care of her, wherever she is now.'

'She'd be good with a mob of grandmas,' said Nathan grinning.

It was hot in the sun, rays blazing down from the heavens. But no one wanted it to end.

Maya said, 'I'd like to recite part of a poem by Maya Angelou. I was taught this by my dads to honour those we've lost.

"Mya the road rise up to meet you. May the wind always be at your back.

May the sun shine warm upon your face. May the rains fall softly on your fields.

Until we meet again, May God hold you in the hollow of his hand."

There was silence for a moment, everyone with bowed heads appreciating Lucy's short life. Then they wandered off, back to the house except Jack and Maya. He bent to shovel the red dirt in the hole.

'This is gut wrenching,' said Maya. 'After all we've been through, I thought we'd all make it.'

'I love animals but it hurts so much that they don't live as long as we do,' said Jack. 'I find it hard to accept you only get 15 precious years before losing them.

'I know what you mean but I think those years are worth it,' said Maya. 'I think life's about learning to accept loss. Surrendering control.'

Jack reached out to take her hand, 'Death tells me that life is precious. I don't want to miss a second.' He leaned forward and kissed her.

Maya's head swum. Her own tsunami of emotions. Perhaps moving faster than she'd like?

18

A clanging sound rang out from the gong on the Veranda. It wasn't the wild, angry gonging of Dr Ted, nor the exuberant musicality of Joy. This was a tentative sound. A shy, 'sorry to bother you' kind of noise.

Maya rushed to the veranda, hearts racing, primed by Lucy's passing. She saw Nathan, red and sweating, tapping at the metal plate. The veranda was cluttered with rubbish. Broken chairs, overturned tables and tree litter. Part of the gabled roof cracked and fallen. Like it'd been hit by an out-of-control truck.

Everyone came within minutes. Nathan flushed when he saw the group and said, 'I was wondering if any of you're willing to help on the property. I've been assessing the damage and we've lost all 50 of the sheep. They're real roamers.'

'Are all the gates and fences down?' said Jack, stepping up to the front.

'Yep. The Homestead's only 150 acres so if we work together, we should be able to rescue them.' said Nathan shuffling his feet and looking at the ground, 'I can't do this on my own.'

'Okay. Of course, we'll help.' said Jack, apparently nominating himself as spokesman for the group.

'I've got three 4-wheeler motorbikes. I know Jack can manage one. Does anyone else know how?' said Nathan, 'We've got four walkie-talkies that we can use to communicate.'

Lydia put her hand up, like a conscientious schoolgirl eager for attention. 'I've been driving these bikes since I was small. I can manage even with the trees down.'

Nathan said, 'Great we can get onto it. Steve you can be my partner. We work well together. We'll pair up Jack and Maya. And then Lydia and Eamon.'

'Sure thing,' said Jack. 'Graham and Sarah can you both keep working together on cleaning up the house?' They nodded.

'That'll work,' said Nathan. 'Graham's handy so he can fix stuff if needed.'

Graham's face lit up, 'Sounds good.'

There was no chatter as they paired up. Unusual for this group. Everyone moved slower with exhaustion and lack of sleep. Eyes glazed. Lydia, Nathan and Jack bent over the map to divvying up the 150 acres.

'Don't worry Nathan. We'll find the sheep. They tend to stick together so it should be pretty easy,' said Jack.

Pleased to be paired with Jack, Maya hopped on the back of the motorbike and put her hands around his waist. She could feel his back muscles as they clenched and unclenched, moving forward and back on the seat. Amazing that a line of muscle could be so seductive.

They headed to the north east corner of the property. It was slow going. The bike slipped on the muddy track as Jack ground the gears, jerking back and forth. The red mud baked in the heat of the day. Like the sun crisping a meat pie, it was sloppy underneath. The bush smelt thick and rotten. Trees were down all over the property after the onslaught of the winds. Branches blocked the gravel track. Maya hopped on and off the bike to help Jack move them. Hard work. Sweat streaming.

Once they reached their search area of the property, they slowed down, walking, taking time to look. Worried about the livestock. Walkie-talkies crackling.

Maya used a stick to stop from sliding over, but was still covered in the hot, sticky clay. 'What's that over there?' she said, standing on tippy toes, pointing to the hazy horizon.

Jack peered through binoculars in that direction. 'Oh my God, I think you've found them. You do have eagle eyes.'

Maya smiled. They walked closer through the slimy mud, aiming to balance on the bushy weeds on the side of the path. The illusion of dirty white creatures in the distance became firmer. Yes, they'd found the sheep.

'Looks like they wandered over the boundary with Omar Station,' said Jack.

'Greener pastures.' Maya laughed in the soupy heat.

Jack spoke into the walkie-talkie and said, 'Nathan wants us to wait here. They're going to come to us.'

Soldier ants swarmed in the heat over the sloppy mud, which meant sitting on the ground was unwise. They moved some branches to sit on in the shade of a surviving tree, fashioning a bench-like structure.

Lydia arrived, driving her bike like a crazy person, spitting up red mud all over. Eamon clung to the back, face pale green. Nathan took the opposite approach, moving with care and caution. Steve smiling, arms loose around Nathan.

They arrived and took their helmets off. Eamon pale and gagging. Maya passed him her bottled water.

'Thanks so much for finding them, Maya. I was worried they'd wander further,' said Nathan.

'She'd make one hell of a tracker if she had the training,' said Jack.

Maya flushed and smiled. She stared at the sheep, who were now about 800m away glaring back, and said, 'How the hell are you going to get these animals back behind the gate?'

Nathan smiled. 'I've already fixed up the stock pen next to the house. The fences there are sturdier than the rest of the property.' He turned to Steve and said, 'Steve's going to lead them home using lupins.'

Steve glowed. 'What are lupins?'

'They're a seed that grows into a purple flower. The grain's like crack cocaine to sheep. They'll do anything to get a fix,' said Nathan opening a hessian sack on the back of the motorbike.

They gathered round the bag of seeds and eyebrows raised. Small, white/grey nuggets that didn't look palatable, let alone addictive.

Nathan said, 'Okay Lydia and Jack take your bikes around the back of the flock. When we pour the lupins in the plastic bucket the sheep will come towards us. Steve, your job is to shake the bucket making as loud a noise as possible, then pour out a few lupins every hundred metres.' Nathan was a quiet man but when he spoke everybody listened. He was a natural leader.

Maya hopped on the back of the bike, eager to see if this unlikely plan worked. They took their positions, then Steve filled the bucket. Immediately the sheep lifted their heads to listen. Steve poured out a few lupins on the ground and the flock thundered towards him, pushing each other out the way to get there first.

Nathan started the bike moving forward at a steady pace. Jack and Lydia had little to do, but follow. The sheep behaved exactly like cocaine addicts. They pushed and shoved, bleating as loud as possible to grab Steve's attention. They moved faster, travelling at a fair clip.

The gate to the stock pen was open. Nathan drove the sheep in, and slipped out the back when they were counted.

Steve's eyes were shining and he grinned hard enough to split his face. 'That was fantastic fun.'

Maya joined in, laughing, 'I couldn't believe it worked. I'm such a city girl. It was amazing that you moved the whole 50 so easily.'

Eamon still looked pale. 'I'm not sure I want to do anything to do with a four-wheeler bike, ever again.'

'Yeah, you were a bit of the wuss,' said Lydia, who then turned to Jack and whined. 'I'm so hungry, what time is it?'

Jack glanced at his wrist, 'It's nearly 6 o'clock. We've been at it all day.' He rubbed his jaw and ignored Lydia, looking directly at Maya, 'Are you hungry?'

Maya's stomach growled. 'Yes, I'm starving. Let's go and see what survived the cyclone.'

The kitchen was set up to manage most power cuts with ease. The cold rooms were built with the best quality insulation. None of the food had spoiled, despite being without power for nearly 24 hours. They found bread, cheese and condiments.

Graham and Sarah had saved as much as possible from Joy's vegetable garden. The shade cloth had fallen in, but they'd managed to collect a box of squashed tomatoes, cucumbers, capsicums and lettuce. A feast. Joy may've been missing but her green thumb and mothering spirit was everywhere.

Maya made herself a sandwich and wandered outside. It was a beautiful, twilight night. The moon, and the stars winking. The heat fading. The sky clear, like the world was taking a breath after the exertion of the cyclone. The breeze carried a cleaned, salty smell from the ocean.

Owls called to each other. Perhaps in relief? The storm had passed. Maya looked at Venus which sat just under the moon, remembering the wishes she made on the first star as a child. Careful what you wish for. The gypsies curse.

The temperature was 27 degrees C, according to the thermometer in the kitchen, and there was a gentle breeze. The world smelled wet. Maya loved the smell of northern Australia. There was a fresh eucalyptus and peppermint flavour to the air, combined with the salt of the ocean.

Red mud was everywhere. Who knew mud had its own distinctive smell? She heard the rustling of the animals around her. The kangaroos were fearless, not caring whether she saw them or not. The emus were much shyer, just seen in the open bush.

There was a sense of timelessness in this landscape. The country ancient, hundreds of millions of years, transcending human existence. The time scale was different. But Maya knew that life was precious. Murder demanded recognition and retribution.

Jack poked his head out the screen door. He said, 'It's a beautiful night. Do you want to go for a walk? Nathan asked me to check a few of the gates and fences on the property.' His legs were muddy to the mid-thigh, face dusty and his wide brimmed hat pushed back on his head. He was a mess but it enhanced his attractiveness. Casual but gorgeous.

Maya smiled at him. 'Yes, but won't it be wet and sloshy?' She was dishevelled too. Muddy, sweaty, dirty in shorts and a T-shirt.

'Some of the water has drained away. We'll just avoid the puddles. Wear shoes you don't care about. It'll be fun,' said Jack, grinning back at her.

They started off down the track to the ocean. There were large muddy red puddles. Maya was soon splashed to her midcalf. But it was fun. The severe temperatures of the day had passed. There was a sense of magic and possibility in the air.

They saw the ripples of the ocean in the distance, sparkling silver. Many of the trees and fences were down on the property. Jack took photos for Nathan to start the insurance claim.

They reached the eucalyptus tree where they had first kissed. It'd survived the onslaught of the cyclone. Standing tall among the flattened landscape. Perhaps a sign?

A low-pitched grating call sounded. Maya jumped. 'What's that noise?'

'I think it's a mopoke. They're a kind of owl who hunt and kill at night,' said Jack.

'Do you have to bring up hunting and killing? I was just feeling safe with you,' said Maya, reaching out for his hand and moving closer to him. Only half joking.

Jack turned and smiled at Maya, looking deep into her eyes. Maya was drawn to the intense green of his, and leaned forward. An energy passed between them. She felt a warm tingling sensation over her body. She smelled his masculine scent. Musky, smoky.

Maya held her breath and gently placed her lips on Jack's. A question. How far might she go? He responded by pulling her in tight to his chest and kissing her hard.

Maya's sensible thoughts left her mind. She was swamped by touch. She ran her hands over his muscular shoulders and down his biceps. He grabbed the lower part of her back and pulled her towards him. Tighter. Close in their intimacy, but not close enough.

She panted with longing for him. Jack pulled off his shirt and pressed against her. Maya threw off her own top. Jack kissed her breasts. She rubbed his chest and back, his hair and stubble.

Maya was possessed by an ancient spirit. Yearning for sexual connection. Her sense of self disappeared. All that was left was sensation. She scrambled to remove the rest of her clothing. Jack followed her lead. Neither of them made a sound. No precautions were taken.

His smell, deep and masculine. His taste, clean, strong with testosterone. Touch. Oh God the touch. Soft and hard. His hair and nipples erect with desire. Touch, sending spasms of yearning to the base of her spine.

Jack picked her up as if she were a doll. He leaned against the surviving white gum tree, and plunged himself deep inside her in one motion. Maya gasped. Staring into his eyes. Wild, pupils dilated. Waves of intense energy swam over her body. Sensations rising. Jack cried out her name. A primitive riot of sexual desire. No rationality. Sex at its most basic.

They came together, like a king wave crashing into a rock face. Echoes of intense pleasure. Both gasping with relief.

A broad, strong beam of torchlight shone over the bushes, straight into their faces. Maya blinked in shock.

'You utter, utter bitch,' said Lydia, between gritted teeth. No jingling of her bangles now.

Lydia kept the torch full on Maya, as she tried to cover her nakedness. Eamon, hidden in the grey shadows, came into the light and attempted to grab the torch from Lydia.

'Give her some privacy, Lydia,' said Eamon. 'Don't be cruel.'

Maya blushed. Her body flushed hot and cold with adrenaline. Jack reacted much faster than Maya. He already dressed in shorts and his T-shirt. How the hell had he managed that? He moved to stand in front of Maya. She dressed as fast as possible.

Jack said, 'Give it a rest Lydia. I'm sure you're not perfect.' Jack's voice was loud but his movements were relaxed and slowed. 'Are you looking for me?'

'No,' said Lydia, 'we couldn't sleep so we decided to take a walk in the moonlight.'

'Given that Dr Ted could be a murderer and running around here, we've all been a little lax with our security,' said Eamon, his face red in the torchlight.

'You didn't want to come anyway,' said Lydia. 'You just agreed because you didn't want me going on my own.'

'Eamon's right,' said Jack. 'We should go back and stick together.'

'I want to have a swim,' said Lydia.

Maya sighed. Lydia loved to cause trouble.

'For God sakes, Lydia, do you have a death wish? Haven't you seen Jaws? Sharks come out to hunt at night,' said Eamon, grabbing her shoulder. 'Not to mention, yet again, there's a murderer running loose around here.'

Maya hadn't managed to say anything. She was more shocked than embarrassed. She went and stood next to Jack. There was something about their sexual connection that bound them. She was angry with Lydia for interrupting the experience that felt sacred to Maya. She could still sense an energy drawing her towards Jack, holding her in this primordial world.

It was dark as they walked. There was one torch, but the moon lit the path. Jack and Maya moved together, holding hands, but walked in silence.

The Homestead was lit up. Steve, in his purple/lime green striped pyjamas, was on the veranda. Moving around the tables and chairs, while chattering to his voices. Cleaning up.

Steve's face brightened as he saw them. 'I turned on all the lights so we'd be safer. I think we could sleep out here. We should stick together. I worry about getting trapped in my room. The house is creepy. Like Dr Ted's hiding behind the furniture, getting ready to murder someone else.'

Maya smiled at Steve and said, 'It's a frightening time. I don't think any of us really know what to do. It's probably important we get a good night's sleep because we'll be busy tomorrow with the search.'

She turned to Eamon and said, 'Could Steve sleep in your room? He might feel safer behind locked doors with someone he knows well. I'll give him a sleeping tablet so you both get a good night.'

'Okay. We've hung together before and we can do it again,' said Eamon. His voice sounded warm and welcoming.

'Thanks so much. You're really kind,' said Maya.

Grateful for the distraction, she bustled off with Steve to organise his sleeping situation and medication. It took a while, moving mattresses, sheets and pillows. Steve glowed with the attention and appeared contented with the arrangement

Maya saw Jack sitting on the veranda alone, amongst the rubble, as she moved through the Homestead. She went outside and stared at him in silence.

Jack smiled, but he looked tired. He said, 'I'm so sorry about what happened. I lost control. I should never have put you in that situation with Lydia.'

'I'm a big girl and can make my own decisions,' said Maya. 'I wanted you as much as you wanted me. I don't regret it.'

'Even so Lydia will make things difficult for you,' said Jack.

Jack's sat phone rang. It had a piercing ring tone which was difficult to ignore, 'I'm sorry I have to take this. We're still trying to coordinate police searchers and the SES. Everyone will be here by tomorrow. We'll start the search then.'

Sarah and Lydia stood in the corridor of the bedroom wing, gossiping. Maya consciously lifted her head to look taller, staring ahead as she tried to walk straight past the women.

Lydia grabbed her arm to stop her. 'You don't know what you're getting into. Jack has a real reputation with women. Love them, then leave them. You're going to get hurt.'

'Thank you for your concern but I can make my own decisions and I'll stand by them,' said Maya, using a low, slow tone of voice.

'Lydia's just trying to help,' said Sarah. 'She grew up with Jack so she knows all about him.'

'We're tired and need to get up early tomorrow to begin the search,' said Maya, trying to distract from the uncomfortable situation. 'Do you want to camp out in one room or go to our own rooms and lock the door?'

'Are you sure you wouldn't prefer to sleep with Jack?' said Lydia with a wicked grin. Maya thought how difficult it must've been for Lydia's two sisters, growing up with her.

'No, I'll be just fine with you both. Jack's busy coordinating the search parties coming up here from Perth,' said Maya.

'I vote for separate rooms,' said Sarah. 'Having people in the same room as me at night freaks me out.'

Maya turned to go to her room. 'Okay. Sleep well.'

'Has Jack told you that he's married and has a twelve-year-old child?' said Lydia, taking her time to articulate every stabbing word.

Maya's stomach skewered her in the throat. She smelt acid. Oh God she might vomit. She willed her muscles to lift her leg and kept moving forward into her room, locking the door.

Alone with her thoughts, her body went shaky and faint. Maya was horrified with what Lydia had just said.

Maya's self-critical, inner voice started up with a hostile creak. "I'm so stupid. They're all talking about me. Why didn't he tell me? He used me.'

She'd never had intercourse outside of a long-term relationship. She was a planner not a risk taker. She'd been caught in such a compromising position.

Tears started to flow down her cheeks. God, she despised herself when she cried. It was so childlike. Her body was a mixture of intense emotions. There was a residual tingling from the sex, the gut punch sickness of shame and embarrassment, and the confusion of what it meant.

Maya tried to ground herself using the five senses. She started with smell, the moist air, eucalyptus scent, sound of the cicadas, warbling of the magpies on their way to bed ... it wasn't working. Her mind darted all over the place. Her hand twitched to her pocket. Looking for her mobile. Nothing, no connection there.

Damn it, she was a grown-up who knew better than this. If only she could talk to her dads they'd help so much. She couldn't bear talking to Jack. He was so distracted with the search.

Her stomach knotted. Did she hate him now? Should she cut him out of her life? Should she talk to him? Could she leave it until the morning?

Her automatic negative voice was having a hay day. Thoughts like 'you should've been more careful', 'you should be smarter'.

God what a mess. Sleep seemed unlikely. She punched the pillow, trying to relieve some of the tension.

The moon shone bright in her room, messing with her circadian rhythm.

Even the clock annoyed the hell out of her. Tick, tick, tick, interrupting her sleep.

She continued to toss and turn. Way beyond the time it would have been sensible to give up and get out of bed.

Tick, tick, tick.

What was she to do? ...

19

Day 12 Post Death

Maya woke with a start and saw Lydia at the end of her bed. Every limb stiffened in shock. How the hell had she got into the room through a locked door? Was Graham at it again?

Lydia was dressed, full of her jingly bracelets and loud colours. A walking nightmare.

Lydia said, 'Everyone from Perth has arrived. It's 5 AM. We're leaving soon. They want to set up headquarters where the four-wheel-drive was last seen. We'll be divided into different sections.'

Maya blinked, not taking in what Lydia said.

'Hurry up sleepyhead. You're going to miss all the drama,' said Lydia raising her voice. A stabbing pain rammed through Maya's forehead.

Maya washed her face and went to the dining room to get coffee. There were people everywhere. The noise was overwhelming. Her head throbbed. She served herself a strong black coffee and ladled in 2 tablespoons of sugar. She needed all the help she could get.

Everything in the dining area had changed. Maps covered the wall space. There were grey-green police uniforms and bright orange SES uniforms everywhere. Everyone was talking at once. People were wearing armbands with one of two colours blue and yellow. A technicoloured, Orwellian version of purgatory.

She was trying to remember where the aspirin was kept, when Jack came over.

Jack said, 'We have put you with the yellow group which I'm leading. Get some good shoes and long trousers. You need a hat and layers of sunscreen.' He was officious and loud. Grey with exhaustion. Not like the gentle person of last night.

'Hurry up,' he said. 'We have to get going as soon as possible.'

Maya's stomach contracted. Oh God Lydia was right. He really did just want sex. Her head hurt.

'Come on Maya. You've got to get moving. You can't go out into the bush in a sundress,' said Jack.

Maya couldn't find words to say how angry she was. She glared at him, hoping this would translate. She stood up, slamming her chair back into the wall.

She went to her room and threw open her suitcase looking for clothing that resembled Jack's advice. She jammed on a pair of jeans, sand shoes and socks.

Back in the eating area she found Jack and said, 'I'm changing myself to the blue group. I don't want to search with you. Lydia told me. I know you used me last night.'

Jack flared his nostrils like an angry horse. 'Fine report to Sgt Bradford over there at the dining table. Just remember you can't believe everything Lydia says.'

'Well, she says that you're married and have a 12-year-old child,' said Maya clenching her jaw.

Jack paled and swayed on his feet.

'Is it true? Why didn't you tell me?' said Maya. Waves of nausea flooded her body.

Jack gulped, looking sick. 'It's sort of true. But it was over years ago.'

'Oh, for God's sake, this is something you should've told me days ago,' said Maya, her face flushed. 'Keep away from me. I don't want anything to do with you.' She turned her back on Jack and stomped away.

Maya headed over to the dining table, which had been turned into the admin center, in order to change groups. Jack stood, looking like he was going to faint. Maya remembered she didn't have sunscreen. She went back to her room and burst into tears. She fell on her bed sobbing. Her head hurt and she really didn't want to search. She'd be burnt to a crisp. Her energy subsided with the sobs and she fell asleep

Maya woke with a start. Her right arm throbbed. There was a burning sensation in her fingers. She flicked them to get back her feeling. She grabbed her worry doll and put it in her pocket. Her bladder ached. She had a desperate urge to pee. She stumbled into the corridor and made her way to the toilet.

The house appeared deserted. The smell of sweat of the dozens of people was all around her. But they'd gone. They'd forgotten her.

A stabbing pain hit her in the stomach and she gasped. She rushed to the sink. She tried to vomit but nothing came. She settled on a sip of lukewarm tap water.

Maya hated being alone in any house. The creaks and cracks amplified, sounding as if a murderer hid behind every door. She went back to her room and looked at the clock, 3 PM. She'd slept for hours.

Her skin prickled at the thought of being abandoned. A primitive fear of waking the demons when alone. The house had old bones and groaned like an elderly woman, trying to move on a hot day.

Maya chided herself. 'Get something to eat. You're just hungry. The fear will pass.' Rubbing her thumb over the worry doll's hair.

She left the room and walked down the corridors to the main eating area. She shuddered at the large windows, in full view of any killer lurking outside. She curled forward and shuffled across the open area.

Her heart raced. Oh God was someone watching her? Maya held her body stiff and tight, trying to minimise the noise she made. She gulped repetitively, pushing back the stomach reflux.

She moved into the kitchen and noticed the light on in the pantry.

Was that where Dr Ted was hiding? She braced for the door to swing open and the attack to begin. But nothing. Silence. More frightening than the noise. Like the house was holding its breath waiting for terror.

Maya opened the fridge and took out the milk. She started clinking and crashing the cutlery. Hoping the normal routine would soothe her. She took the long way round the island Determined to avoid the pantry light. She put on the kettle.

All her limbs were tingling with anxiety. She swayed back and forth, back and forth, like a mother reassuring a babe in arms. Her stomach was so tense she wasn't sure she could swallow, but she rustled in the tins looking for a sugar fix. She found a chocolate chip cookie and took a large bite washing it down with milk.

There was a crash. Unmistakable. Something glass had broken. Shattered against the floor.

Maya startled and dropped the milk, spilling over the floor. The noise echoed round the empty room. Her whole body stiffened and she looked for a place to hide.

She moved to the pantry. She saw the knives and took one, somehow strengthening, with her decision to take a weapon. She flung open the door but it was empty. No one there. She turned off the light and moved inside.

Her thoughts raced. Oh God oh god, I'm going to die. The suspense was unbearable. The seconds moved so slowly, as if going backwards.

She heard footsteps. Step, step, step. Coming towards the kitchen. Moving inch by inch, persistent. The kitchen door creaked as it moved open.

Maya held her breath. There were slats in the pantry door but it was hard to see. A sudden movement and the door flung open.

'Joy,' said Maya stiffening with shock.

Joy said, 'Hello dear I've been wondering where you were.'

Maya's chest tightened. 'Oh my God. We've been looking for you. There are search parties out there. Where the hell have you been? Where's Dr Ted? How did you get away?'

Joy said, 'I really don't know what you are talking about dear. I've been here the whole time. I'm getting the guest room ready in case Sam wants to visit. The university holidays are coming up and he has done so well this semester. I'm so proud of him.'

Maya tensed. She noticed that Joy was bedraggled, messy. Oily hair scraped in a pony tail. Like she was imitating sanity. The skin on the back of Maya's neck prickled. Nausea rose in her throat, as if she'd swallowed poison.

Maya backed away, and went outside onto the veranda to take a breath. Her panic mounted. The tingling in her neck spread to her fingers, which trembled. Her body screamed to run after Jack. Who cared that he'd let her down? She would've run but she had no idea where anyone had gone.

The screen door opened behind her and Maya jumped in. Every muscle in her body stiffening. Joy came out and stood there staring at Maya.

Joy said, 'I'm so excited for you to meet Samuel. He's such a lovely boy. You could be a role model for him. I've always hoped he might do Medicine.' She spoke like she was a robot, reciting her lines.

The sickness in Maya's stomach mounted and twisted. She said, 'But Dr Ted told me that Sam died. You lost him years ago. It's why you work here. You made the white group room his shrine.' Maya was babbling with fear, never a wise strategy.

Joy's face went red and contorted. She tensed her arms and gritted her teeth.

Maya's heart raced and stomach clenched. She saw Joy had a meat hammer in her right hand and a small black box in her left. Was she going to attack her? Surely not?

Maya's muscles froze. She tried to backtrack 'I'm so sorry. I didn't mean to upset you. It must've been a terrible loss.' Joy stared beyond Maya, breathing heavily, expanding like a dart frog, eyes bulging.

Maya had been protected from this level of fury her whole life. She didn't know how to respond. She backed towards the edge of the veranda, stumbling on the wooden surface. Bumbling muscles refusing to coordinate. Limb shaking, heart racing. Maya clenched her jaw and gritted her teeth. Every muscle tight with tension.

Joy rushed forward, rising up and struck at Maya's head with the hammer. Maya moved both her arms forward to ward off Joy's attack. But the momentum pushed them off the veranda in a tangle of limbs.

Maya fell hard. Sharp pains spread from her hip over her body. Tears welled in her eyes.

Joy landed on top of Maya. She hit out with the meat hammer again. Joy was strong. Years of hard physical work. But the position was awkward and she missed Maya's head. Joy's teeth bared and she snarled like a trapped wolf.

With a burst of adrenaline, Maya started to fight back. Pushing with all her might. Pulling hair, clawing, pinching. Maya saw that Joy was trying to get a better grip on the box in her left hand. She struck out with all her limbs to drive Joy away. Kicking, pushing, hitting.

A jarring bolt of electricity exploded through Maya's body. An explosion from her chest outwards. Oh God a Taser. She gasped attempting to force air into her lungs.

Out of the corner of her eye Maya saw Joy raise the meat hammer to strike. Pain radiated from her head, as she slipped into darkness

∾

MAYA WOKE with the threads of pale sunlight kissing her cheek. Her head throbbed and her hip ached. She gasped. The fight with Joy. Her hands and feet pounded. Oh God she was tied. Where the hell was she?

She felt her worry doll in her pocket. Her mum and dads were cheering her on. She would fight, no matter what.

Maya peered out at the world around her, forcing open her swollen eyes. She turned her head left and right, trying to orientate herself. There was a rocky overhang. Dark. The deeper areas smelled of bat shit. A rough cave in the red rock. Joy was outside shouting. Dr Ted was tied up beside her, unconscious, beaten, possibly dead.

Her throat tightened with an awful taste in her mouth. As Maya breathed in, she inhaled the red dust on the cavern floor. She stifled a cough. Her heartbeat echoed in her eardrums, compounding the sense of suffocation.

Maya's hairline prickled and a creepy feeling moved up her body. She felt her bowels clench. Oh God, now she needed to go to the toilet.

What the hell could she do? Both she and Dr Ted were trussed up like turkeys, with their hands tied behind their backs and legs bound together.

She focused on her dads and tried to draw strength. The rough, stony floor, cold beneath her. She wiggled. How could she loosen these ropes? She had to get away.

Dr Ted opened his eyes and stared into the distance. There but not there. He coughed and croaked, 'Joy has gone completely mad.'

Maya could see Joy talking to herself. Waving her arms and arguing with unseen companions. Her shirt and trousers covered with red dirt, mixed with sweat, blood and tears.

Maya said, 'What should we do?'

Dr Ted spoke, a raw dry sound. 'How the hell do you think I know?'

'You're a God damn psychiatrist with decades of experience. You have to know something,' said Maya, her pulse racing. 'Maybe we should scream for help?'

'We're in the Cape Range. It runs for hundreds of kilometres. No one ventures out here in the wet. It's too hot,' said Dr Ted, face red. 'I haven't worked with a psychotic person for years. You're the one who's more likely to have a clue.'

Maya stared at him. Her muscles tensed. Ready to hit him, if she could move these damn ties. She needed to get him thinking about escape. This pathetic, given-up state was no use to anyone. She said, 'How did you cope with the cyclone?' Maybe she could get him thinking about survival?

'We were already here when the storm hit. Joy brought her meat trolley and pushed me deep into the cavern, like a pig carcass,' said

Dr Ted, jaw clenched. 'Being inland, up high and undercover, helped. Not that it's any use now.'

Maya sighed, jigging to and fro, trying to loosen the ties. She found a sharp stone on the cave floor and manoeuvred her body to scrape at the ropes tying her ankles. It was an awkward position, but she had youth and flexibility on her side.

'Don't even bother. I've trying to loosen the ropes for at least a day. Joy must've been one hell of a scout. She's good with knots,' said Dr Ted.

Maya wrinkled her brow. 'Well, I refuse give up. I have a good life and I'm determined to get back to it.' She gritted her teeth and kept scratching at the ties.

'How did you end up here?' said Dr Ted.

'I was left at the Homestead by the others and Joy found me,' said Maya. 'They were out organising the search in the Range. She must've come back to find something. She used a Taser to overpower me.'

'She tricked me,' said Dr Ted, dropping his voice to a whisper. 'She told me she had come to rescue me from the police, so I went with her. She put a vial of haloperidol solution in my drinking water. It's tasteless so I didn't know what she had done, until I collapsed.'

'Have you tried talking to her?' said Maya.

Dr Ted said, 'Joy's been ranting about Samuel ever since I woke up. She doesn't seem to understand that I regret what happened but I can't change it.' He closed his eyes and slumped, as if moving back into his own little world.

An energy coursed through Maya's body, giving a sense of strength and purpose. She refused to roll over and give up. She kept sawing at the knot of the ropes binding her ankles.

Her voice strained as she said to Dr Ted, 'Help me.' Sweat ran down her face, 'Don't just lie there like a bloody coward.'

Dr Ted's eyes sprung open, his face grimaced, and he shouted at her, 'You're such a little Miss Perfect. Always pleasing everybody. No one would miss you if you died.'

Outside of the cave, Joy jumped as Dr Ted's words reached her. She rushed in the cave and hit Dr Ted in the chest with the Taser.

Dr Ted made an un-godly sound as he seized, then lay unconscious. Or was he dead? Maya's gut contracted, as she thought she'd vomit.

Joy turned to her and said, 'Shut up and lie there. I'm thinking and can't be disturbed. If you make a noise, I'll knock you unconscious.' She went outside the cave once again and started pacing back and forth, talking to herself.

Maya went straight back to her efforts to free herself. She was determined to hold fast to hope. She would fight no matter what.

Everywhere in the canyon life was stirring. Out the corner of her eye, Maya saw the wallabies coming out and moving around in small family groups, down their tracks. She heard the magpies singing. The kookaburras joined the noise competition and their laughter was winning. She smelt the freshness of a new day. The world around was cheering her on.

Finally, with a jerk, the ties on her ankles gave way.

Joy shifted back into the view. She moved in a way that was stiff and awkward. The physical fight yesterday must have taken a toll on her body.

She turned to stare at Maya. 'This is all your fault, you stupid child. I told you not to get involved but you never listen. You made me hurt you, and now I have no choice but to kill you.'

Maya's mind froze and she couldn't think what to say. She knew the theory was to make a connection with her attacker and try to build feelings of empathy. But Joy's behaviour was Jekyll and Hyde, that Maya couldn't think where to begin.

'I just can't think how to kill you,' said Joy. 'You're too big and too strong for me to push you over the edge here. I knocked you unconscious with a hammer yesterday, but it's a much more difficult job to kill you with a rock. I wish I'd bought my cooking knives but I forgot them in all the drama you caused. I'm so mad with you, you thoughtless, thoughtless girl.'

Maya heard the *whoop, whoop, whoop* of a search helicopter. Her heart lifted. Maybe she could hope for rescue. Joy heard it too and came under the rock shelter. She stared at Maya confused.

'I wish you'd never come here,' said Joy. 'I was so pleased when I first heard you were arriving but you're such a disappointment to me. I thought you would help us but you've just made it worse.'

Joy was ranting. She'd created a whole truth for herself which didn't link to reality.

Maya's head throbbed as she tried to pull herself together. Madness was very familiar to her. She knew how to talk to delusional people, but she had to think clearly first. She could do this. She was strong and brave, and would find a way to survive.

20

The memory of her dads reading to her, was strong in Maya's mind. Even after she learnt to read for herself, she found the rhythm of their voices comforting. One of her favourite books was the *One Thousand and One Nights*. If Scheherazade could come up with 1001 stories on the fly, then Maya could create just one to fool Joy.

Maya softened her face and lowered her voice, trying to sound as hypnotic as possible. 'I'm so sorry to have ruined your plans. The care you give everyone here is amazing. I know that you were just trying to protect the participants and Dr Ted,' She pulled herself to sitting and edged towards the granite walls of the cave. Her feet had come loose so she moved slowly.

Joy appeared to be listening. Maya continued. 'Right from when I arrived, I saw that your role in the Homestead was central. I know you've been here more than 10 years. No wonder, Dr Ted and the participants have so much faith in you.'

Maya slipped another small sharp stone flake into her right hand as she moved across the cave. 'The fact that you've chosen to make this your career is remarkable. I think you're saving people's lives. Dr Ted's so lucky to have you. You're the heart of the Homestead.' Joy had used the ropes from the veranda furniture to tie Maya. They were old. Maya had already cut one. She'd find a way to cut them all.

Tears started running down Joy's cheeks. Soon she was weeping from every orifice, mouth and nose, even ears, sobbing.

'I appreciated your kindness to me when I first arrived,' said Maya keeping her voice low and slow. 'The food and the housekeeping were both amazing. You make the Homestead a special place.'

Maya was cutting the ropes binding her wrists, trying to keep her body steady. 'I can see how poorly the world has treated you. No wonder you felt like you had to take control. I can see how Daniel betrayed your trust.'

Joy stopped crying and wiped her face on her shirt. More snot and dirt. 'He was such a bastard. Daniel never appreciated everything that Dr Ted did for him. He was going to bring us down. I didn't have a choice. I had to kill him.'

Maya kept the tone of her voice gentle. 'Yes, I can see that now. You did the right thing. It makes sense why you had to act.' All her efforts aimed at distracting Joy and keeping her calm. The tension in the ropes gave way. Her heart rate soared. She was untied.

They both heard the helicopter. Joy stood up and paced across the entrance to the cave. She had to be aware they were closing in on her. Maya hoped that whatever good was in Joy, would be enough to save her.

Joy muttered to herself as she walked, weighing every option, looking for a solution. The ropes untangled, Maya planned her next move. Joy sat and put her head in her hands. Rocking back and forth.

The rock flake Maya had in her hands was cool, hard and very sharp. Maya realised that, even in this situation, it was much easier to murder with poison, than to physically stab someone to death. She would cut Joy and then run like hell. She was tall, slim and athletic, despite her pampered upbringing. It was her best option.

Part of her listened to the *thuck, thuck, thuck* of the helicopter and hoped for rescue. She knew that Jack would be doing everything he could to find them. Thinking of Jack gave her courage and settled her nervousness. She visualised her moves to escape, trying to imprint the physical motions into her unconsciousness. It was now or never.

Maya leapt to her feet and went barrelling across the cave floor, screaming as loudly as she could. Electric, angry energy pulsed through her body. This woman was not going to take her away from her dads. Maya was quick on her feet and much younger than Joy. The element of surprise was in her favour.

Joy let out a yell. She was hit in the side by Maya's power. Maya stabbed the sharpened flint stone into Joy's upper back again and again. Joy fell forward and screamed in pain. Blood pouring from her shoulders. Everything went red.

Maya did not stop. She took off down the gravel path leading from the cave. The path was narrow. Worn down by kangaroos over many years. The path of least resistance. Prickly, spiky, but better than death.

Afraid of snakes, Maya slammed her feet on the ground. Trying to make as much noise as possible. She heard Joy following her, but Maya had a head start and was stronger. Down she went into the canyon. Pounding along the gravel. Driven by a desire to get away, anywhere but the cavern.

There was no hiding from Joy, who could see her easily from the higher position, so Maya shouted and screamed. She could still hear the helicopter but couldn't see its position. Trying to cause so much disturbance, that she drew attention to herself.

She rounded a white gum, tripped over a ledge and fell forward into Jack, bowling him to the ground. He landed hard but cushioned her fall. Maya shrieked.

'Where the fuck have you been?' said Jack, 'We've been looking for you as well as the others?'

Maya gasped for breath and struggled to tell the story, 'Dr Ted was kidnapped by Joy. You're looking for the wrong murderer. Joy's the one who killed Daniel. She just told me.'

Jack went red. His eyes widened. 'How did you find this out? Where's Joy now?'

'Joy attacked me on the veranda at the Homestead. She hit me over the head with a meat hammer and tied me up. I was in a cavern with Dr Ted. He's unconscious. Or maybe dead. She wanted to kill me but couldn't bring herself to do it. She didn't have a weapon, like a knife or a gun or poison, thank God,' said Maya, words spilling out of her, barely able to breathe. 'I escaped and she's been chasing me along this path. She must've seen you and gone back to the cave.'

'Where is she going?' said Jack, muscles tense, ready for action.

'It's only about a kilometre along that wallaby trail to your northeast. She came from the North in a four-wheel-drive. She'll probably go back that way to escape. God knows what she'll do to Dr Ted.' said Maya, by now wheezing with exhaustion, unable to go on.

Jack looked up the track then back at Maya. Back and forth like watching a tennis match. He appeared torn between staying with Maya or trying to find Joy. They heard voices below and a pair of searchers came into view.

Jack moved forward to take control of the situation. 'It appears we've been looking for the wrong killer,' he said, with authority in his voice. 'Maya has just escaped from Joy who admitted she's the murderer. Joy doesn't have a weapon but she's hidden a four-wheel-drive. She's probably trying to escape.'

The small search party moved forward to support Maya. She was dizzy and exhausted. The world darkening at the edges of her vision.

Jack appeared to know and trust the searchers. 'I'm going after her. Can you two stay here and help get Maya out of this area?' he said. He moved off quickly and was soon out of sight in the rocky scrubby landscape.

Maya was crying hard. Unable to think. Terrified for Jack. She tried to make the couple understand. 'You have to go with him. She overpowered me. He needs back up. She could run him over with the car or push him over the edge.'

The female searcher said, 'I'm Simone and this is Jonathan. We're in our 60s and not in any shape to chase up rock faces. I know Jack well. He's very clear that our job's to look after you. I'm not going to be distracted by chasing after murderers.'

Jonathan moved towards the canyon's edge. He had a walkie-talkie and Maya heard him giving out information to the others. She was relieved that everyone knew Joy was the murderer.

Maya was dizzy and shaky. Simone helped her sit down and put her head between her knees. 'It's the adrenaline that's making you feel unwell.'

Simone rustled in her pack and gave Maya a water bottle. 'Sip this slowly. It's really cold and will help you calm down.'

Maya surrendered to this gentle mothering. She was exhausted but grateful to be safe. She drank and Simone helped her up, beginning the walk down to the floor of the canyon. One step at a time.

The area was warming. The walls of the canyon reflected that heat in all directions increasing the severity of the temperature. Compounding the situation was the humidity. Maya was overwhelmed.

'It's heating up. It'll be in the high 40's by lunch time,' said Simone. But she smiled, appearing calm and in control.

It took an hour but Maya and Simone made it back to base camp. Jonathan followed behind talking back and forth on the walkie-talkie, keeping the information flowing.

Maya was sobbing again.

'It's the effect of the adrenaline rush. It tends to come and go for hours,' said Simone. 'Sit here and rest. I'll find the medical officer to look at your head.'

Maya was hot and distraught, leaking like a bucket someone'd shot with buckshot. She realised through her sobs however, that her stomach had stopped hurting. Perhaps for the first time since the abduction?

The SES had set up a village of tents among the gum trees. Grey-green canvas, like a military operation. Busy, sweaty people rushing around.

Maya went to the first aid station with a chatty volunteer. It was manned by a retired doctor who was calm and reserved. He examined Maya and declared her dehydrated but otherwise fine. Her head wound was bandaged and he gave her ice-water to sip.

Maya was drained. But her busy mind kept worrying about Jack. Going over and over potential disasters, like a broken record.

People carried walkie-talkies that hissed with distorted voices. Crackling, noisy but indecipherable. Maya needed information but the workers were busy, important and difficult to catch.

The kind doctor brought her a cheese sandwich and jellybeans. Starving, Maya fell on the food. He gave her aloe vera cream for her sunburn. Excellent field medicine.

Maya was soon feeling much better and ventured out of the tent.

She heard the *thuck, thuck, thuck* of the helicopter. That sound had given her hope earlier in the day. She followed the noise to a clearing where it landed.

The first person to jump out was Jack. Maya burst into tears. Embarrassed by her reaction. Overwhelmed by everything.

Jack, covered by red dust, ran up to Maya and kissed her hard on the lips. He said, 'Thank God you're okay. I've been so worried.'

Maya looked at his dirt lined face and bright green eyes. Gummed up with sweat and tears, she said, 'I think I'm going to be sick.'

'Oh God, I hope that's not because I kissed you,' said Jack smiling. He grabbed hold of her and moved towards a shady gum tree.

'I can't stop shaking,' said Maya, tears pouring down her face. 'I was terrified Joy would hurt you.'

'Your directions were excellent. I found the cavern easily,' said Jack helping her sit in the gravel, checking for errant solider ants. 'Joy was in the four-wheel-drive about to leave. I shot out the tyres. She tried to run but I caught her. She was strong and fast for an older lady.'

'Is Dr Ted okay?' said Maya stumbling over her words. There was so much stuff she needed to know, but she surprised herself with that question. She didn't think she cared.

'Yep. He was still in the cave, tied up. Our police wagon met me at the cave and have taken him back to Exmouth,' said Jack, his arm around Maya, holding her tight. 'He'd just given up and isn't saying much. It's like he's shrunk back into himself. He looks old. Not one spark of the powerful guru.'

'What about Joy? She was psychotic. Is she okay?' said Maya, tensing up her jaw. More questions out of nowhere.

'We ended up with two vehicles so we sent her back to Exmouth separately from Dr Ted. She was ranting when I last saw her,' said Jack. He was all over Maya, touching her as if to check she was real. He'd given up any pretence of impartial professionalism. Maya was aware of her red, sunburnt skin, sweaty hair and dank smell. But she sunk into his touch, like she'd come home.

Simone came up to them, smiling and with cold rehydration fluid. She said, 'Here you go, you two. Get this into you. We're going to be nagging at you both to drink for the rest of the day.'

Jack looked at the ground and scuffed his feet. He hesitated for a moment, then said, 'Maya, you were right to be angry with me. I owe you an apology and an explanation.'

Maya stared at her shoes, as if her shoelaces were doing the talking.

Jack said, 'Lydia told you the truth when she said I was previously married and had a twelve-year-old son.'

Tears came unbidden to Maya's eyes.

'The girl's name is Elissa. I got her pregnant when we were both 17. I insisted on marrying her to give the child a real father, but we never lived together. She stayed with her mum who helped raise my son. His name's Jacob. He's a great kid and I see him regularly,' said Jack, sitting straighter in the dirt.

'But I don't understand why you didn't tell me.' said Maya, lifting her head and looking straight on at Jack's face. Challenging him.

'I guess this last week has been like a fantasy to me. As if we were on a magic island. The real world faded and I didn't want to think about anything other than this,' said Jack furrowing his brow.

Jack kicked at the red dirt. Maya said, 'That just doesn't make sense to me. Didn't you trust me? Were you ashamed of them?'

'No, I couldn't be prouder of Jacob. He's an amazing kid. But growing up in the country is different from the city. The values are old-fashioned. I copped a lot of criticism for what happened. I was told to be ashamed of the pregnancy,' said Jack, tensing.

Maya sipped her water while she thought for a moment. She said, 'I do understand that the social morals are different here. But my impression's that children are welcomed and loved no matter how they arrive.'

'My dad's a complicated man. On one side he's a rigid Catholic who attends church weekly, on the other he's a raging alcoholic who was violent to my mum,' said Jack, tearing up himself. 'He's the one who pushed the sense of shame on me.' Every muscle in his body was straining to be heard.

'Well, that makes more sense,' said Maya moving forward to touch Jack's hand. 'Children of alcoholics learn to cope by compartmentalising. They put thoughts in boxes to try and protect themselves. But it's not going to work if you want to have a relationship with me.'

Jack breathed in and out through pursed lips. 'I really want a relationship with you, but I can't move to Perth. I have to stay near Jacob. It feels really complicated.'

Maya smiled and said, 'These things can be worked out if we communicate. I'm almost used to the heat. But I wish I had your olive skin.'

Jack moved forward and kissed her. Maya kissed back. It was going to be difficult but she could make it work.

'Do you want to come back to Exmouth with me in the helicopter? I want to keep an eye on you,' said Jack. He had put his arm around Maya as if he wasn't going to move it ever again.

Maya laughed. 'I've a weird feeling that I don't want you out of my sight either.' Maya kept grinning, she liked the strength of Jack's touch A joyride in a helicopter was a bonus.

The helicopter was like a giant dragonfly. The body was flimsy with floppy rotors on top. Didn't look like it'd fly. Maya belted herself in tight and put on the ear muffs. She liked rhythmic sound of the blades spinning. Reassuring, a reminder of the possibility of rescue.

As she flew over the land, Maya could see its vastness. The startling colours, red earth, blue sky and silver- green eucalyptus. A world of contrasts. Amazing she'd been found in that wilderness and was safe.

Exmouth was a shock. Striking colours, incoherent shouting and the sweat of too many bodies. Being off grid had rebooted Maya's brain and everything was too bright and too loud. She was swept into the assembly line of never-ending uniforms, both police and SES. Orange and green. Armbands everywhere. Busy, important people hustling around. Everyone shoved fluids at her, as if trying to stop her melting.

Jack stepped into his police sergeant role and was being congratulated for his bravery. Maya had her fair share of fist bumps and back slaps herself. It was too much. She longed for quiet. Time to sort out her emotions.

21

Maya and Jack were taken to the station. The now-familiar, square building. Pumping with volunteers. Too much colour, light and noise. Country towns always step up to help others, when there's a need. But this was chaos.

Blood curdling screams came from the interview room.

'If that's Joy,' said Jack. 'She's pretty upset.'

Upset was an understatement. The noise was gut wrenching and never ending.

One of the constables came up to Jack. Maya had never got it straight whether she was dealing with Mitch or Dave, but he said, 'The doc's gone out to the hospital to check on everyone there. He was pretty keen to leave. I don't think he knew what to do with this one.'

Maya remembered Joy's kindness to her when she first arrived and thought for a moment. She said, 'As long as she is handcuffed to a chair and Jack's in the room, I'm willing to go to try and interview her. I think she's sick and needs psychiatric help.'

Jack stood, taking a dominant position. Maybe without realising it? He said, 'No. You've been through too much. I won't let you.'

'I've been cleared by the first aiders. I have the most psychiatric training of anybody here. And I know my own mind,' said Maya. She was calm, firm and strong.

When Maya walked into the interview room with Jack, her jaw clenched with the memories of violence. The room was unpleasant. Hot, stifling, with peeling paint. Smelling of unwashed generations of criminals. Sticky grey-green chairs around a yellow laminated table. Depressing.

Joy was distraught. Brown/grey hair matted with dirt. Trousers and shirt askew. Blood stains down her front. Her face distorted, not human. She shouted, but the words were garbled, not making sense. Jack moved to stand behind Joy, watching her every move.

Maya sat in Joy's direct eyeline and waited. She was the mountain duck, gliding through the still water, calm. Paddling frantically below the water line.

Joy shrieked and wailed, but began to settle. Her face was red and sweating. Eyes filled with tears. Hands twisted and spasming.

'Joy, would you like a drink? It's ice cold and refreshing,' said Maya. She pushed forward the plastic container she'd collected for this purpose. She waited.

Time passed, but eventually Joy took it and sipped. A win.

Maya mirrored Joy's moves, drinking her own water. She breathed slowly, calming herself and calming the room.

'I have jelly beans as well. You must be starving,' said Maya, continuing to mirror Joy's moves. Joy took some and ate. Maya mimicked her action.

'Can you tell me what happened to you?' said Maya.

'The world's not safe. Nowhere's safe,' said Joy, tears running down her face. 'I have to save Samuel. He's in trouble.'

Maya leaned forward in her chair. Her movements, calm and gentle. She said, 'Joy have you been sleeping lately?'

Joy frowned, as if surprised by the question, and said, 'No, not for weeks. I'm very tired.'

'Could I give you a simple sleeping tablet to help? You need some rest,' said Maya.

Joy stared at Maya for a long moment. Then she nodded and took the medicine Maya had organised. Within minutes her eyes went heavy. Ready for sleep.

Joy went back to the cells with Mitch or Dave and fell dead asleep on the small bed. Maya spoke to the constables to organise a shower and some food and coffee for when Joy woke.

Maya's body relaxed. A job well done. She'd managed to help Joy, even if it was only a little.

Maya went to the station kitchenette, looking for food herself. The Country Women's Association had taken over to feed the huge numbers of volunteers. Maya knew this was excellent news. The CWA is full of great cooks. Probably where Joy did her apprenticeship?

Maya found beef and salad sandwiches and ate. The sandwiches were nutritious, delicious and plentiful. She kept sipping at her water bottle, mindful of dehydration. Her main complaint was the sheer number of people crammed into this tiny building. It was hot, humid and sweaty.

Lydia appeared out of the crowded room and approached Maya. She was as energetic and loud as ever. Sarah followed behind, a khaki waif, looking lost.

Maya's eyes ached to look at them. Lydia was dressed in tight, bright exercise gear, inappropriate to the extreme conditions required by the search. But maybe it was better karma if everyone was true to themselves?

Lydia said, 'Oh my God. You're alive. I was sure that Dr Ted had murdered you.'

Sarah stared blankly at the wall. Even in her exhaustion Maya rescued, saying, 'Sarah, have some of this rehydration fluid. It'll help you stay present and cope with all the chaos.' Sarah took the bottle and drank.

Lydia said, 'What happened to you? Jack said you'd had a fight but you just disappeared.' She used her excess emotional energy to rock back and forth. Maya felt seasick.

Maya focused her attention. 'Dr Ted wasn't the murderer. It was Joy. She abducted Dr Ted and then me. I managed to escape.'

Lydia said, 'OMG. Are you sure? She could've been set up by him.'

'No,' said Maya. 'I'm sure. She admitted it to me.' Lydia's eyes wide and mouth opened. Silenced for the first time, since Maya had known her.

Eamon appeared in bland grey shirt and trousers, with Graham dawdling behind, wearing a prominent blue arm band. Eamon said, smiling broadly, 'Our little detective group is getting back together.'

'I think we made a significant difference with our research,' said Lydia bouncing up and down. Recovered from the shock. 'But Maya tells me the murderer was Joy, not Dr Ted.'

'Yeah, we know that,' said Graham. 'It's been flying over the walkie-talkies all morning. We were looking for the wrong murderer.'.

'Nobody told me,' said Lydia, her face darkening. Sarah found a chair but Maya noticed she kept her eyes focused on Lydia. Perhaps Lydia was Sarah's transitional object helping her cope in the outside world?

'Well Lydia, as we've said before it's not always about you,' said Eamon, softening his comments with a grin.

'Was that Joy who was screaming earlier?' said Graham.

'Yes. She's become unwell. I'm not sure why. Had any of you noticed?' said Maya.

'It's strange but Joy seemed to fade into the background. She was a mother figure, who you never thought about, but always expected to be there,' said Graham.

'I feel like we've let her down, not noticing she was in trouble,' said Eamon.

'In psychiatry training, they teach us that we're not God. You can't know everything,' said Maya, leaning forward towards Eamon.

'It's drawn my attention to how selfish I have been,' said Graham, moving his chair into the circle. 'I was so preoccupied by my misfortune, I couldn't see anyone else's suffering.' Maya made room for him. Graham was positioning himself as if he wanted to belong to the group.

Sarah hiccupped. Lydia put her arm around her shoulders, and said, 'It's all going to be okay.'

Maya stared at Lydia. It was a spontaneous, unselfish, kind gesture. Perhaps everyone had made changes?

'What are you all going to do now this is over?' said Maya.

'We've been talking about renting a big house together in Perth. We've grown close to each other through this drama. We know each other well and might really help each other,' said Eamon.

'We've become like brothers and sisters. We still get on each other's nerves but we want to be together,' said Lydia.

'It's also true that we are all on our own and don't have family support,' said Eamon. 'And rental costs in the city are astronomical.'

'I'm going to study to become a support worker,' said Lydia, sucking up attention as per usual.

'They usually discourage people who've been through extreme experiences from trying to live together. It's difficult to translate the bonding to ordinary life,' said Maya shifting on her stool to get comfortable. 'So if you are going to stick together remember to get a short lease and a big house.'

Lydia rolled her eyes but Eamon nodded. It was possible they could make it.

Steve came up to them, his face lit up. He said, 'Hi everybody. I missed you all. It's nice to see you're okay, Maya.' He moved forward. Maya thought he might hug her, but he veered left and grabbed some sandwiches.

'Where have you been Steve?' said Eamon.

'Constables Mitch and Dave made me their right-hand man. I was with them the whole time. They said I was a terrific help. We were in the central control unit. Like on Star Trek,' said Steve, helping himself to a slice of a huge sponge cake. 'Where were all of you?'

'We were searching in Shotgun Gulley. It's right on the other side of Exmouth,' said Eamon.

'Yes. It was bloody hot and bloody useless,' said Graham. 'But I guess someone had to do it.'

Jack came through the crowd. He was flushed and sweaty but he grinned at the group, 'You've got the gang back together again.'

'We did an amazing job, didn't we?' said Lydia, puffing out her chest. Maya was relieved that Lydia had chosen support work rather than the police force. She wasn't subtle.

'Yup, you sure did,' said Jack. 'We would never have sorted it out without all of you.'

'Is Dr Ted okay?' said Eamon wrinkling his forehead.

'He's fine. He's a bit dehydrated so he's spending time in hospital,' said Jack, his eyes darting left, an obvious tell.

'I knew it wasn't him,' said Graham. 'But I get that the police need to do their own research. Sorry I was such a pain.'

'No worries, mate. We've all got our own journey,' said Jack.

'Yes, milage can be rough,' said Maya, leaning back in her chair with a sigh.

Jack moved towards Maya, perched on a counter chair as close as possible to the tired air-conditioner. Maya's strength continued to return with the food and water.

Jack said, 'Are those good?'

'You betcha,' said Maya. 'Do you want one?' She'd piled four of the sandwiches on a single plate like practising for an "all you can eat" buffet. Jack smiled and took one.

'Thanks for your help with Joy. You were really great with her. She's sleeping now,' said Jack.

Maya was in a good mood and smiled, her mouth too full to answer.

'We're going out to interview Dr Ted. Will you be all right on your own?' said Jack.

Maya closed her eyes to think for a moment. She was proud of herself for facing her demons. Her absent stomach pain had shifted into a warm feeling of achievement since interviewing Joy. After all that had occurred, she wanted closure. Maybe there was another demon to face?

'Could I come to see him as well? I need to understand everything that happened to me,' Maya said.

Jack raised his eyebrows. He said, 'Are you sure? It might bring up bad memories. We really needed your help with Joy but we'll be fine with Dr Ted.'

Maya pursed her lips and thought about the question. 'Every research paper on PTSD pushes the importance of facing your traumatic memories. Avoidance doesn't work. It's the easy way out but leads to longer term problems. I want a sense of resolution. Trust me. I know my own strength.'

'Okay. I guess I'm a face your fears kind of a person anyway,' said Jack, reaching to hold Maya's hand. 'We can go when you have had enough sandwiches. I'm off to find this scones, jam and cream. Do you want one?' Maya nodded with enthusiasm. The food was great.

When they drove to the hospital, Maya was struck by how flat and dusty the town was. The hospital was this squat and flat. The mythical giant that had squashed the police station had been here too. The building had been refurbished by an enthusiastic State government, but still showed its 1960s bones underneath.

Although the hospital looked like a structure out of a time warp, the people inside were wonderful. Maya was welcomed and thanked by everyone. They were polite and kind about Dr Ted's admission, and focused on maintaining his privacy. Maya was there as an observer, not in a professional capacity.

Maya was shocked when she entered the small room and saw Dr Ted. He'd shrunk into himself. The power and strength he'd exhibited in the past, had evaporated. He was dressed in one of the ridiculous hospital nighties that open from the back. He was showered and his hair combed, like a small boy prepared for bed by his mother. The strongest smell in the room was hospital disinfectant. The loudest noise, the laughing of distant kookaburras.

Jack said, 'Hi Dr Ted, we need to get an interview from you to finish up the paperwork.'

Dr Ted closed his eyes and sighed. Gone was the alpha male posturing. Gone was the Guru archetype. A tired, old, burnt-out man was left in his place.

'I don't remember much,' said Dr Ted. 'My mind keeps focusing on the past.'

Jack sat in the visitor's chair and indicated to Maya to do the same. Maya kept behind, out of Dr Ted's eyeline.

Jack said, 'Well start in the past and see if the present catches up'

Dr Ted smiled wanly and said, 'I keep focusing on Samuel's death.'

'Are you sure it was suicide?' said Jack

'Definitely, I cut him down. It was horrific. I felt I'd failed him,' said Dr Ted. 'And then Joy arrived like an angel of mercy. She hasn't left Exmouth since. She was my right-hand man and I trusted her.'

'When do you think everything went wrong?' said Jack, leaning forward, listening intently.

'I guess she wasn't herself for about a month before Daniel died,' said Dr Ted. 'But she was always such a private person, I didn't like to enquire.'

Dr Ted sat with his thoughts for a moment, closing his eyes. Then he said, 'I really was shocked. I never thought Joy was capable of murder or abduction. She drugged me and by the time I woke up, I was tied up in a cavern. She'd moved me there using a meat trolley, for God's sake.'

Dr Ted turned to look at Maya, and said,' I have no idea why I gave up. I froze. When you fought back, I couldn't believe it.'

Jack said, 'Everyone responds differently in emergency situations. Plenty of people freeze or run away. No one can predict how they'll respond.'

Maya leaned towards Dr Ted and said, 'I was shocked that I acted as well. It was like part of my unconscious just wouldn't give up. I got lucky. I am glad that you're safe too.'

Jack touched Dr Ted's shoulder, directing his attention back to himself. He said, 'Do you think that Joy was psychotic?'

Dr Ted clenched his fists. 'Yes, but it just doesn't make any sense. She doesn't have a personal or family history of psychosis. Samuel was depressed not mad.'

Maya intervened. 'What about stress? People can develop a stress induced psychosis.'

'Yes,' said Dr Ted. 'I've thought about that but I still don't understand it. Why now? The stress was no different to the past retreats.'

Jack said, 'I'll have another opportunity to interview Joy when she wakes, but sometimes we never figure out what happened.'

A nurse bustled into Dr Ted's room and set about taking blood pressure and temperature. Jack and Maya left.

Maya and Jack met back with Joy in the interview room, after she'd slept for 4 hours. It was early evening. Joy was less agitated. No longer screaming and her movements slowed. She was showered and smelled fresh. The constables had managed to get her clean clothes and feed her. Even the room was fresher. The small window had been opened giving some crisp air as the heat of the day evaporated.

Maya smiled at her across the table. She said, 'You were very kind to me when I first came to the Homestead. I'd like to return the favour now.'

Joy's expression remained flat. Maya continued. 'I know you've been through a terrible time. I'm just trying to find out what happened to you.'

Joy closed her eyes and a tear escaped. 'It's all confusing. I can't remember. It's so disjointed.'

'When did the problems start?' said Maya, leaning forward, her forehead lined in concentration.

'Samuel's old girlfriend sent me a wedding invitation two months ago. She's getting married,' said Joy, pausing for a moment. 'I was devastated. It's like everyone is moving on now and forgetting him.'

Maya nodded, trying not to direct Joy's story.

'I couldn't sleep, which meant I started not coping with my job. There's always so much to do,' said Joy. 'I was ashamed.'

Joy looked down and the tears flowed fast. She said, 'Dr Ted always trusted me. I had the keys to the drug cabinet. I took some MDMA and LSD tabs. I knew it was stealing but Dr Ted never kept records and I was desperate to feel better.'

Joy had her hands clasped over her stomach and was rocking

back and forth. She said, 'It worked at first. I was so productive and didn't miss the sleep. But then everything got muddled. My head got paranoid. Like something bad was going to happen but I didn't know what, or how to stop it.'

Joy stopped rocking and looked directly into Maya's eyes, 'I never would have taken drugs if I hadn't heard about the benefits of psychedelics from working here. I didn't think it through. I should've known it could make me paranoid.'

Maya had not moved during Joy's story. Now she shifted further forward in her chair and said in our low, slow voice, 'What about Daniel? What happened there?'

'Dr Ted showed me a printout of the email confirming Daniel was spying on us. He intended to confront Daniel on the retreat at Omar Station,' said Joy. 'I couldn't stand the deception. I was angry. I was determined to stop him whatever the cost.'

Maya said, 'Go on.'

Joy started to speak robotically, cut off from normal emotions. 'I was staying on the station to organise the food. I've been there many times over the years and knew the set up.'

She flexed and extended her right hand, looking down. 'I think it was wrong now. But I took the strychnine powder and put it in Daniel's drink container. No one else knew that he was taking electrolyte solution because of his intolerance to the heat. He had a special individual container that only he used.'

She gritted her jaw and clenched her fists. 'I was furious. He was obnoxious and irritating. I felt righteous, powerful, like an avenging angel. Right was on my side. I was so sure.'

Maya listened, moving her body forward, nodding her head with the flow of words and watching Joy's face. She said, 'But why did you abduct Dr Ted? You were trying to protect him.'

'He's behaved like an idiot since this happened,' said Joy. 'I worshipped the ground he walked on. But since Daniel's death he has behaved like a namby pamby baby.'

Although cuffed, Joy banged her fists on the table. 'He'd come to the kitchen and just whine. As if I didn't have my own problems. The power he shows is pretend. He hides behind a mask. He's a weak, weak man.'

Maya said, 'Did you intend to kill him?'

'I don't know what I wanted. He fell asleep with the haloperidol, then I tied him up and moved him into the cavern,' said Joy. 'I was sick of his whingeing. I just wanted to shut him up. I came back to the Homestead to get the Taser so I could control him better.'

Joy stared at Maya as if seeing her for the first time in the interview. She said, 'When you found me in the kitchen, I was sure I was caught. I wanted to kill you but I just couldn't.'

Joy slumped back in her chair, appearing exhausted. She said, 'I guess that means I'm a good person.' She closed her eyes, shut her lips, and refused to say another word.

Maya's head whirled. She hadn't got the resolution she craved but she recognised the interview was over for Joy. The constables came to take Joy back.

Jack stood alongside Maya and held her hand. Joy looked up and said, 'I knew you two would suit each other.'

Jack and Maya walked out of the station and across the street to the café. The food smelled terrible. No match to Joy or the CWA. A strong, pungent smell of marijuana in the air. But all Maya wanted was a coffee, in some quiet.

Jack put his arm around Maya's shoulders, recognising she was exhausted. He said 'Thank you for doing that. I think it helped Joy to talk it through. The story's much clearer now.'

'It bothers me that people think psychedelics only do good. The psychosis they cause can be dreadful,' said Maya closing her eyes.

'You can't fight the world. There's good and bad in alcohol and that's legal,' said Jack.

'Yes but at least people know about the bad. Everyone seems to think that marijuana and the psychedelics have superpowers and no problems,' said Maya.

Jack tucked a stray strand of Maya's hair behind her ear. She moved forward to touch his hand. A reminder that there was good in the world. A sense of hope. Important for the future.

Jack said, 'Thanks for being my partner in the investigation. I'm sorry that I'm impulsive at times. I know I can be hard to work with.'

'But it gives you strength. You're quick to adapt to change. The way you ran after Joy, may have saved Dr Ted's life,' said Maya.

Jack stared at her.

Maya ran her fingers down his dusty forearm. 'I think everyone's broken in their own way. Some people are just more honest about it. There can be good in the broken bits. I get anxious but it makes me careful and thorough.'

The humidity mounted until there was a crack of lightning to the north. The rain started. Maya leaned forward and kissed Jack. It poured. Fat wet drops drenching the landscape. As if the world was taking a giant breath of oxygen. The earth was renewed.

THANK YOU

Thank you for reading this book.
    Reviews are the lifeblood of new books.
    I would really appreciate a review of Goodreads or Amazon.
    Your opinions matter to me.

ACKNOWLEDGMENTS

Writing a book is a difficult process. I would like to acknowledge my first reader Sally Cook who has loyally read everything I have thrown at her. Thank you Sally for your encouragement. My book club team were my wonderful beta readers who really helped me develop the manuscript, Nina Lyhne, Sue Nielson, Jeanne Walczac, Kath Daniel, and Gaye Moses. I am grateful to you all.

Printed in Great Britain
by Amazon